ANN M. MARTIN

THE BABY-SITTERS CLUB®

MARY ANNE SAVES THE DAY

A GRAPHIC NOVEL BY
RAINA TELGEMEIER

WITH COLOR BY BRADEN LAMB

Library of Congress Control Number: 2015935841

ISBN 978-0-545-88617-8 (hardcover)
ISBN 978-0-545-88621-5 (paperback)

10 9   19 20 21

Printed in Malaysia   108
First color edition printing, November 2015

Lettering by John Green
Edited by David Levithan, Sheila Keenan, and Cassandra Pelham
Book design by Phil Falco
Creative Director: David Saylor

This book is for Beth McKeever Perkins, my old baby-sitting buddy.
With Love (and years of memories)
A. M. M.

Thanks to David Saylor, Cassandra Pelham, Ellie Berger,
Marion Vitus, Alisa Harris, Alison Wilgus, Zack Giallongo, Steve Flack,
Phil Falco, Braden Lamb, and John Green. And of course, thanks to
Dave Roman, for always encouraging me to do my best.
R. T.

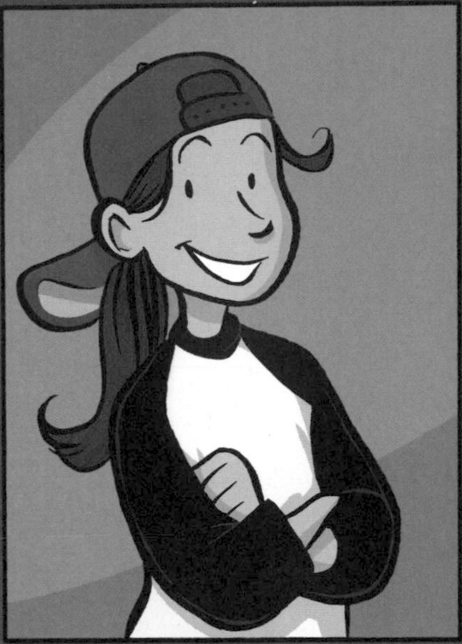

KRISTY THOMAS
PRESIDENT

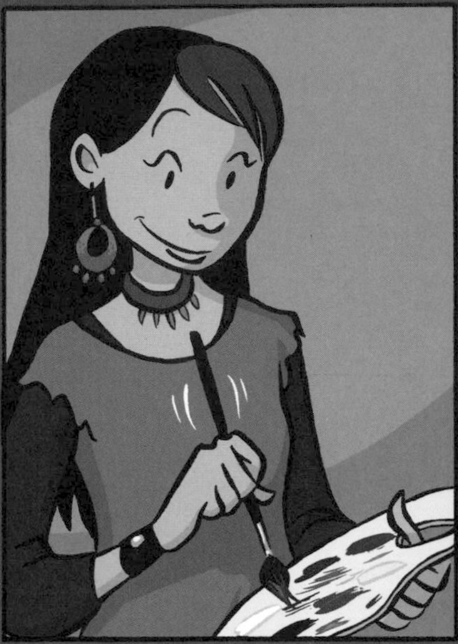

CLAUDIA KISHI
VICE PRESIDENT

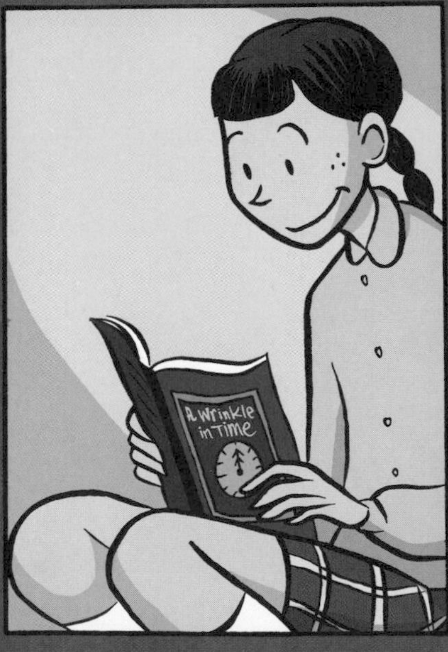
A Wrinkle in Time

MARY ANNE SPIER
SECRETARY

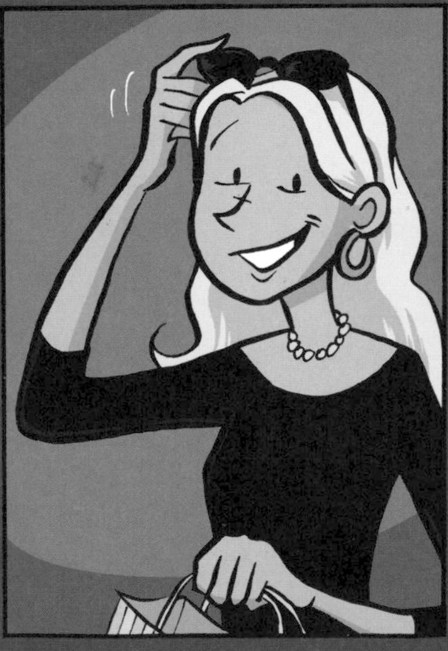

STACEY MCGILL
TREASURER

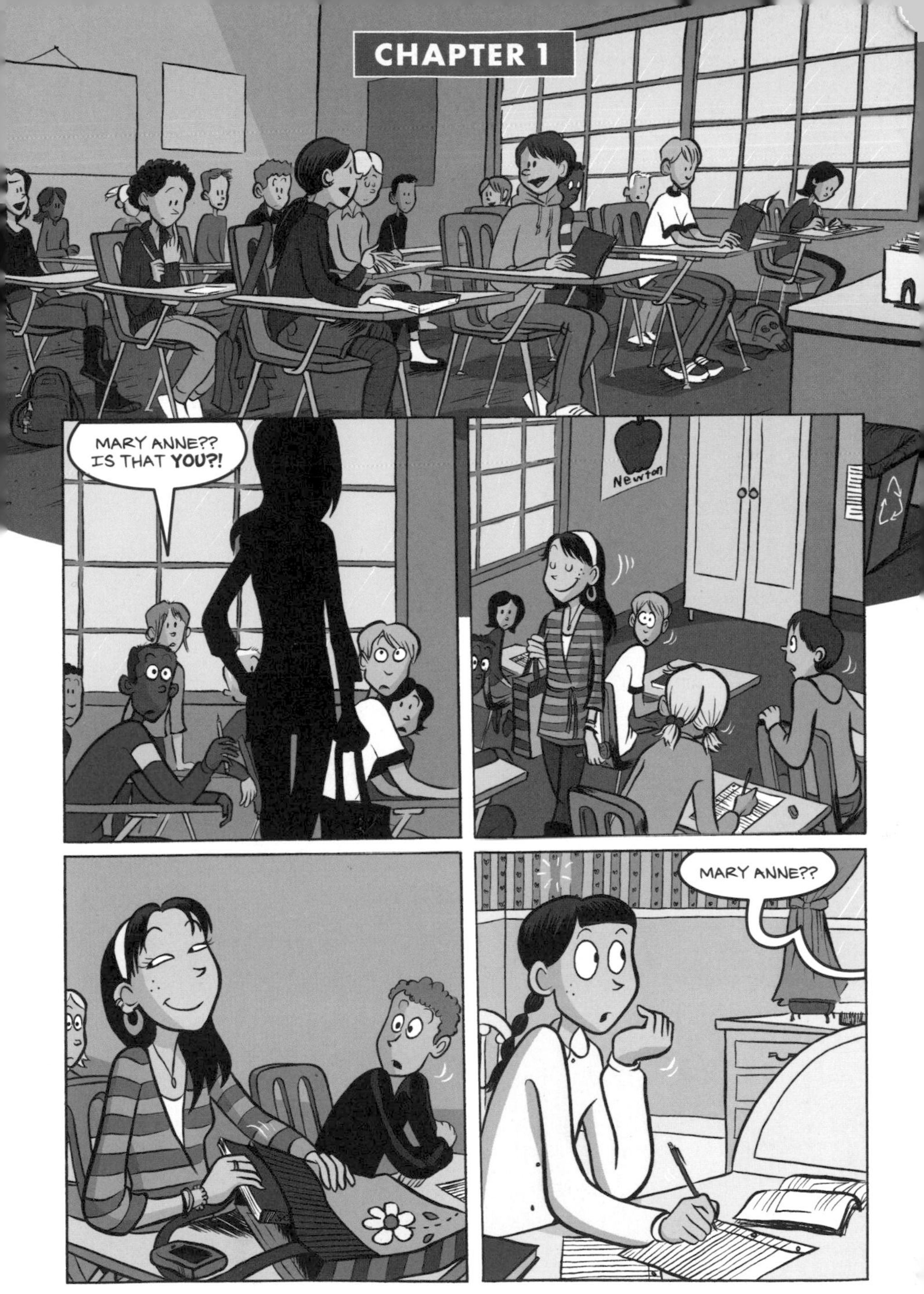
CHAPTER 1
MARY ANNE?? IS THAT YOU?!
Newton
MARY ANNE??

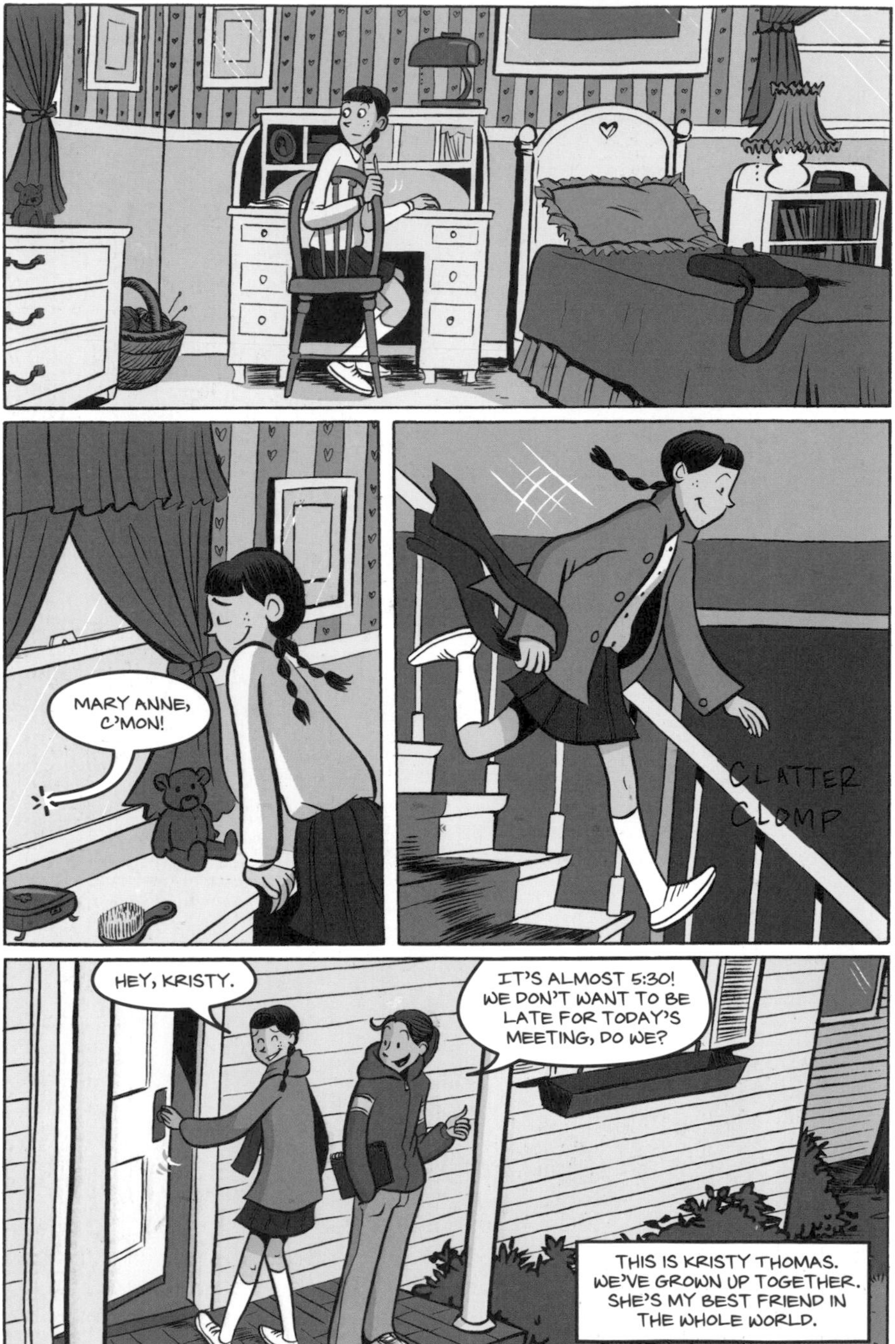
MARY ANNE, C'MON!
CLATTER
CLOMP
HEY, KRISTY.
IT'S ALMOST 5:30! WE DON'T WANT TO BE LATE FOR TODAY'S MEETING, DO WE?
THIS IS KRISTY THOMAS. WE'VE GROWN UP TOGETHER. SHE'S MY BEST FRIEND IN THE WHOLE WORLD.

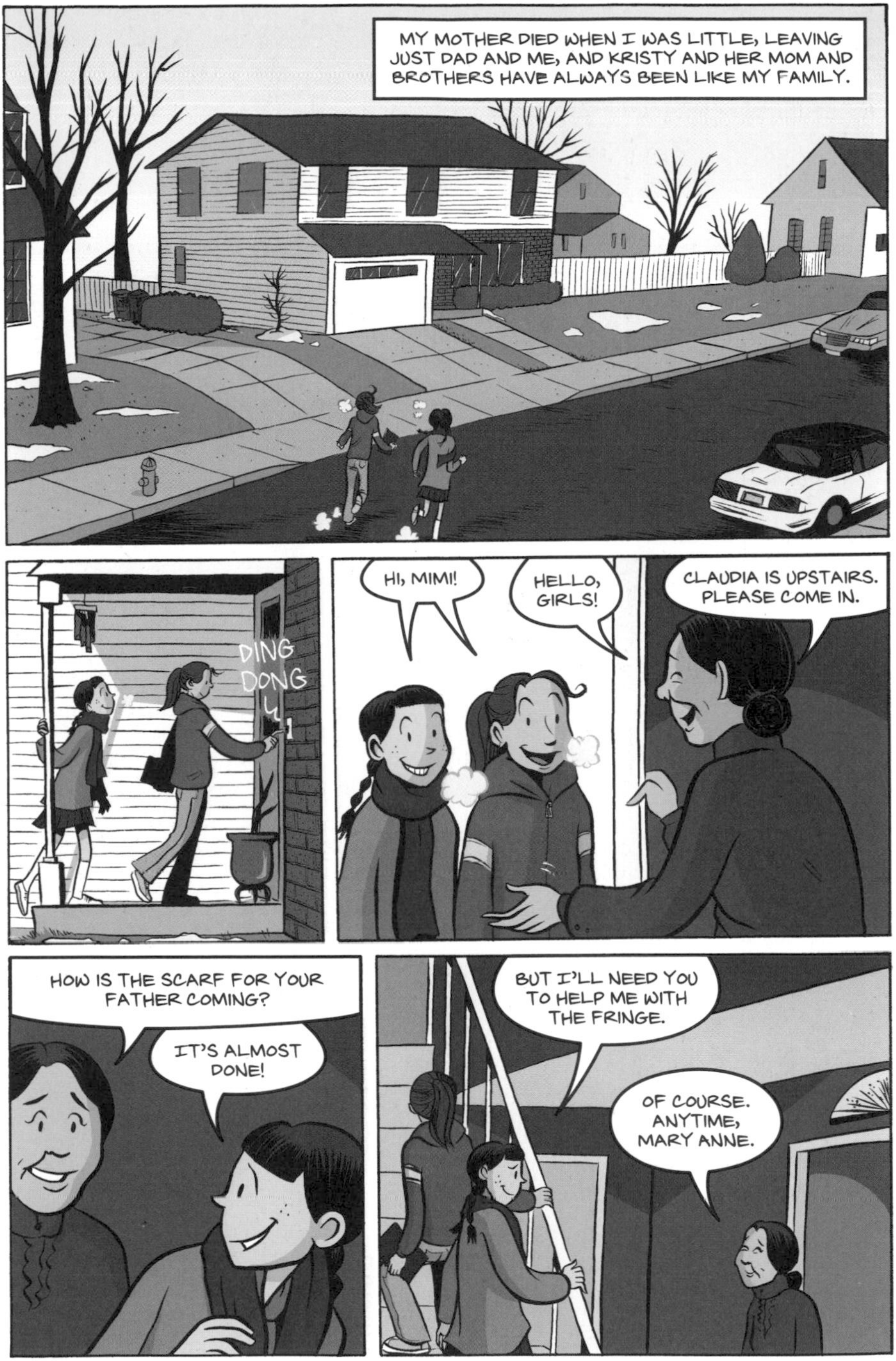
MY MOTHER DIED WHEN I WAS LITTLE, LEAVING JUST DAD AND ME, AND KRISTY AND HER MOM AND BROTHERS HAVE ALWAYS BEEN LIKE MY FAMILY.
DING DONG
HI, MIMI!
HELLO, GIRLS!
CLAUDIA IS UPSTAIRS. PLEASE COME IN.
HOW IS THE SCARF FOR YOUR FATHER COMING?
IT'S ALMOST DONE!
BUT I'LL NEED YOU TO HELP ME WITH THE FRINGE.
OF COURSE. ANYTIME, MARY ANNE.

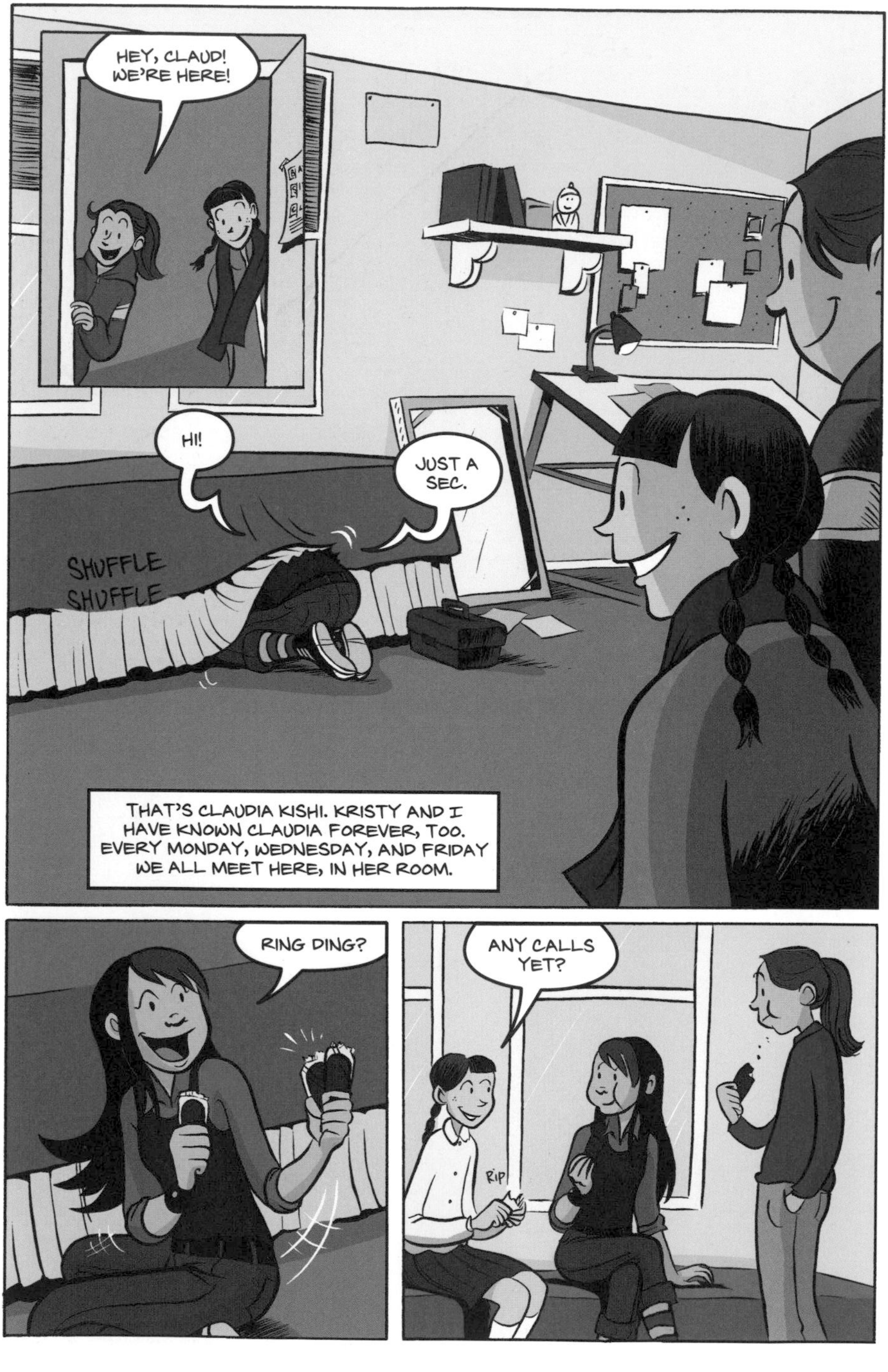
HEY, CLAUD! WE'RE HERE!
HI!
JUST A SEC.
SHUFFLE SHUFFLE
THAT'S CLAUDIA KISHI. KRISTY AND I HAVE KNOWN CLAUDIA FOREVER, TOO. EVERY MONDAY, WEDNESDAY, AND FRIDAY WE ALL MEET HERE, IN HER ROOM.
RING DING?
ANY CALLS YET?
RIP

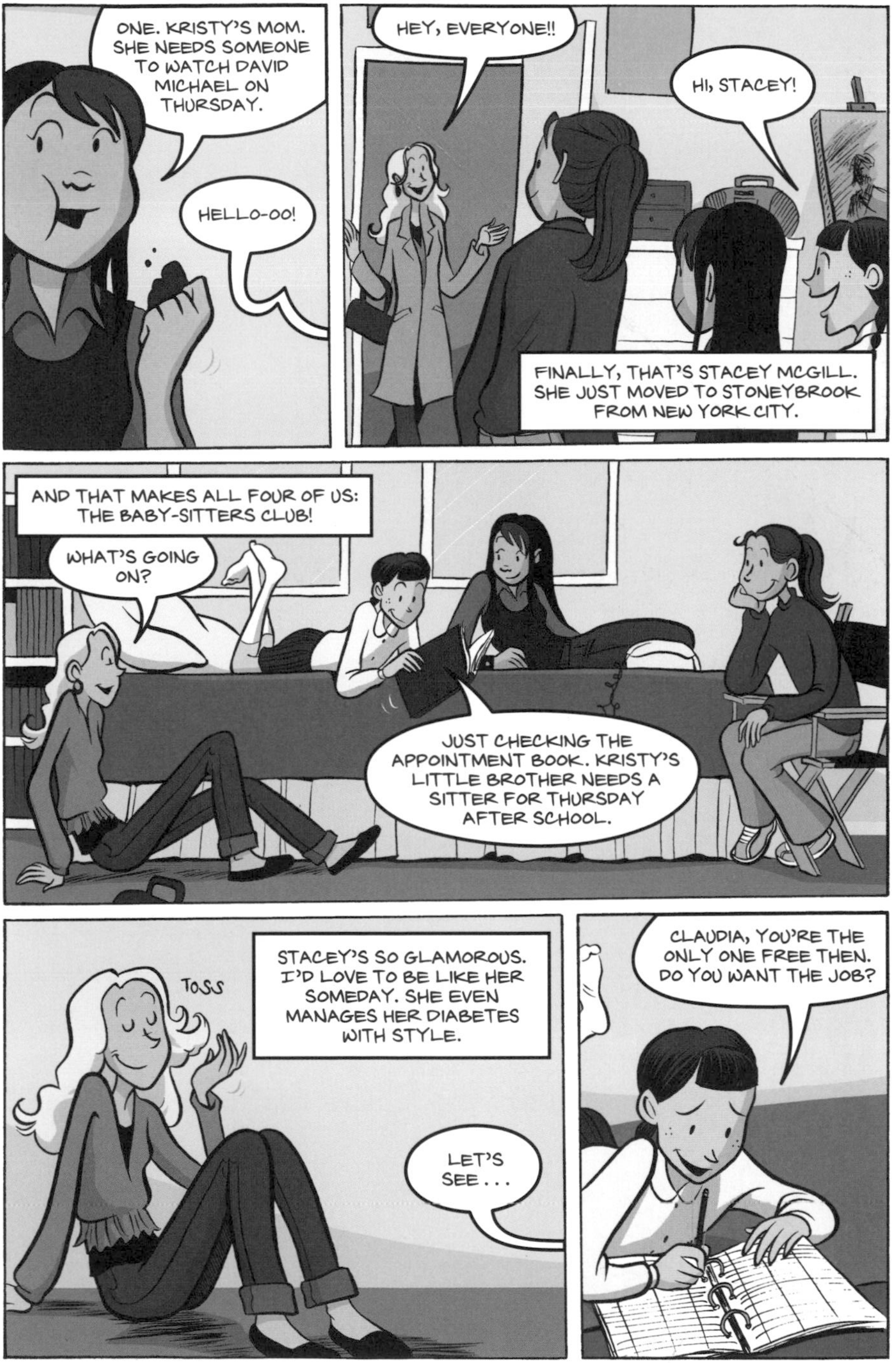
ONE. KRISTY'S MOM. SHE NEEDS SOMEONE TO WATCH DAVID MICHAEL ON THURSDAY.
HELLO-OO!
HEY, EVERYONE!!
HI, STACEY!
FINALLY, THAT'S STACEY MCGILL. SHE JUST MOVED TO STONEYBROOK FROM NEW YORK CITY.
AND THAT MAKES ALL FOUR OF US: THE BABY-SITTERS CLUB!
WHAT'S GOING ON?
JUST CHECKING THE APPOINTMENT BOOK. KRISTY'S LITTLE BROTHER NEEDS A SITTER FOR THURSDAY AFTER SCHOOL.
STACEY'S SO GLAMOROUS. I'D LOVE TO BE LIKE HER SOMEDAY. SHE EVEN MANAGES HER DIABETES WITH STYLE.
TOSS
LET'S SEE . . .
CLAUDIA, YOU'RE THE ONLY ONE FREE THEN. DO YOU WANT THE JOB?

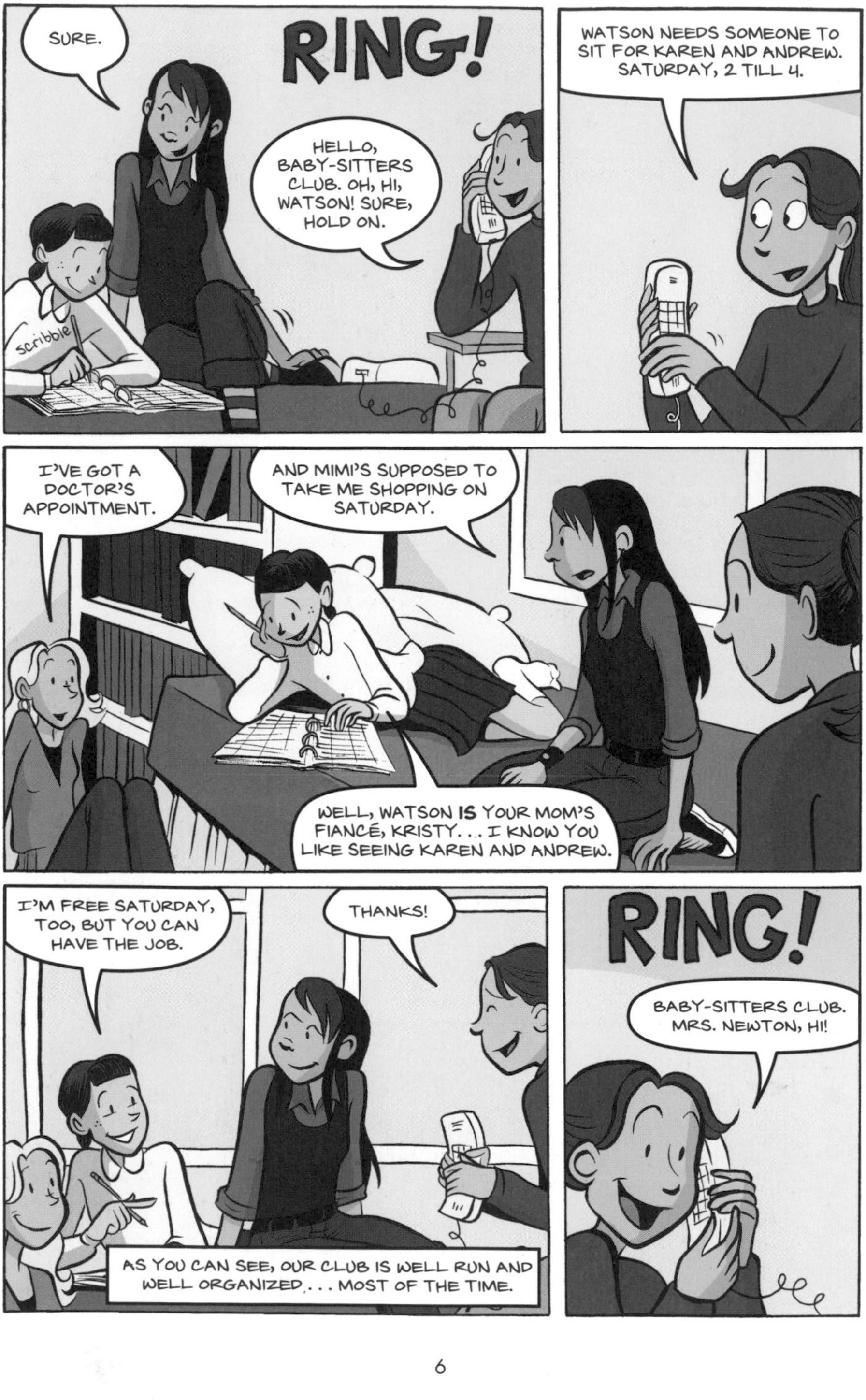
SURE.
RING!
HELLO, BABY-SITTERS CLUB. OH, HI, WATSON! SURE, HOLD ON.
scribble
WATSON NEEDS SOMEONE TO SIT FOR KAREN AND ANDREW. SATURDAY, 2 TILL 4.
I'VE GOT A DOCTOR'S APPOINTMENT.
AND MIMI'S SUPPOSED TO TAKE ME SHOPPING ON SATURDAY.
WELL, WATSON **IS** YOUR MOM'S FIANCÉ, KRISTY. . . I KNOW YOU LIKE SEEING KAREN AND ANDREW.
I'M FREE SATURDAY, TOO, BUT YOU CAN HAVE THE JOB.
THANKS!
AS YOU CAN SEE, OUR CLUB IS WELL RUN AND WELL ORGANIZED. . . MOST OF THE TIME.
RING!
BABY-SITTERS CLUB. MRS. NEWTON, HI!

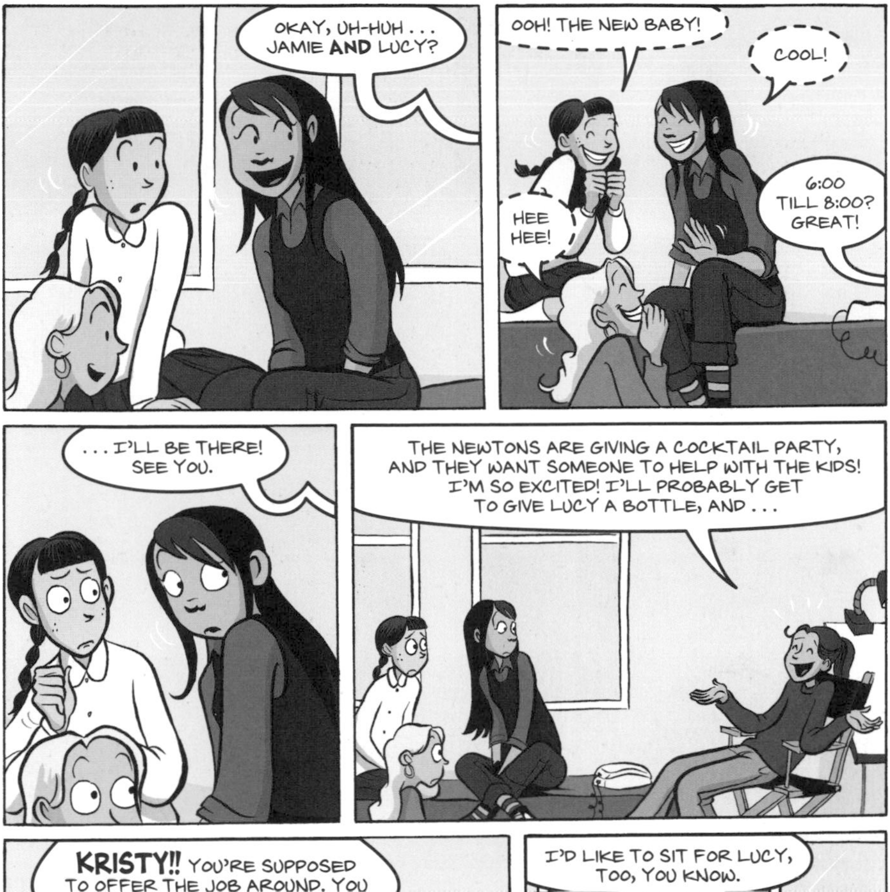
OKAY, UH-HUH . . . JAMIE AND LUCY?
OOH! THE NEW BABY!
COOL!
HEE HEE!
6:00 TILL 8:00? GREAT!
. . . I'LL BE THERE! SEE YOU.
THE NEWTONS ARE GIVING A COCKTAIL PARTY, AND THEY WANT SOMEONE TO HELP WITH THE KIDS! I'M SO EXCITED! I'LL PROBABLY GET TO GIVE LUCY A BOTTLE, AND . . .
KRISTY!! YOU'RE SUPPOSED TO OFFER THE JOB AROUND. YOU KNOW THAT. IT'S YOUR RULE.
OH, YEAH . . .
SORRY.
I'D LIKE TO SIT FOR LUCY, TOO, YOU KNOW.
ME, TOO.
ME, TOO.

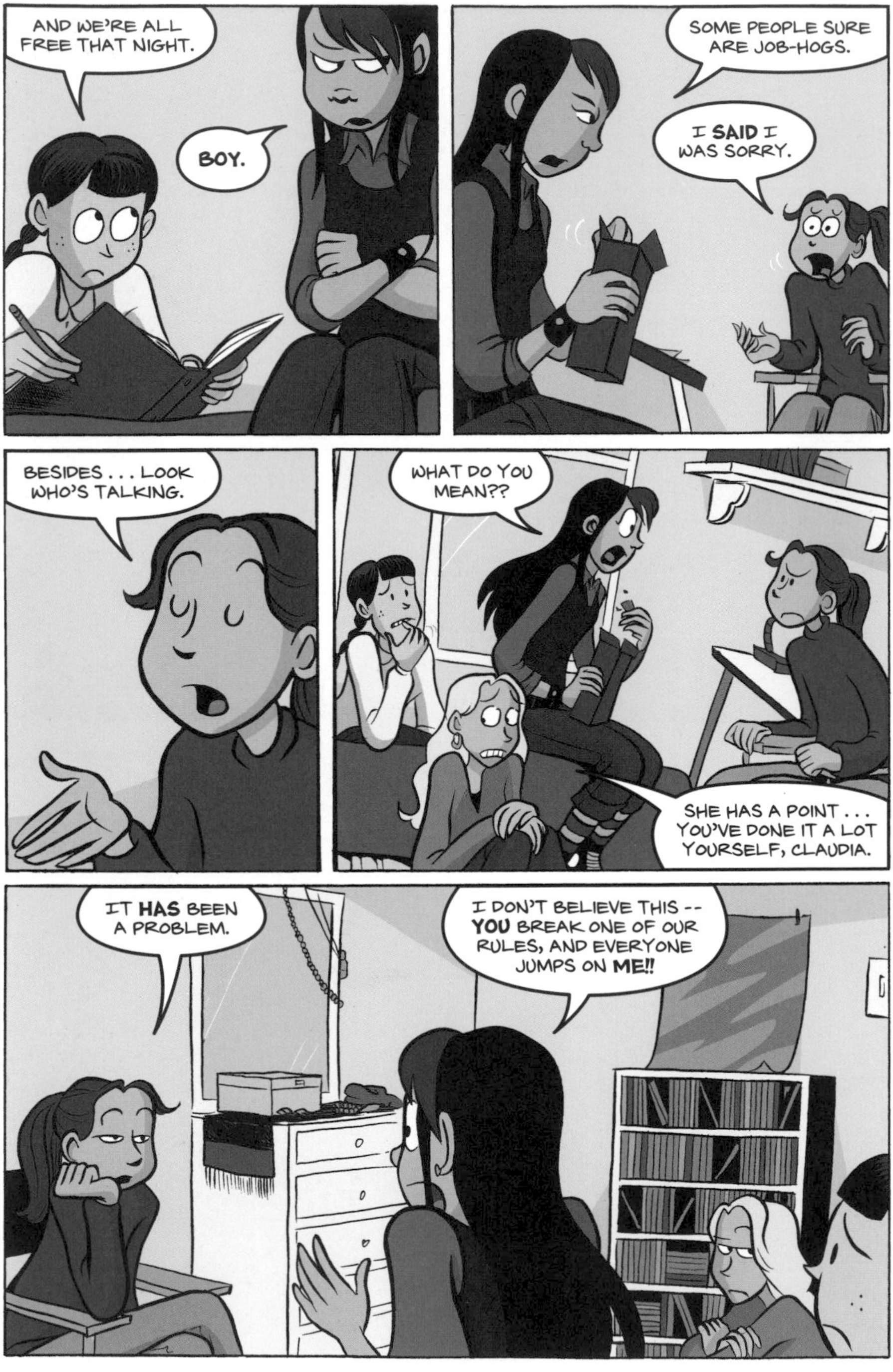
AND WE'RE ALL FREE THAT NIGHT.
BOY.
SOME PEOPLE SURE ARE JOB-HOGS.
I **SAID** I WAS SORRY.
BESIDES . . . LOOK WHO'S TALKING.
WHAT DO YOU MEAN??
SHE HAS A POINT . . . YOU'VE DONE IT A LOT YOURSELF, CLAUDIA.
IT **HAS** BEEN A PROBLEM.
I DON'T BELIEVE THIS -- **YOU** BREAK ONE OF OUR RULES, AND EVERYONE JUMPS ON **ME!!**

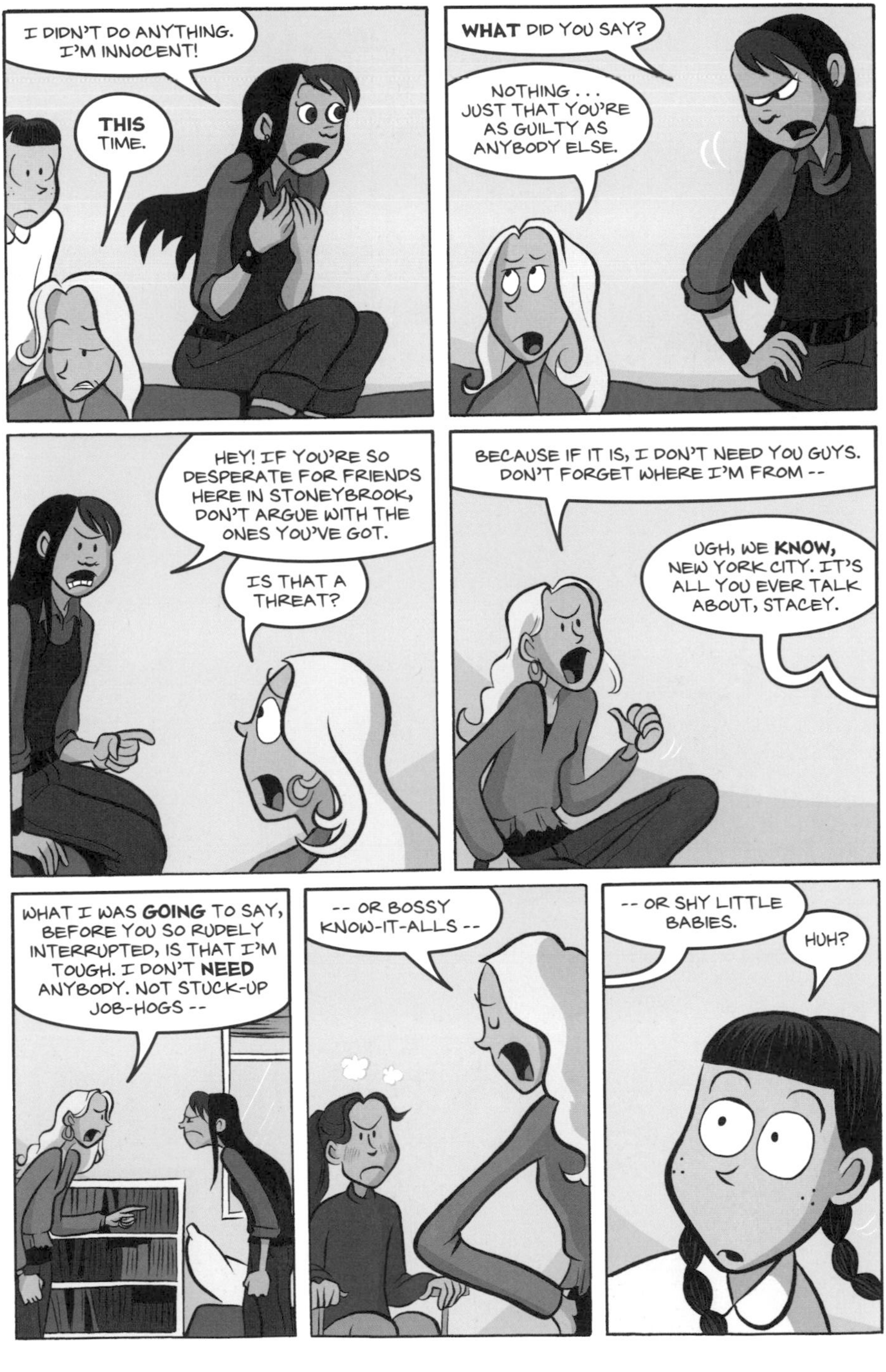
I DIDN'T DO ANYTHING. I'M INNOCENT!
THIS TIME.
WHAT DID YOU SAY?
NOTHING . . . JUST THAT YOU'RE AS GUILTY AS ANYBODY ELSE.
HEY! IF YOU'RE SO DESPERATE FOR FRIENDS HERE IN STONEYBROOK, DON'T ARGUE WITH THE ONES YOU'VE GOT.
IS THAT A THREAT?
BECAUSE IF IT IS, I DON'T NEED YOU GUYS. DON'T FORGET WHERE I'M FROM --
UGH, WE **KNOW,** NEW YORK CITY. IT'S ALL YOU EVER TALK ABOUT, STACEY.
WHAT I WAS **GOING** TO SAY, BEFORE YOU SO RUDELY INTERRUPTED, IS THAT I'M TOUGH. I DON'T **NEED** ANYBODY. NOT STUCK-UP JOB-HOGS --
-- OR BOSSY KNOW-IT-ALLS --
-- OR SHY LITTLE BABIES.
HUH?

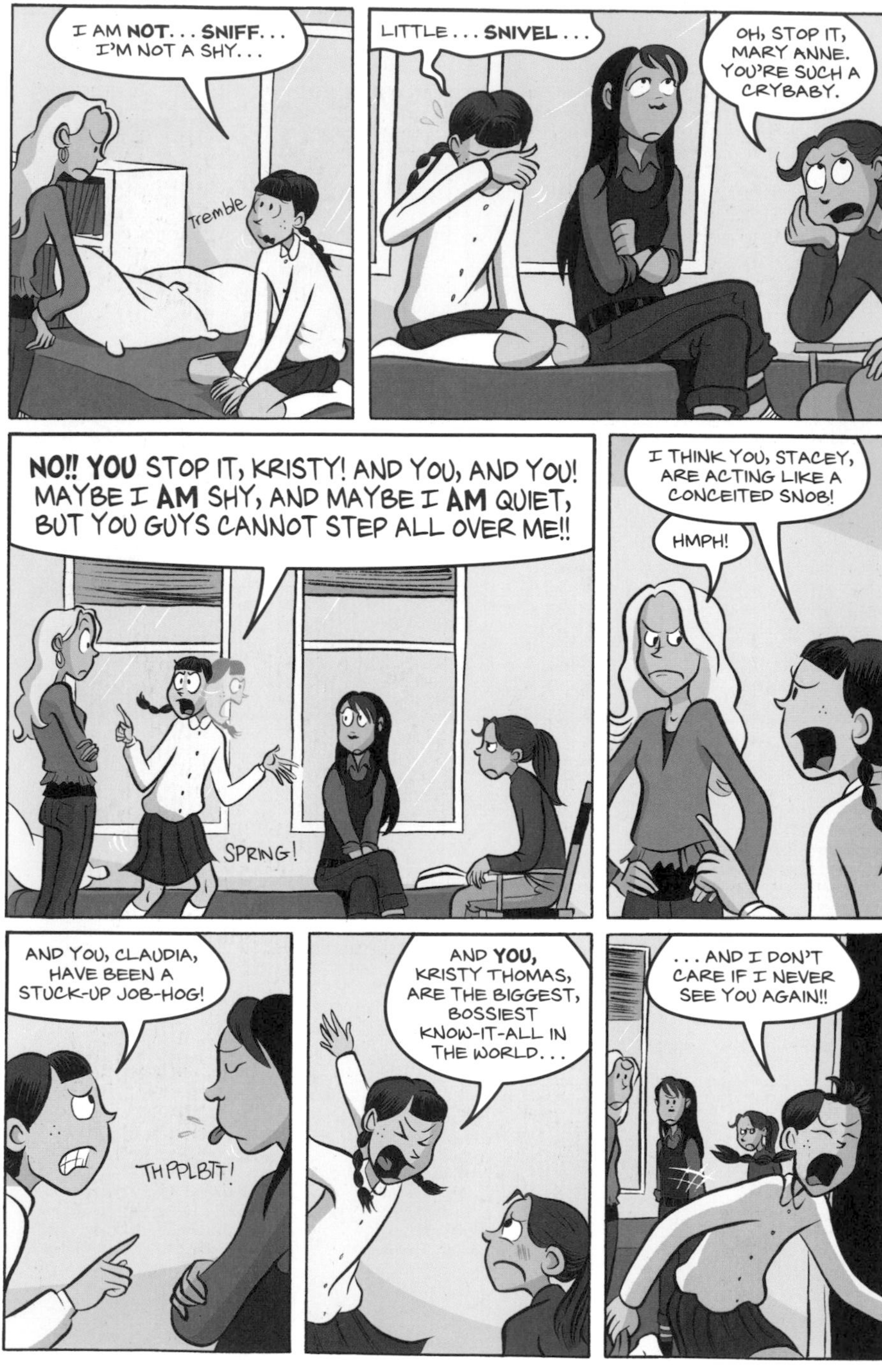
I AM NOT . . . SNIFF . . . I'M NOT A SHY . . .
TREMBLE
LITTLE . . . SNIVEL . . .
OH, STOP IT, MARY ANNE. YOU'RE SUCH A CRYBABY.
NO!! YOU STOP IT, KRISTY! AND YOU, AND YOU! MAYBE I AM SHY, AND MAYBE I AM QUIET, BUT YOU GUYS CANNOT STEP ALL OVER ME!!
SPRING!
I THINK YOU, STACEY, ARE ACTING LIKE A CONCEITED SNOB!
HMPH!
AND YOU, CLAUDIA, HAVE BEEN A STUCK-UP JOB-HOG!
THPPLBTT!
AND YOU, KRISTY THOMAS, ARE THE BIGGEST, BOSSIEST KNOW-IT-ALL IN THE WORLD . . .
. . . AND I DON'T CARE IF I NEVER SEE YOU AGAIN!!

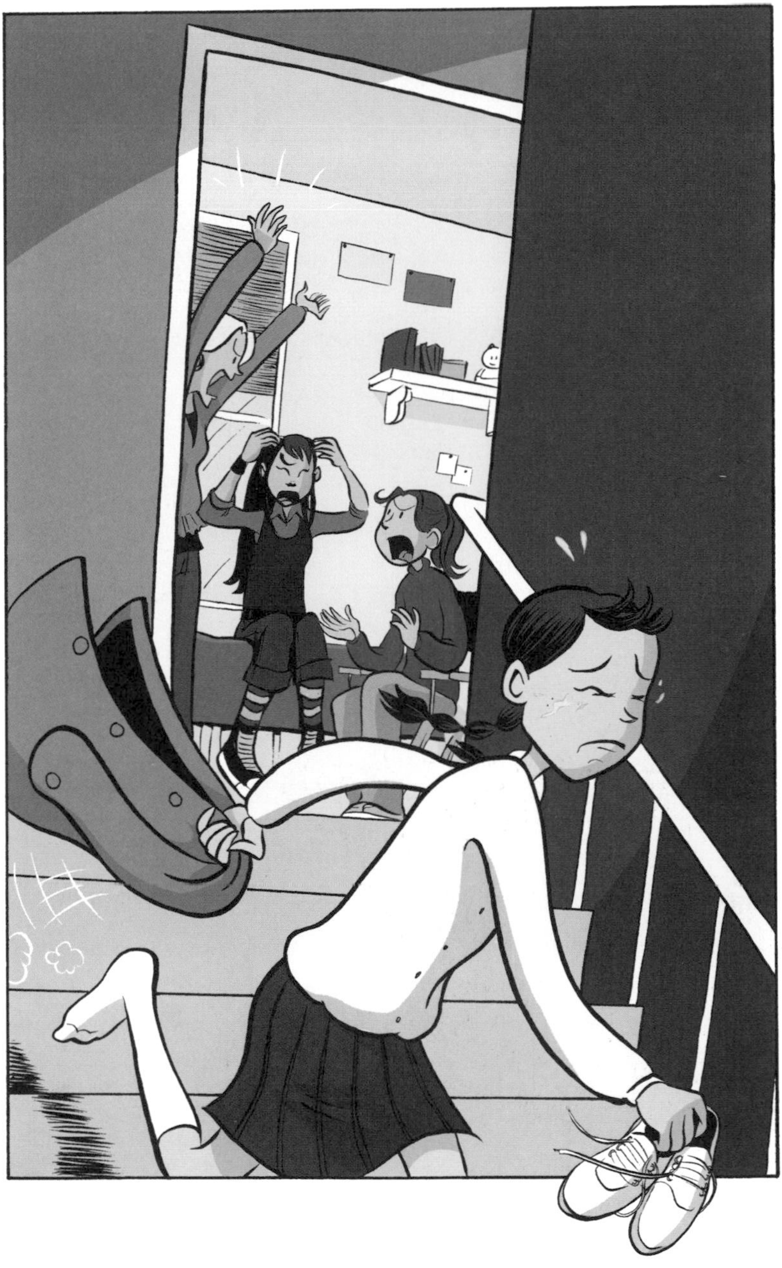

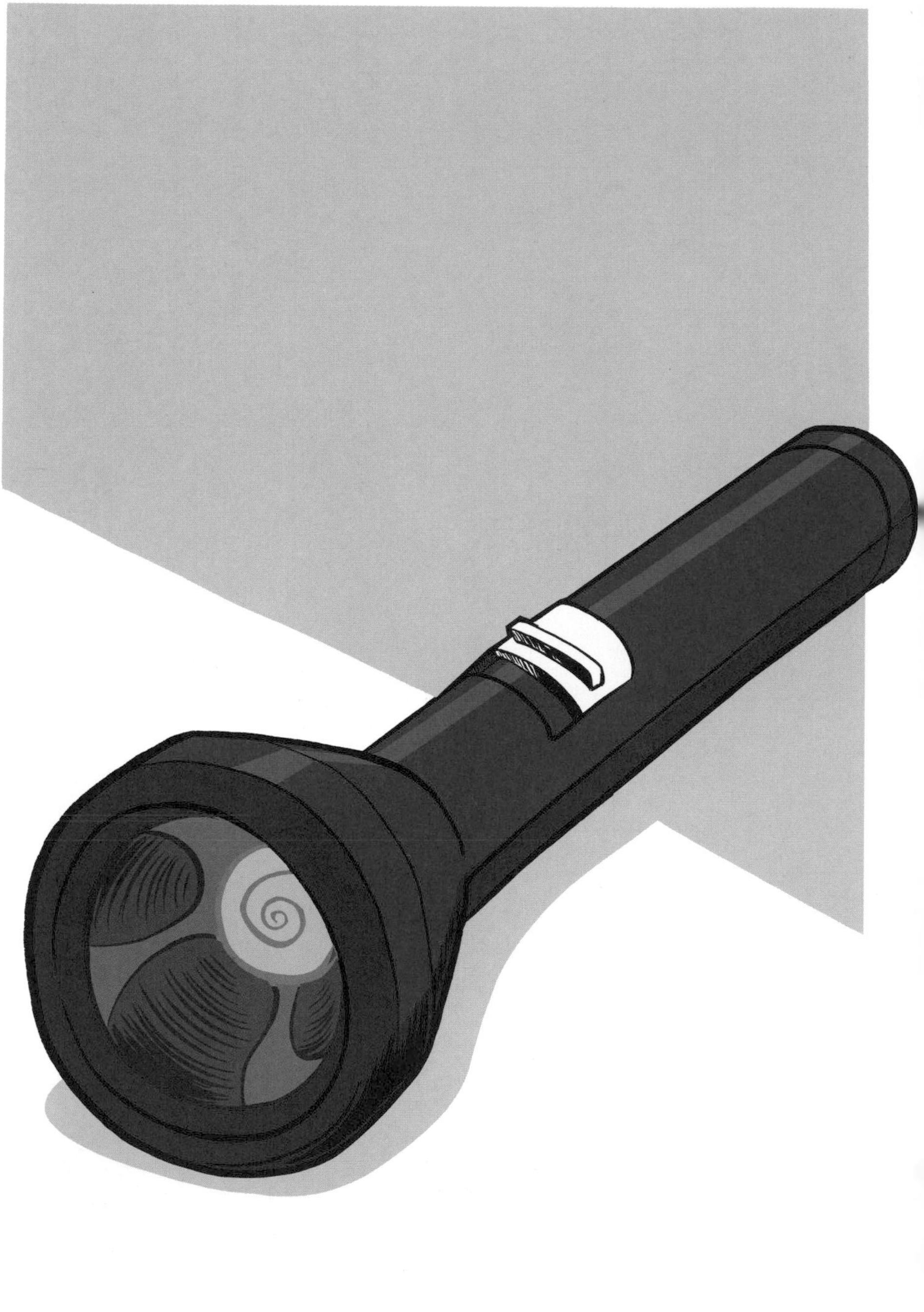

CHAPTER 2

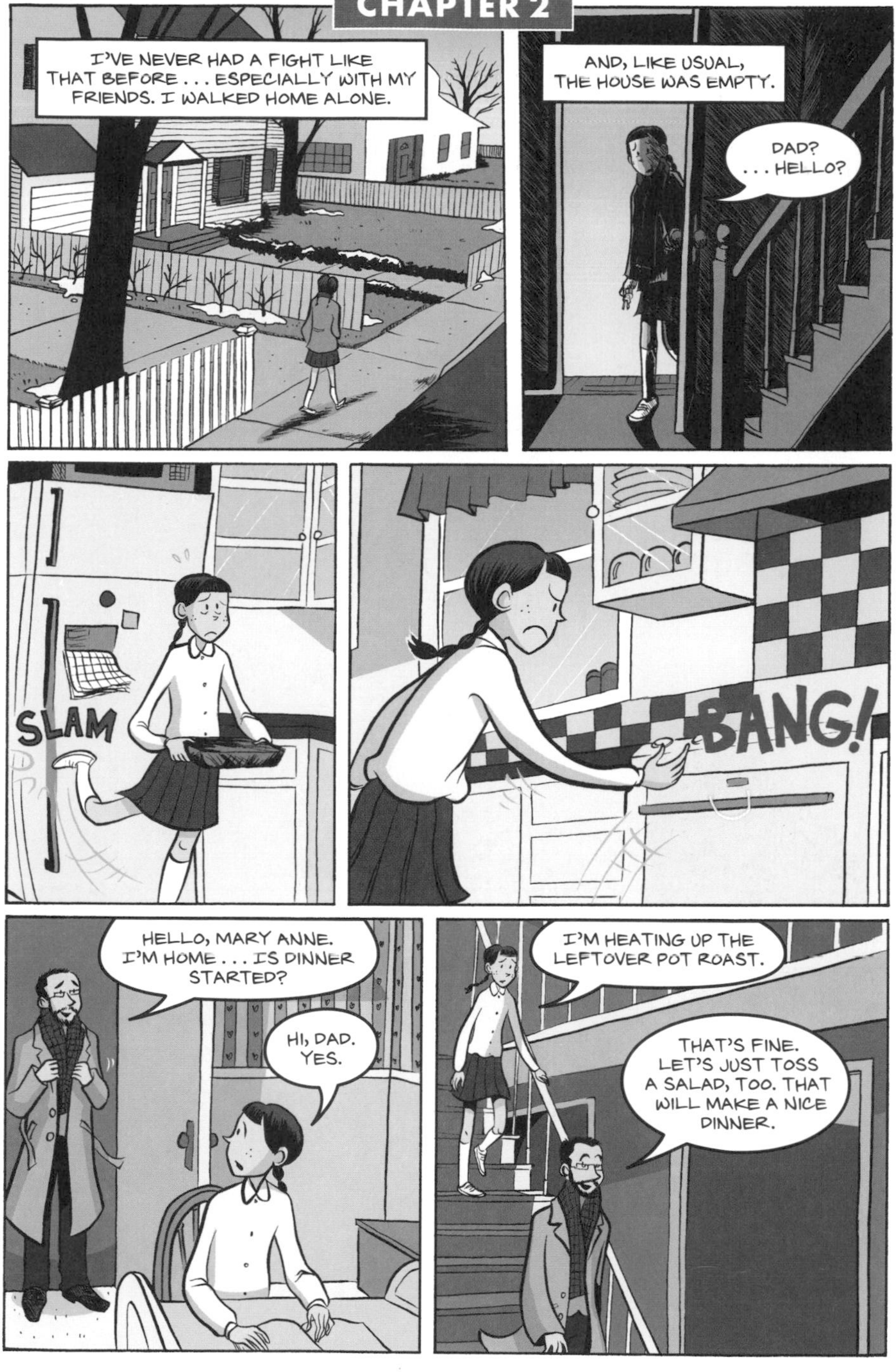

I'VE NEVER HAD A FIGHT LIKE THAT BEFORE . . . ESPECIALLY WITH MY FRIENDS. I WALKED HOME ALONE.
AND, LIKE USUAL, THE HOUSE WAS EMPTY.
DAD? . . . HELLO?
SLAM
BANG!
HELLO, MARY ANNE. I'M HOME . . . IS DINNER STARTED?
HI, DAD. YES.
I'M HEATING UP THE LEFTOVER POT ROAST.
THAT'S FINE. LET'S JUST TOSS A SALAD, TOO. THAT WILL MAKE A NICE DINNER.

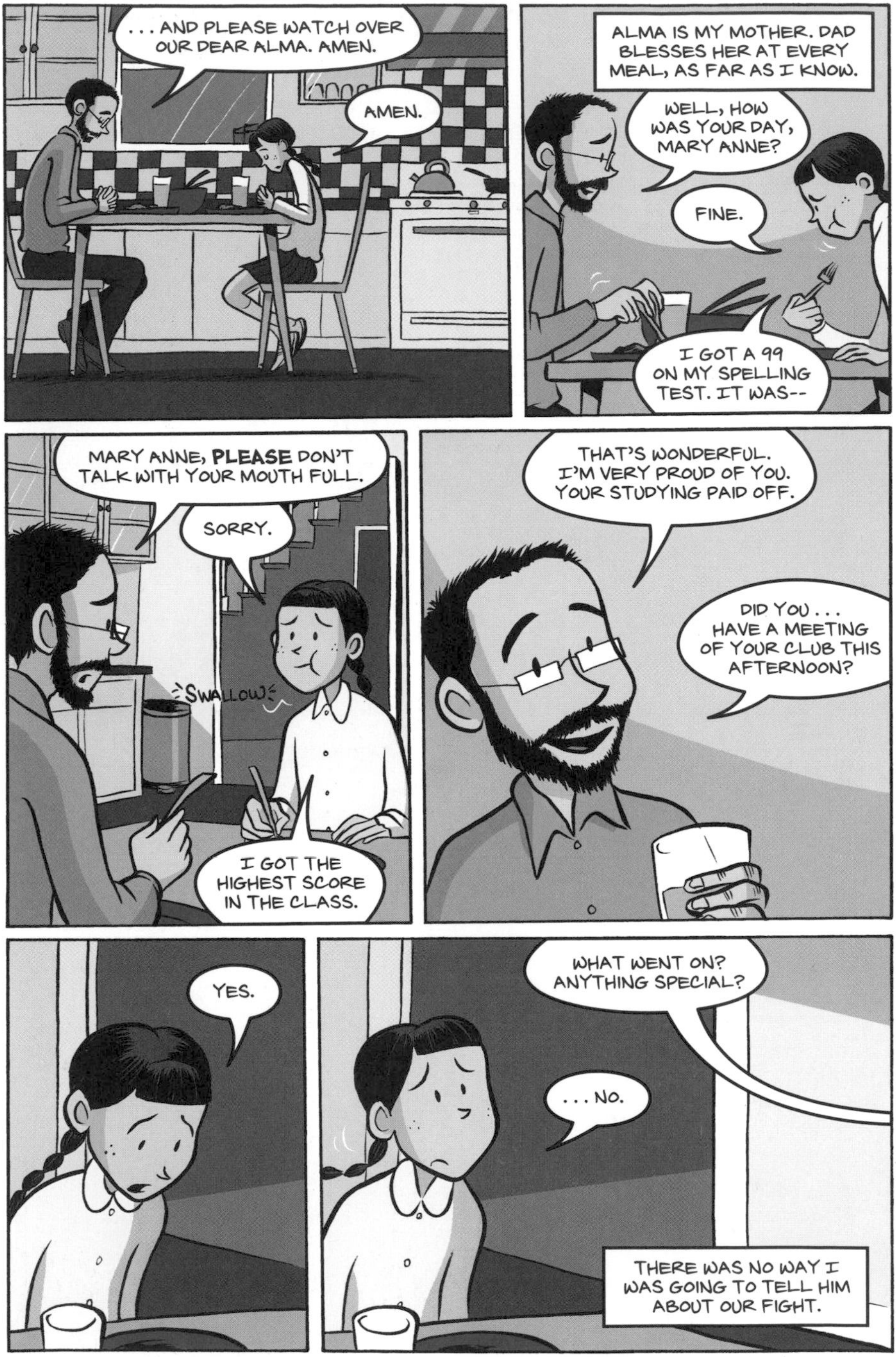
. . . AND PLEASE WATCH OVER OUR DEAR ALMA. AMEN.
AMEN.
ALMA IS MY MOTHER. DAD BLESSES HER AT EVERY MEAL, AS FAR AS I KNOW.
WELL, HOW WAS YOUR DAY, MARY ANNE?
FINE.
I GOT A 99 ON MY SPELLING TEST. IT WAS--
MARY ANNE, **PLEASE** DON'T TALK WITH YOUR MOUTH FULL.
SORRY.
SWALLOW
I GOT THE HIGHEST SCORE IN THE CLASS.
THAT'S WONDERFUL. I'M VERY PROUD OF YOU. YOUR STUDYING PAID OFF.
DID YOU . . . HAVE A MEETING OF YOUR CLUB THIS AFTERNOON?
YES.
WHAT WENT ON? ANYTHING SPECIAL?
. . . NO.
THERE WAS NO WAY I WAS GOING TO TELL HIM ABOUT OUR FIGHT.

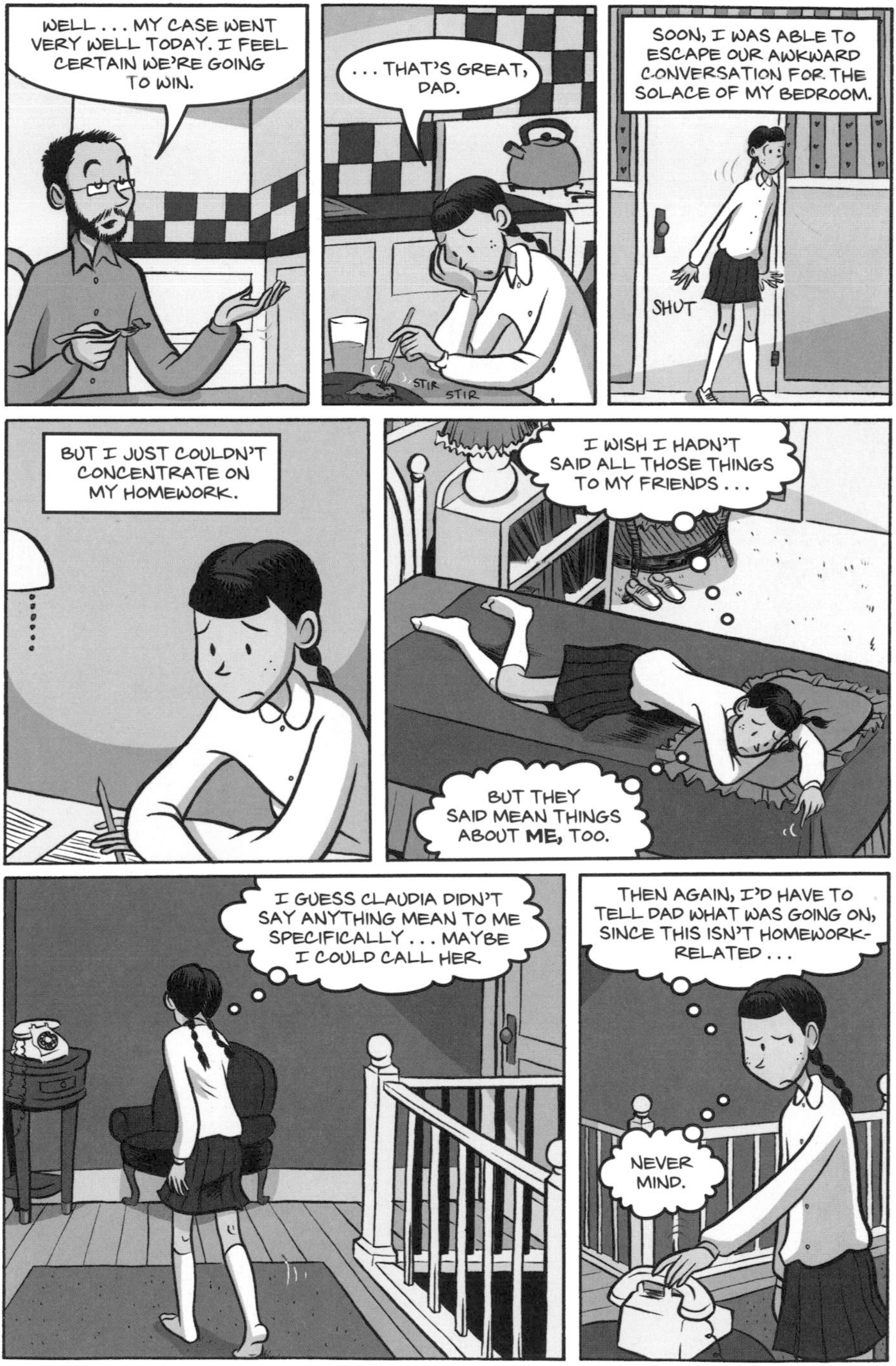
WELL . . . MY CASE WENT VERY WELL TODAY. I FEEL CERTAIN WE'RE GOING TO WIN.
. . . THAT'S GREAT, DAD.
STIR
STIR
SOON, I WAS ABLE TO ESCAPE OUR AWKWARD CONVERSATION FOR THE SOLACE OF MY BEDROOM.
SHUT
BUT I JUST COULDN'T CONCENTRATE ON MY HOMEWORK.
I WISH I HADN'T SAID ALL THOSE THINGS TO MY FRIENDS . . .
BUT THEY SAID MEAN THINGS ABOUT **ME,** TOO.
I GUESS CLAUDIA DIDN'T SAY ANYTHING MEAN TO ME SPECIFICALLY . . . MAYBE I COULD CALL HER.
THEN AGAIN, I'D HAVE TO TELL DAD WHAT WAS GOING ON, SINCE THIS ISN'T HOMEWORK-RELATED . . .
NEVER MIND.

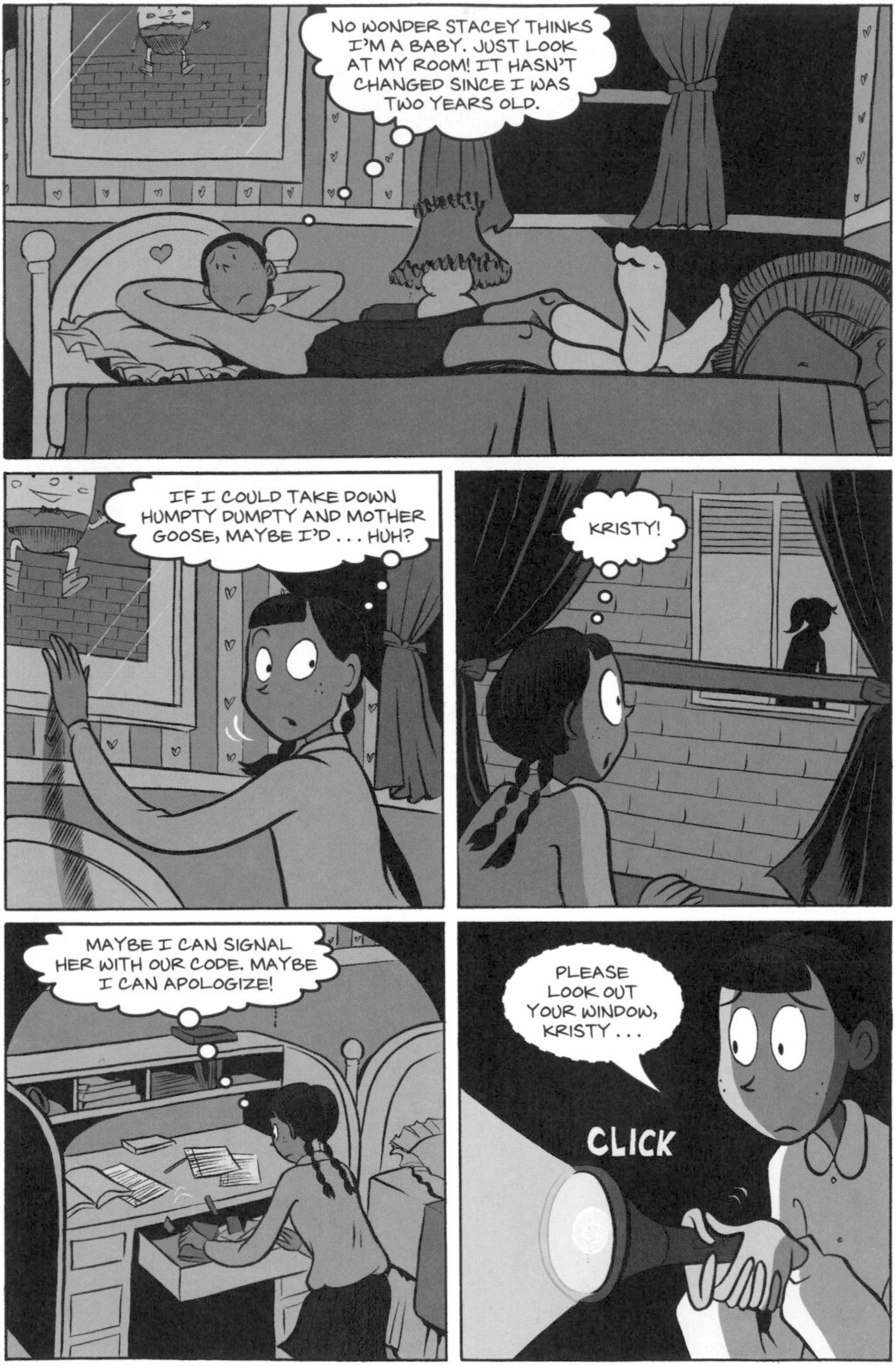
NO WONDER STACEY THINKS I'M A BABY. JUST LOOK AT MY ROOM! IT HASN'T CHANGED SINCE I WAS TWO YEARS OLD.
IF I COULD TAKE DOWN HUMPTY DUMPTY AND MOTHER GOOSE, MAYBE I'D . . . HUH?
KRISTY!
MAYBE I CAN SIGNAL HER WITH OUR CODE. MAYBE I CAN APOLOGIZE!
PLEASE LOOK OUT YOUR WINDOW, KRISTY . . .
CLICK

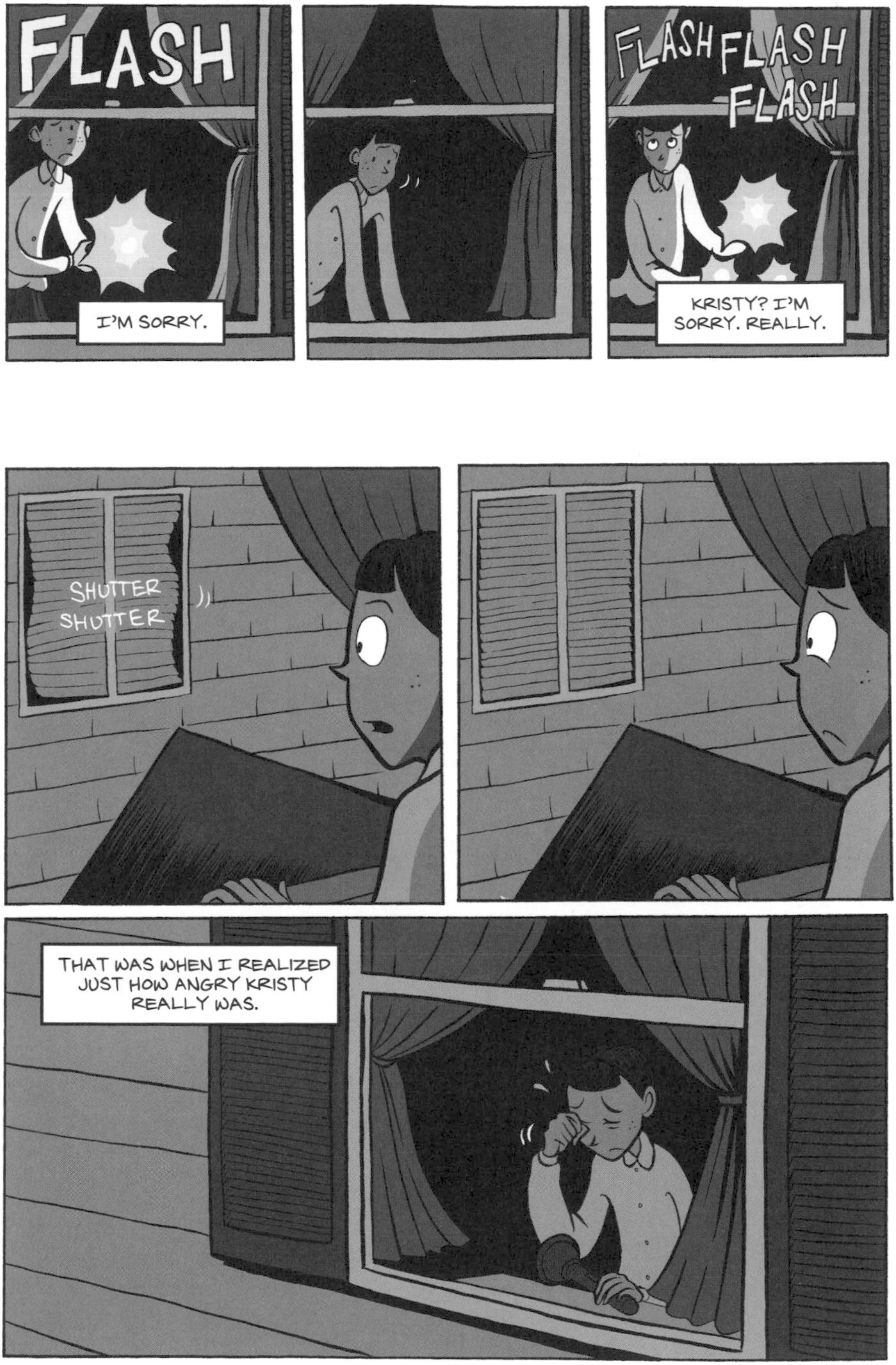
FLASH
I'M SORRY.
FLASH FLASH
FLASH
KRISTY? I'M SORRY. REALLY.
SHUTTER
SHUTTER
THAT WAS WHEN I REALIZED JUST HOW ANGRY KRISTY REALLY WAS.

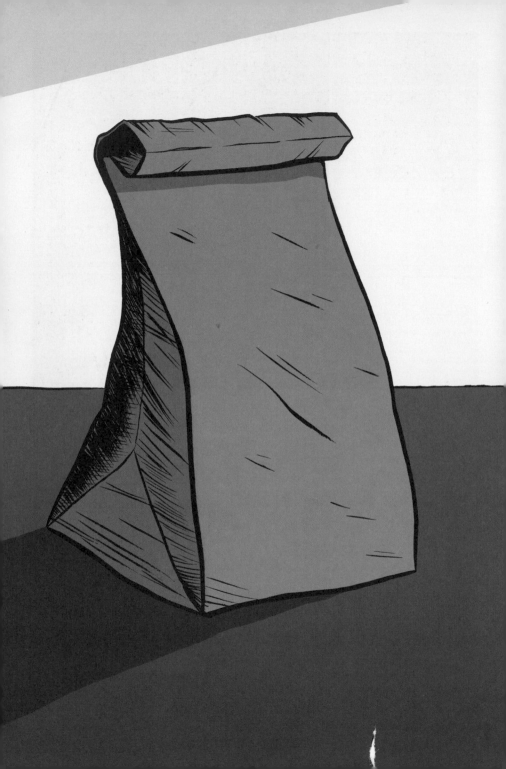

CHAPTER 3

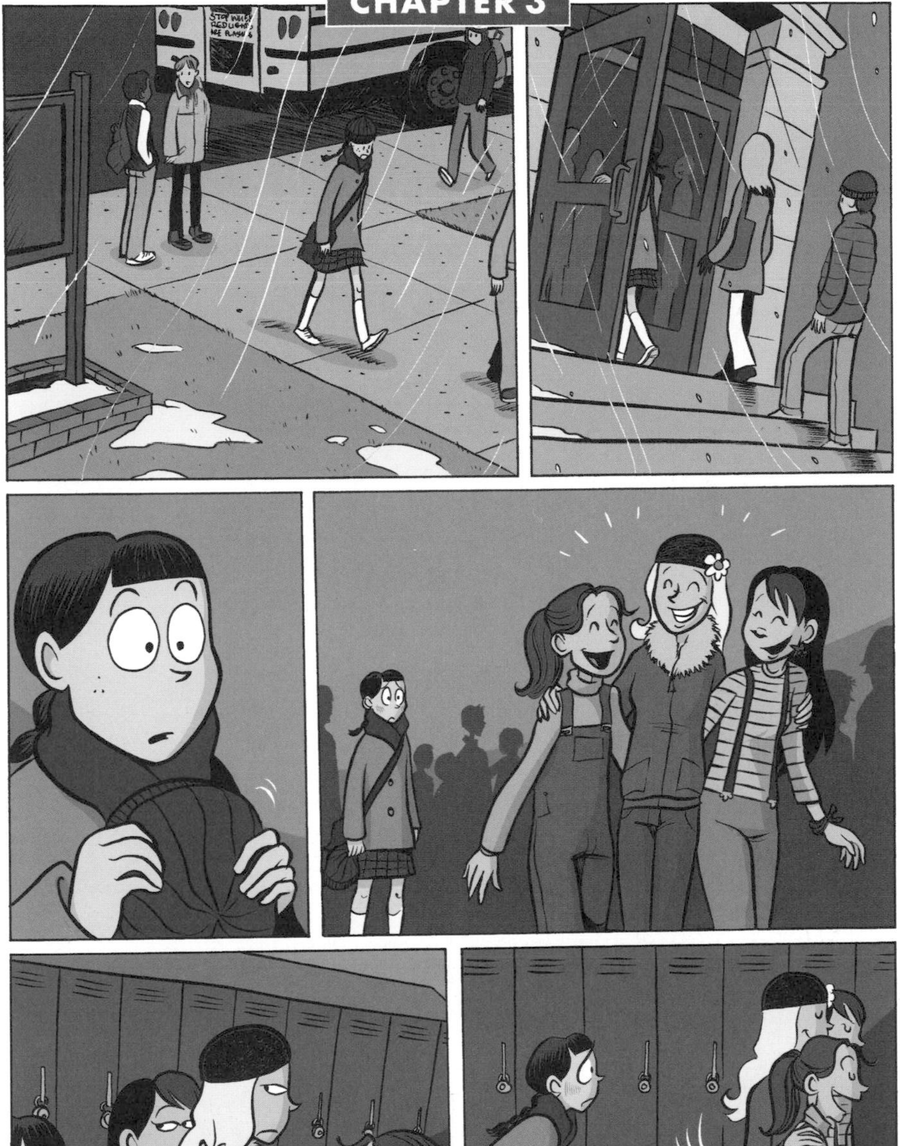

STOP WHEN
RED LIGHTS
ARE FLASHING

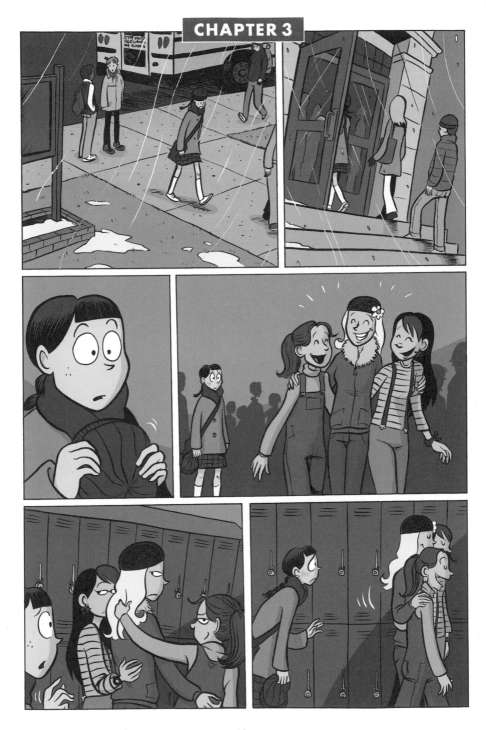

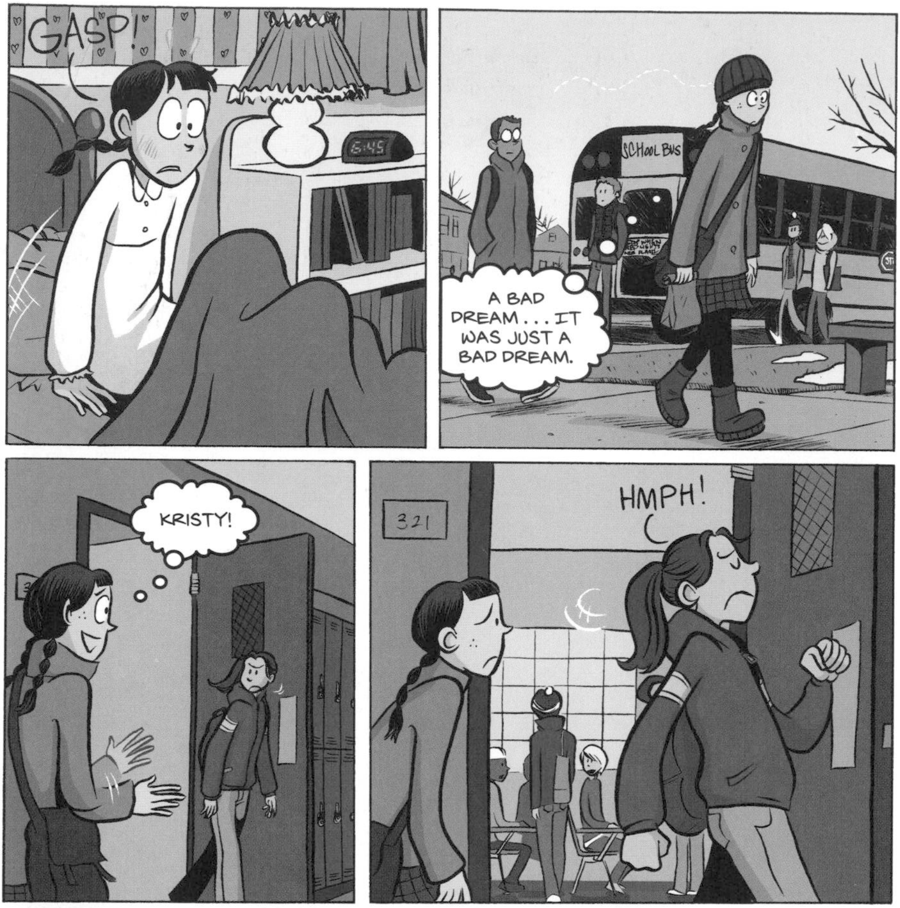
GASP!
6:45
SCHOOL BUS
A BAD DREAM . . . IT WAS JUST A BAD DREAM.
KRISTY!
321
HMPH!
HEY! KRISTY!
ARE YOU TALKING TO **ME?** OR SOME OTHER JOB-HOG?
NO, YOU'RE THE ONLY JOB-HOG I SEE AT THE MOMENT.

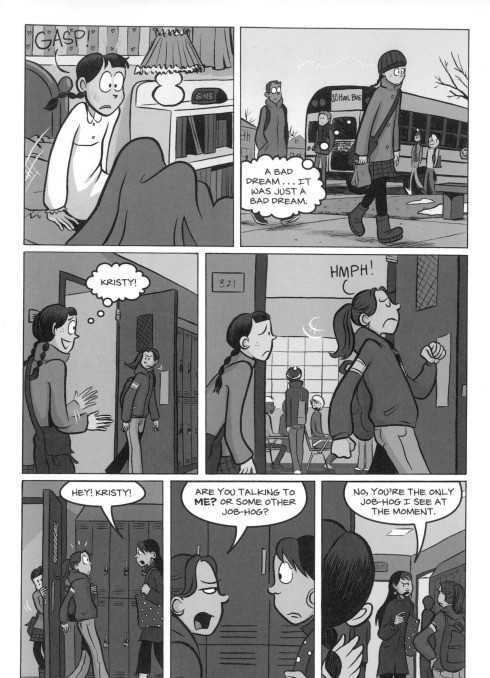

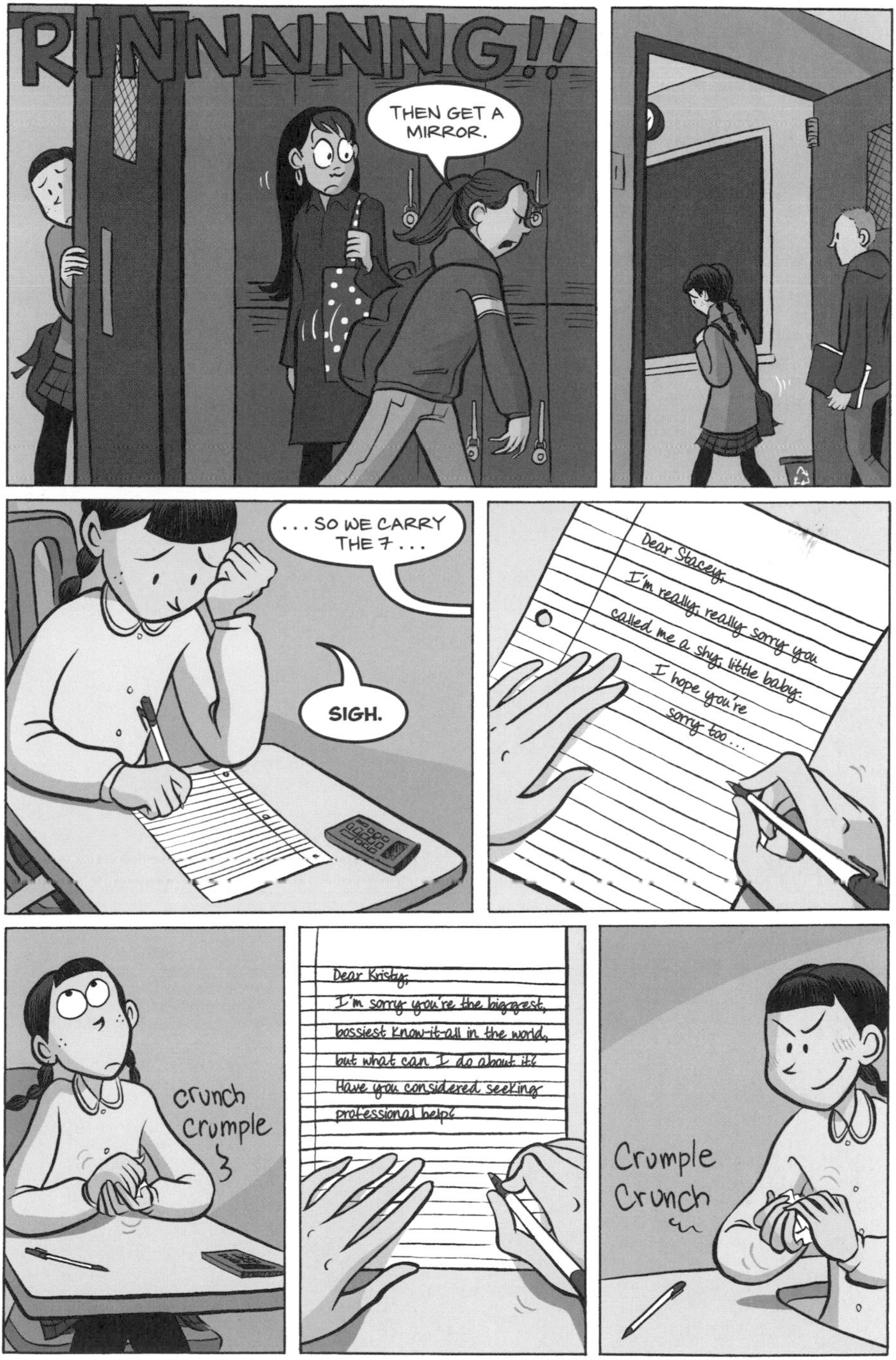
RINNNNNG!!
THEN GET A MIRROR.
. . . SO WE CARRY THE 7 . . .
SIGH.
Dear Stacey,
I'm really, really sorry you called me a shy, little baby.
I hope you're sorry too . . .
crunch crumple
Dear Kristy,
I'm sorry you're the biggest, bossiest know-it-all in the world, but what can I do about it? Have you considered seeking professional help?
Crumple Crunch

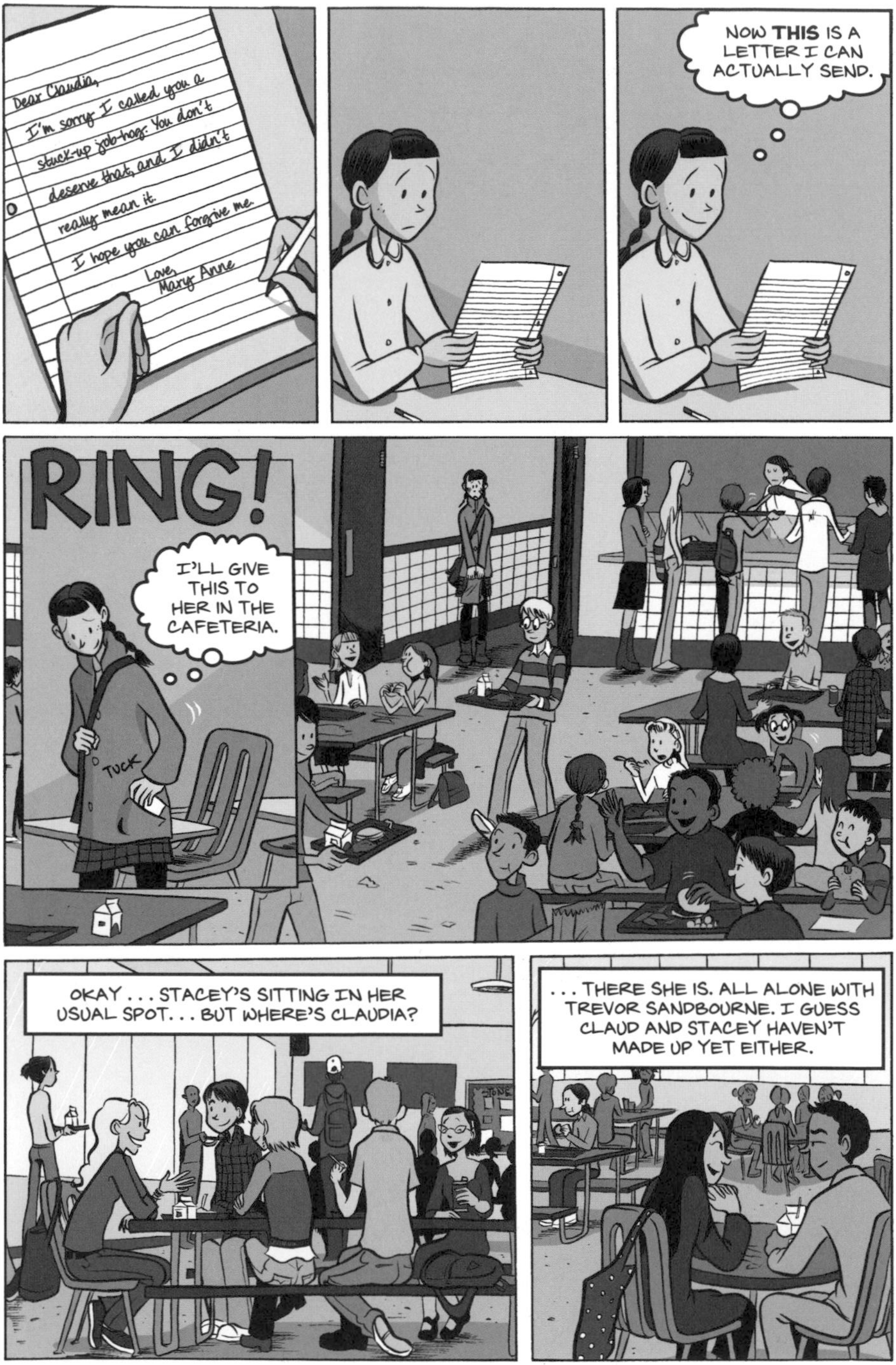
Dear Claudia,
I'm sorry I called you a stuck-up job-hog. You don't deserve that, and I didn't really mean it.
I hope you can forgive me.
Love,
Mary Anne
NOW THIS IS A LETTER I CAN ACTUALLY SEND.
RING!
I'LL GIVE THIS TO HER IN THE CAFETERIA.
TUCK
OKAY . . . STACEY'S SITTING IN HER USUAL SPOT. . . BUT WHERE'S CLAUDIA?
. . . THERE SHE IS. ALL ALONE WITH TREVOR SANDBOURNE. I GUESS CLAUD AND STACEY HAVEN'T MADE UP YET EITHER.

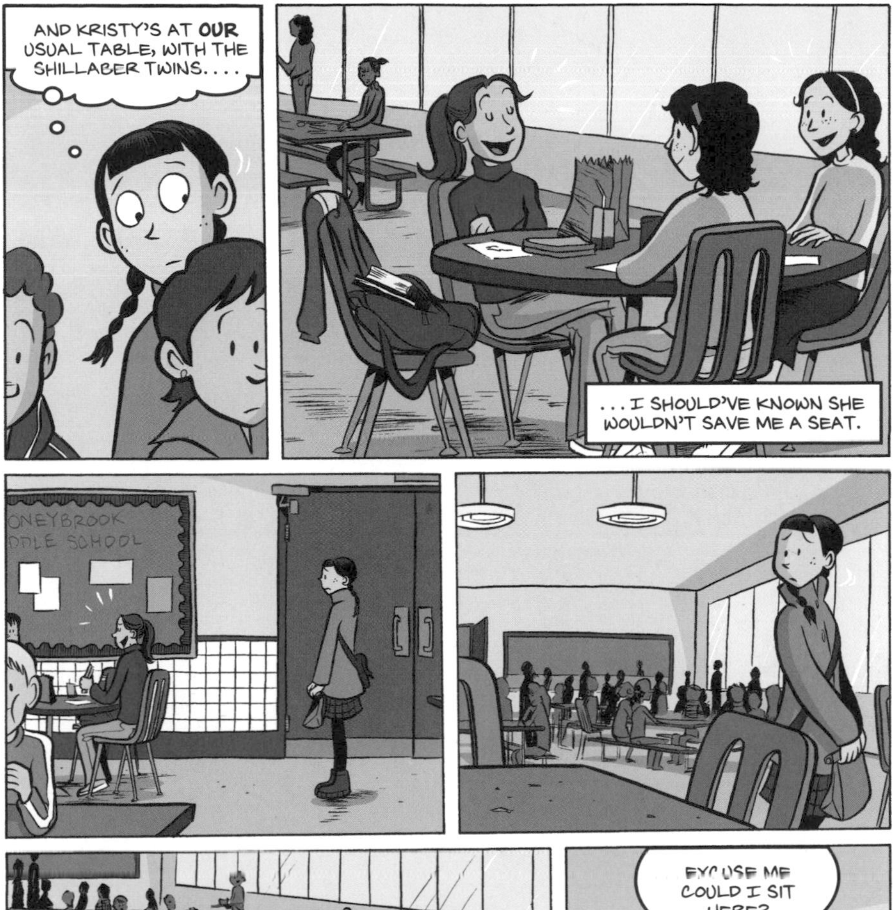
AND KRISTY'S AT **OUR** USUAL TABLE, WITH THE SHILLABER TWINS. . . .
. . . I SHOULD'VE KNOWN SHE WOULDN'T SAVE ME A SEAT.
ONEYBROOK
DDLE SCHOOL
EXCUSE ME
COULD I SIT HERE?

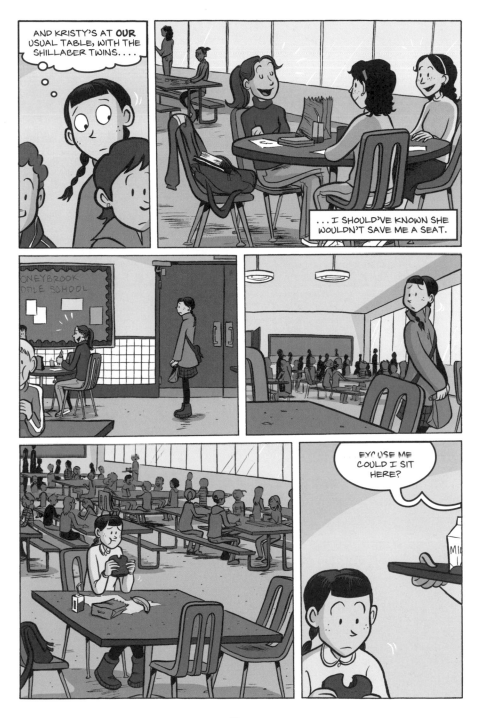

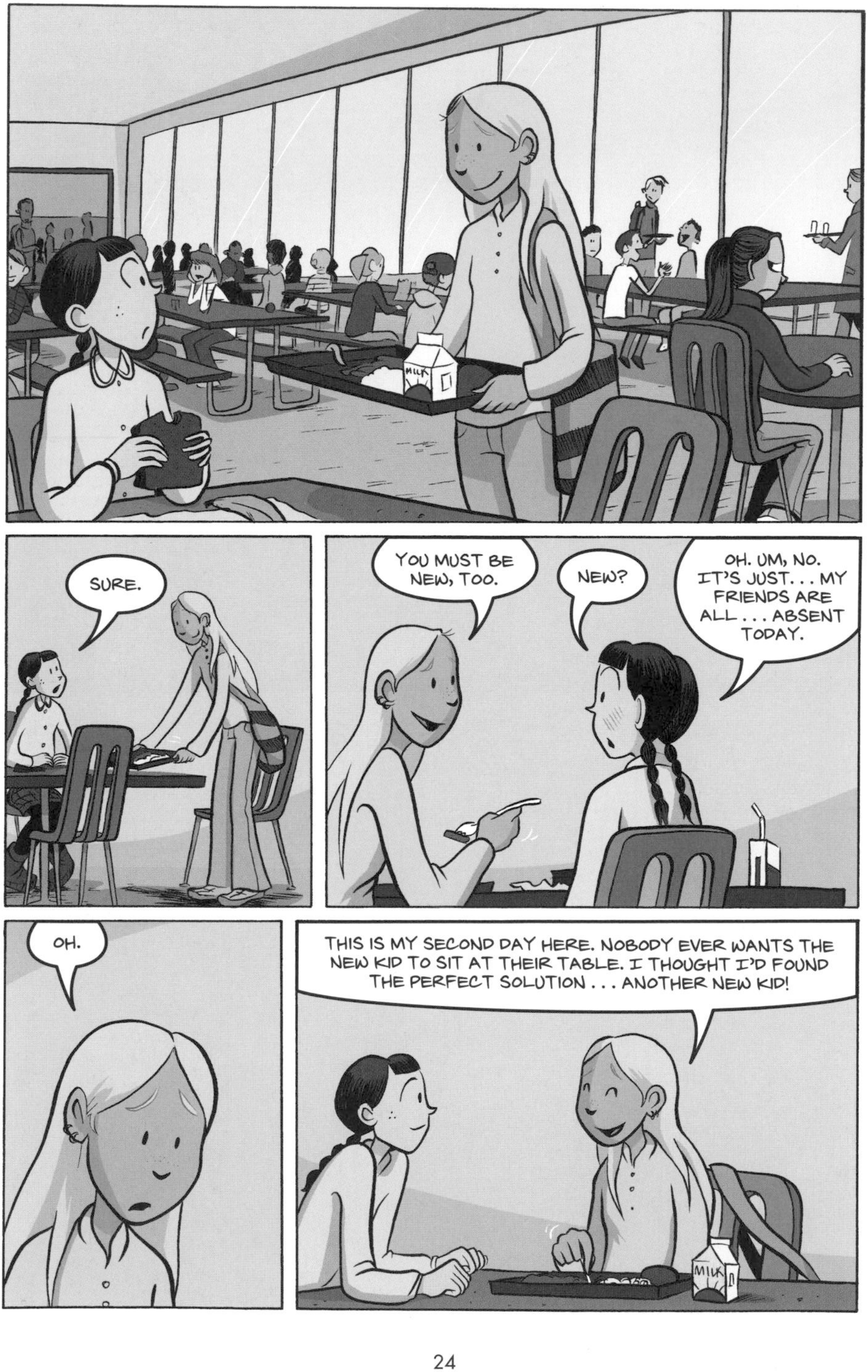
MILK
SURE.
YOU MUST BE NEW, TOO.
NEW?
OH. UM, NO. IT'S JUST. . . MY FRIENDS ARE ALL . . . ABSENT TODAY.
OH.
THIS IS MY SECOND DAY HERE. NOBODY EVER WANTS THE NEW KID TO SIT AT THEIR TABLE. I THOUGHT I'D FOUND THE PERFECT SOLUTION . . . ANOTHER NEW KID!
MILK

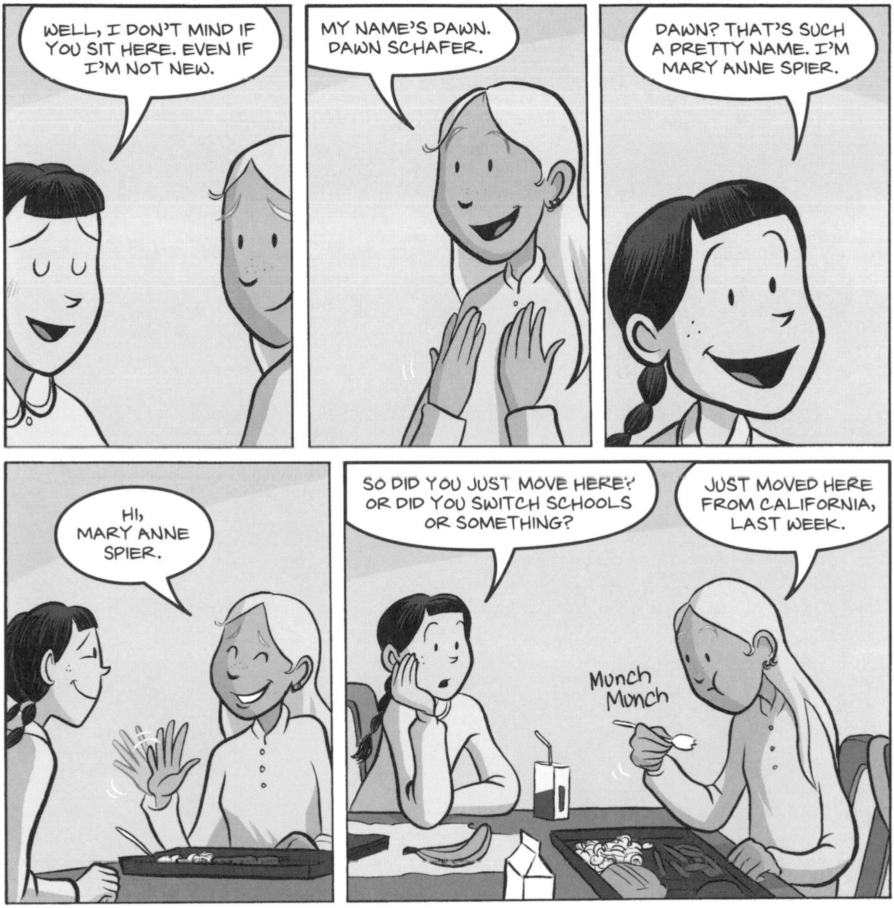
WELL, I DON'T MIND IF YOU SIT HERE. EVEN IF I'M NOT NEW.
MY NAME'S DAWN. DAWN SCHAFER.
DAWN? THAT'S SUCH A PRETTY NAME. I'M MARY ANNE SPIER.
HI, MARY ANNE SPIER.
SO DID YOU JUST MOVE HERE? OR DID YOU SWITCH SCHOOLS OR SOMETHING?
JUST MOVED HERE FROM CALIFORNIA, LAST WEEK.
Munch Munch
OUR HOUSE IS STILL A MESS -- PACKING CARTONS EVERYWHERE. YESTERDAY, IT TOOK ME 20 MINUTES TO FIND MY BROTHER FOR DINNER.
Hee Hee!

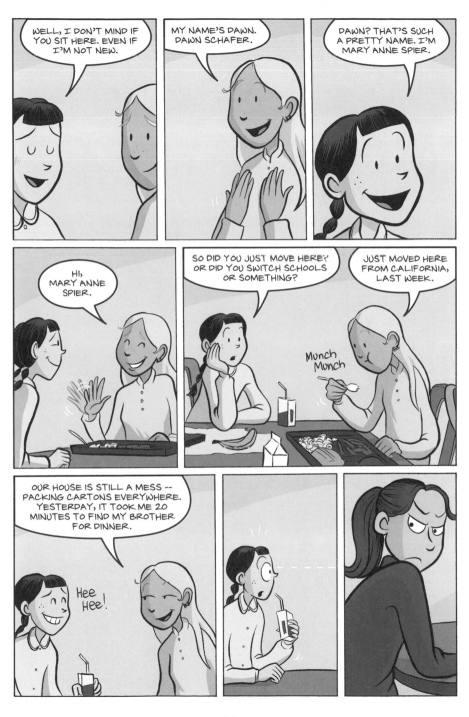

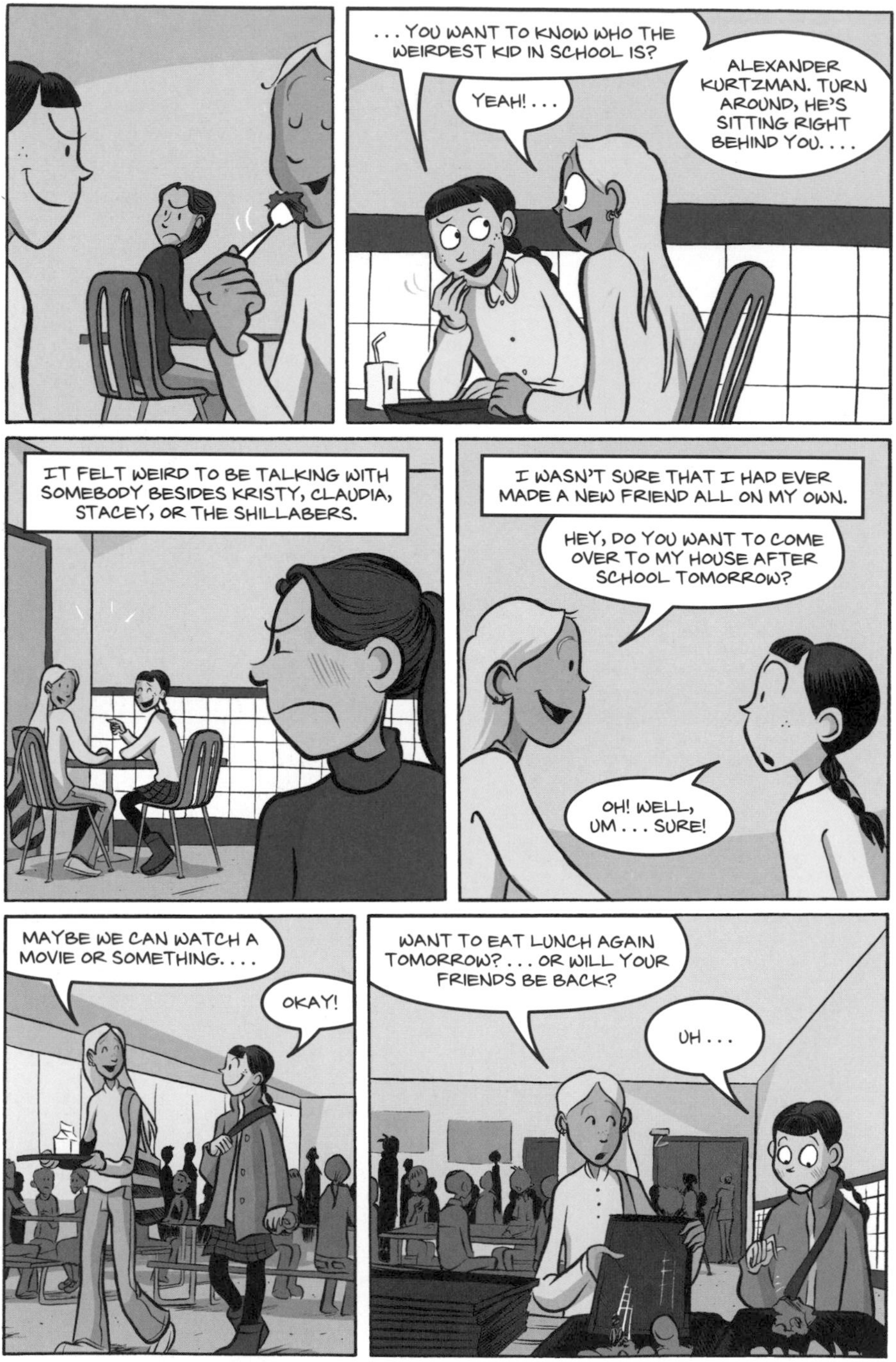
. . . YOU WANT TO KNOW WHO THE WEIRDEST KID IN SCHOOL IS?
YEAH! . . .
ALEXANDER KURTZMAN. TURN AROUND, HE'S SITTING RIGHT BEHIND YOU. . . .
IT FELT WEIRD TO BE TALKING WITH SOMEBODY BESIDES KRISTY, CLAUDIA, STACEY, OR THE SHILLABERS.
I WASN'T SURE THAT I HAD EVER MADE A NEW FRIEND ALL ON MY OWN.
HEY, DO YOU WANT TO COME OVER TO MY HOUSE AFTER SCHOOL TOMORROW?
OH! WELL, UM . . . SURE!
MAYBE WE CAN WATCH A MOVIE OR SOMETHING. . . .
OKAY!
WANT TO EAT LUNCH AGAIN TOMORROW? . . . OR WILL YOUR FRIENDS BE BACK?
UH . . .

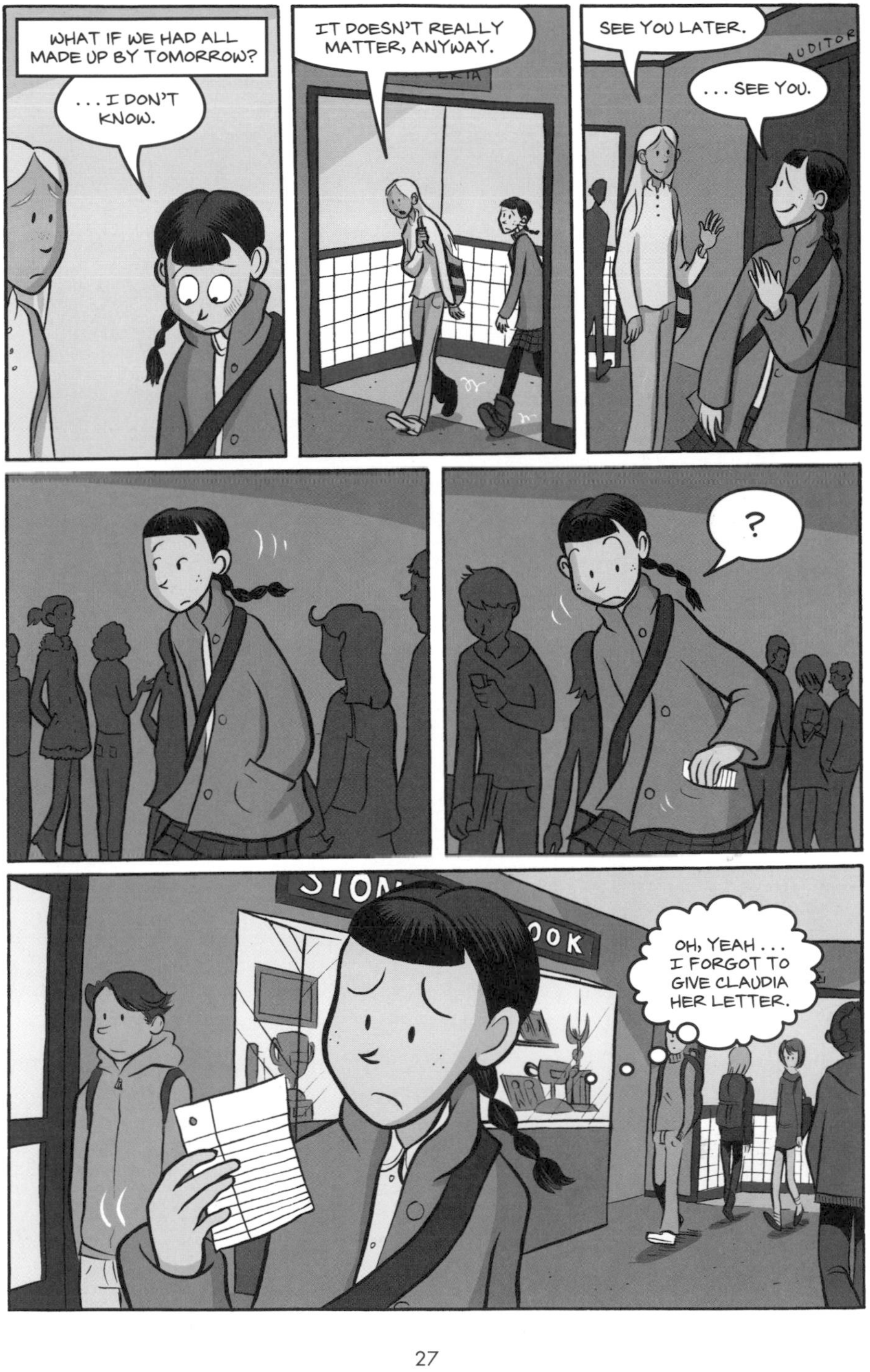
WHAT IF WE HAD ALL MADE UP BY TOMORROW?
. . . I DON'T KNOW.
IT DOESN'T REALLY MATTER, ANYWAY.
SEE YOU LATER.
. . . SEE YOU.
AUDITOR
?
OH, YEAH . . . I FORGOT TO GIVE CLAUDIA HER LETTER.

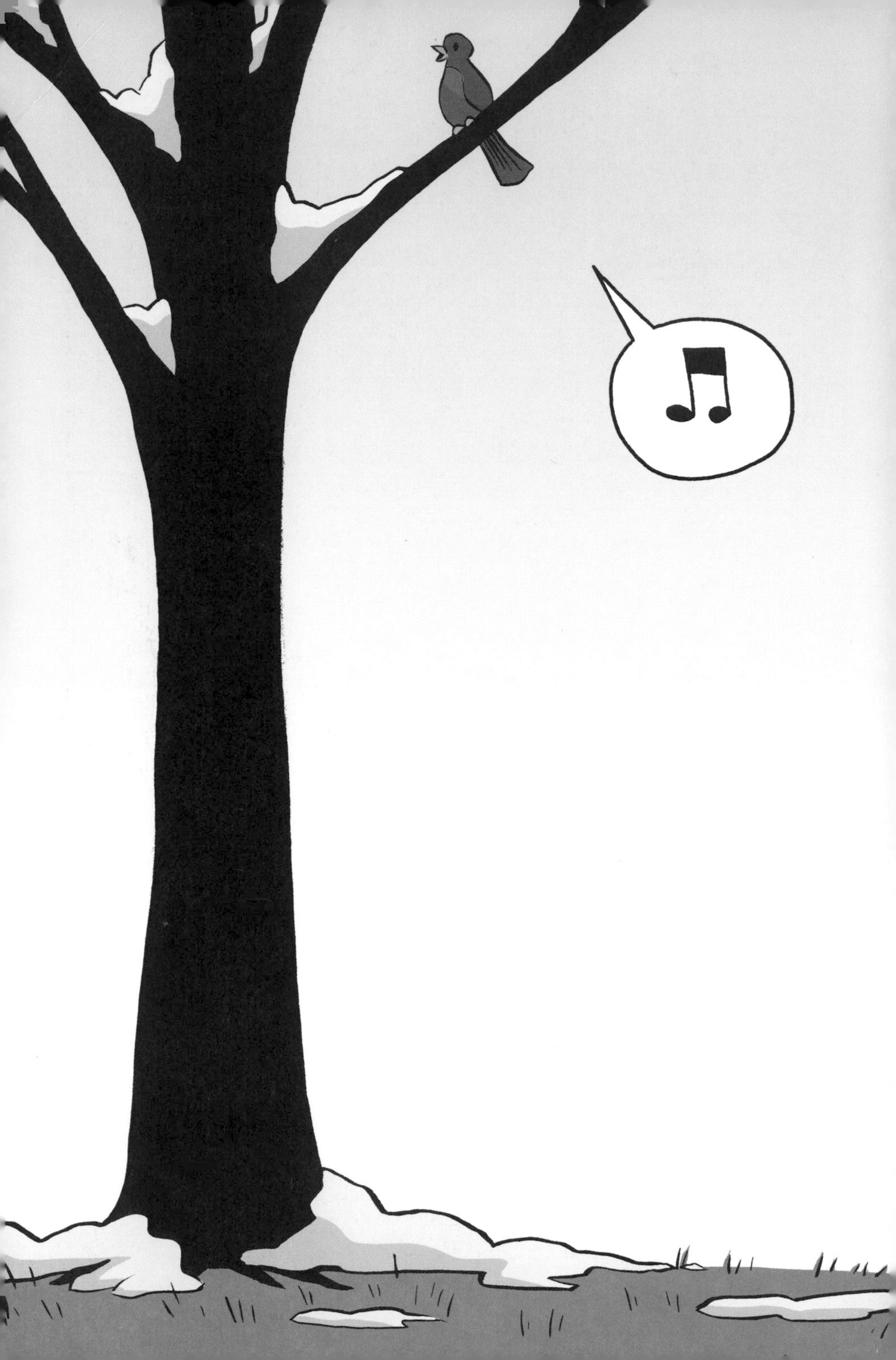

CHAPTER 4

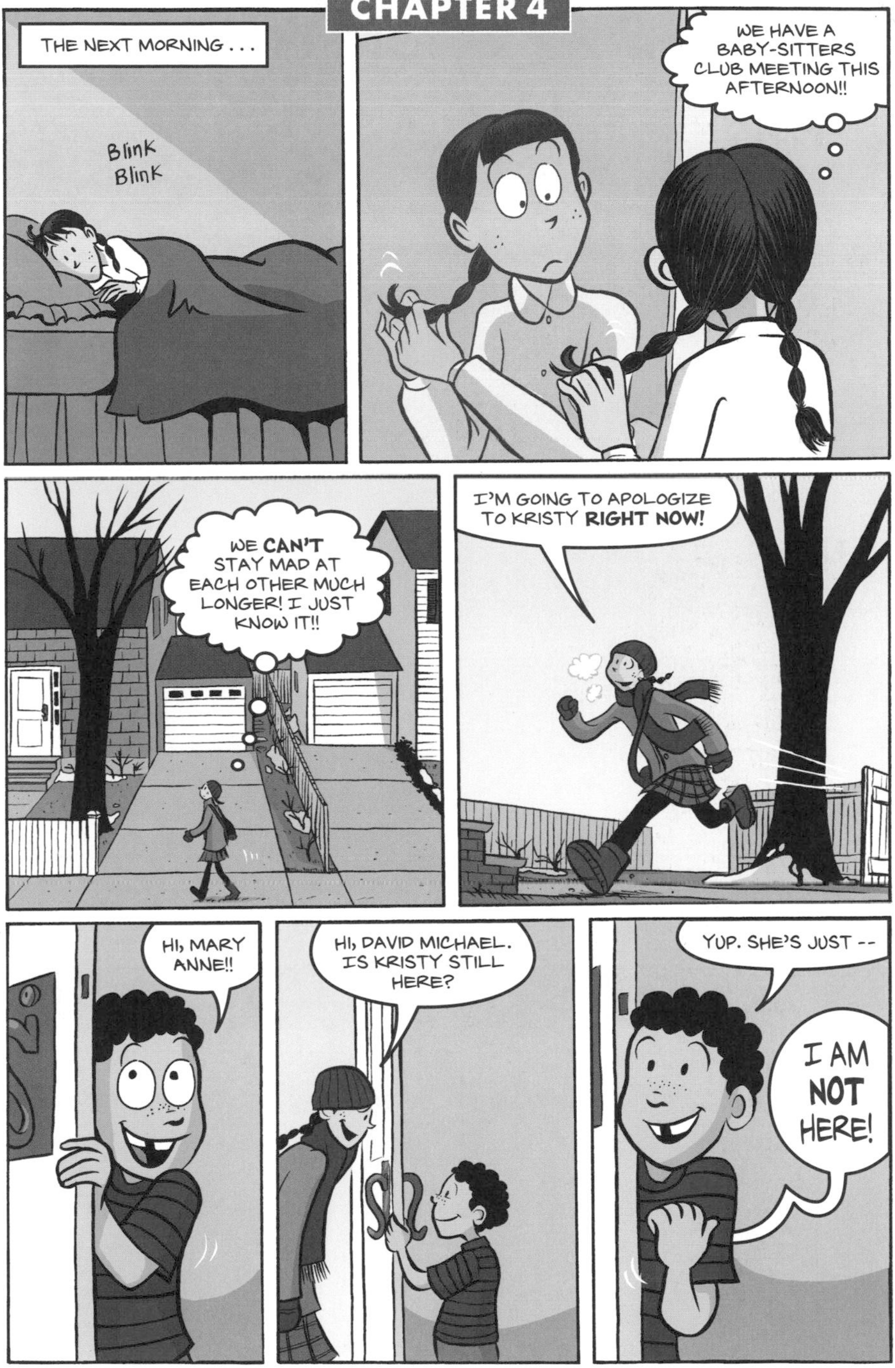
THE NEXT MORNING . . .
Blink
Blink
WE HAVE A BABY-SITTERS CLUB MEETING THIS AFTERNOON!!
WE CAN'T STAY MAD AT EACH OTHER MUCH LONGER! I JUST KNOW IT!!
I'M GOING TO APOLOGIZE TO KRISTY RIGHT NOW!
HI, MARY ANNE!!
HI, DAVID MICHAEL. IS KRISTY STILL HERE?
YUP. SHE'S JUST --
I AM NOT HERE!

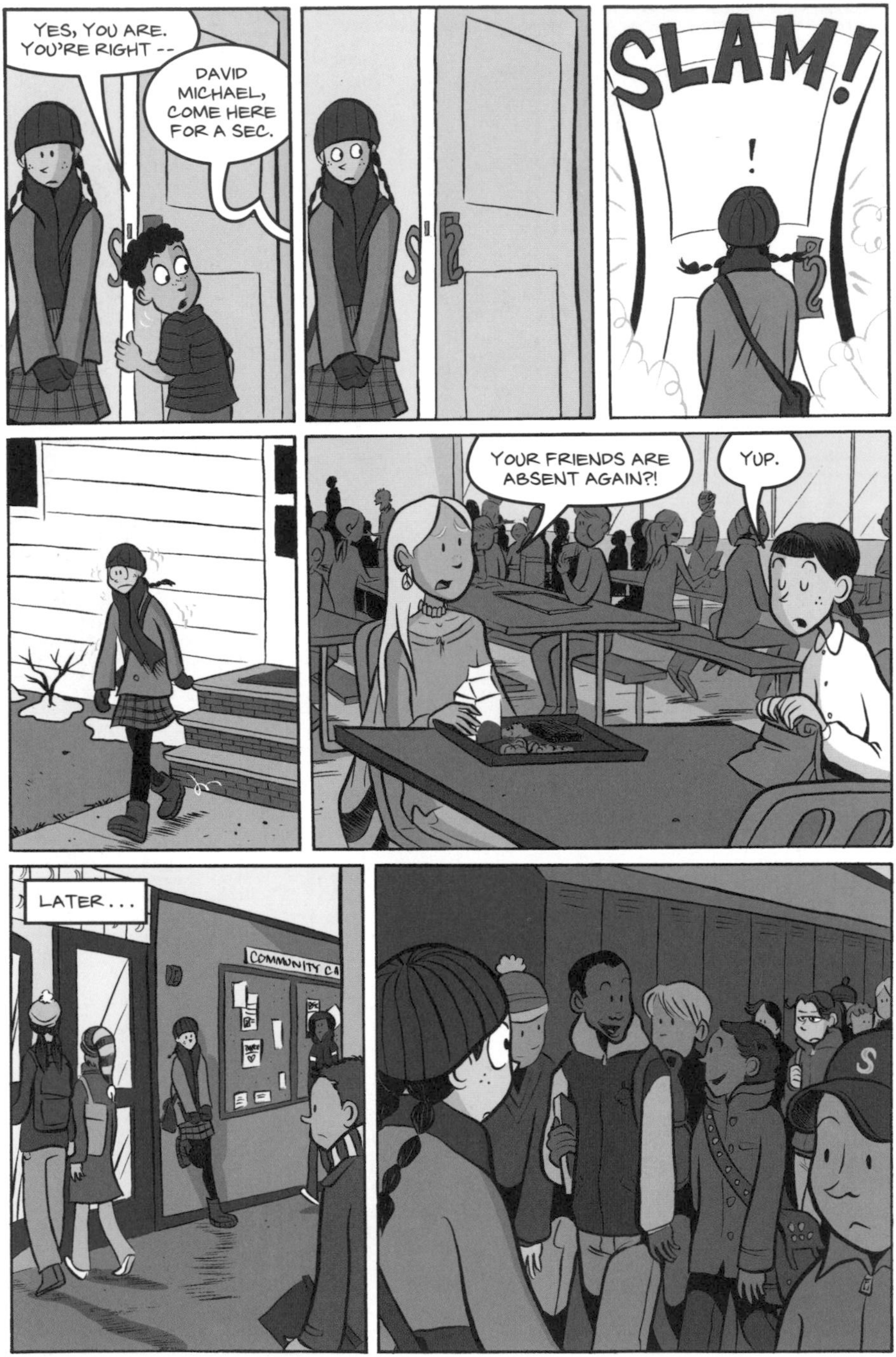
YES, YOU ARE. YOU'RE RIGHT --
DAVID MICHAEL, COME HERE FOR A SEC.
SLAM!
!
YOUR FRIENDS ARE ABSENT AGAIN?!
YUP.
LATER...
COMMUNITY CA

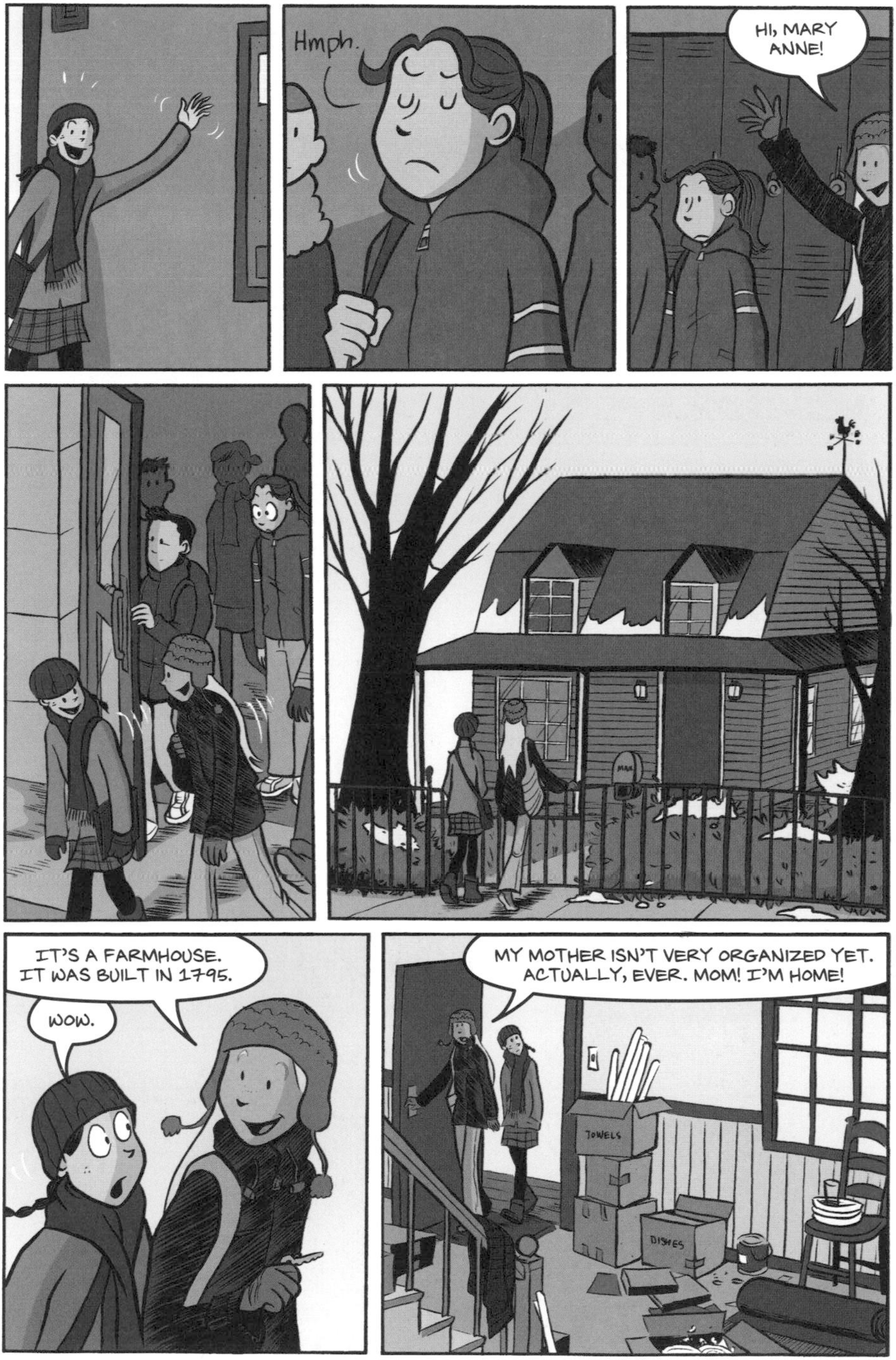
Hmph.
HI, MARY ANNE!
IT'S A FARMHOUSE. IT WAS BUILT IN 1795.
WOW.
MY MOTHER ISN'T VERY ORGANIZED YET. ACTUALLY, EVER. MOM! I'M HOME!
TOWELS
DISHES

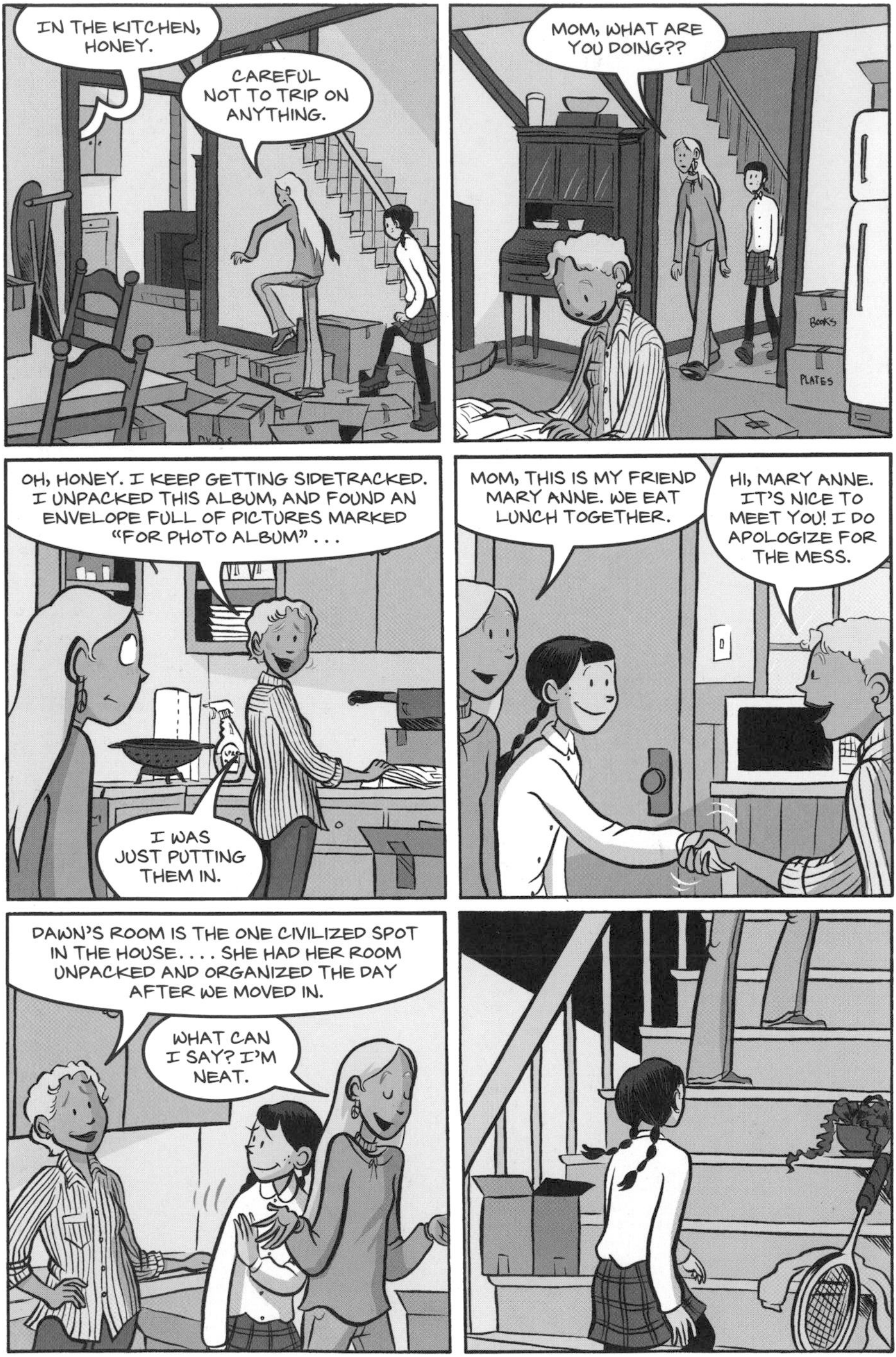
IN THE KITCHEN, HONEY.
CAREFUL NOT TO TRIP ON ANYTHING.
MOM, WHAT ARE YOU DOING??
BOOKS
PLATES
OH, HONEY. I KEEP GETTING SIDETRACKED. I UNPACKED THIS ALBUM, AND FOUND AN ENVELOPE FULL OF PICTURES MARKED "FOR PHOTO ALBUM" . . .
I WAS JUST PUTTING THEM IN.
MOM, THIS IS MY FRIEND MARY ANNE. WE EAT LUNCH TOGETHER.
HI, MARY ANNE. IT'S NICE TO MEET YOU! I DO APOLOGIZE FOR THE MESS.
DAWN'S ROOM IS THE ONE CIVILIZED SPOT IN THE HOUSE. . . . SHE HAD HER ROOM UNPACKED AND ORGANIZED THE DAY AFTER WE MOVED IN.
WHAT CAN I SAY? I'M NEAT.

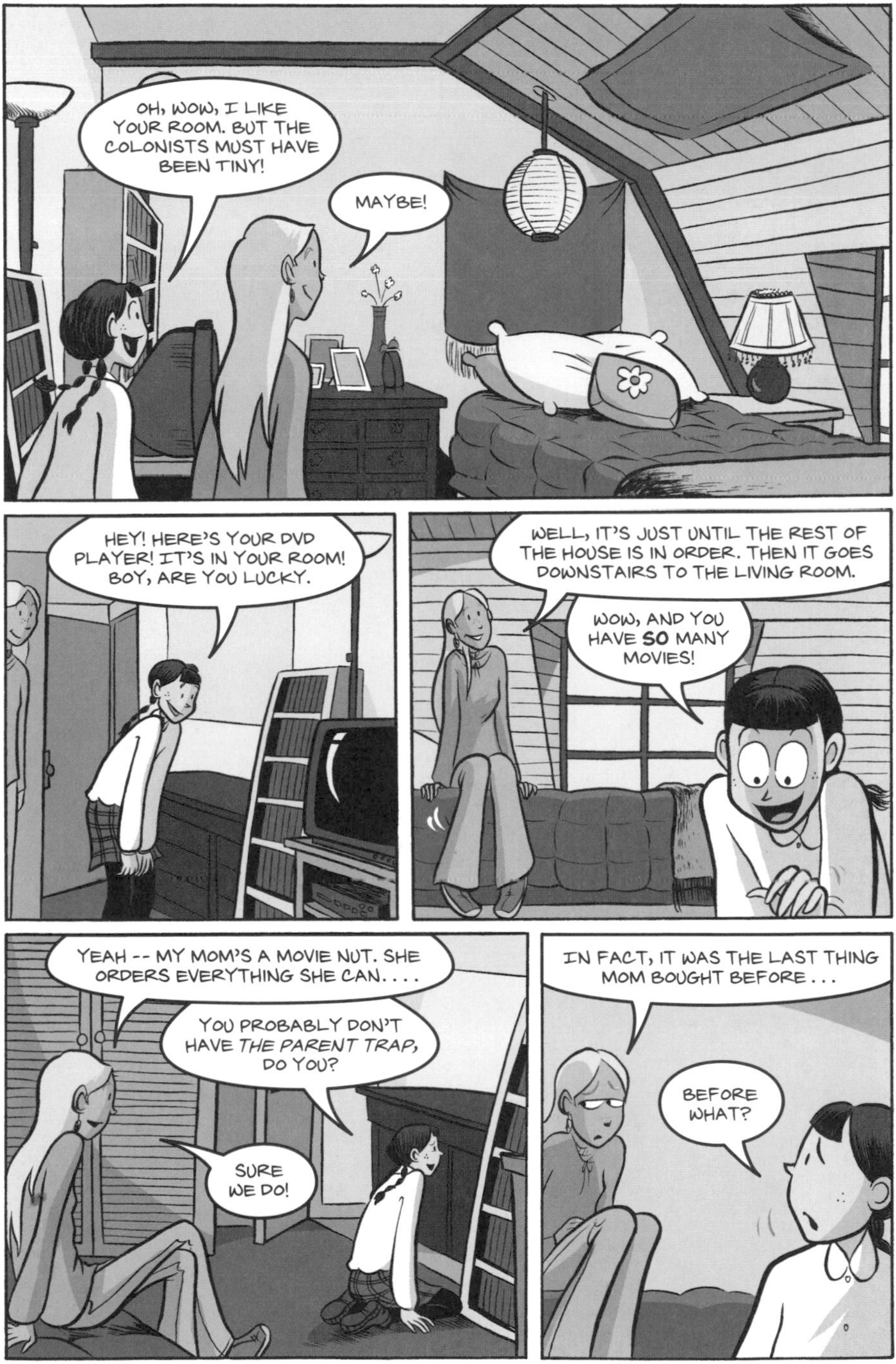
OH, WOW, I LIKE YOUR ROOM. BUT THE COLONISTS MUST HAVE BEEN TINY!
MAYBE!
HEY! HERE'S YOUR DVD PLAYER! IT'S IN YOUR ROOM! BOY, ARE YOU LUCKY.
WELL, IT'S JUST UNTIL THE REST OF THE HOUSE IS IN ORDER. THEN IT GOES DOWNSTAIRS TO THE LIVING ROOM.
WOW, AND YOU HAVE **SO** MANY MOVIES!
YEAH -- MY MOM'S A MOVIE NUT. SHE ORDERS EVERYTHING SHE CAN. . . .
YOU PROBABLY DON'T HAVE *THE PARENT TRAP*, DO YOU?
SURE WE DO!
IN FACT, IT WAS THE LAST THING MOM BOUGHT BEFORE . . .
BEFORE WHAT?

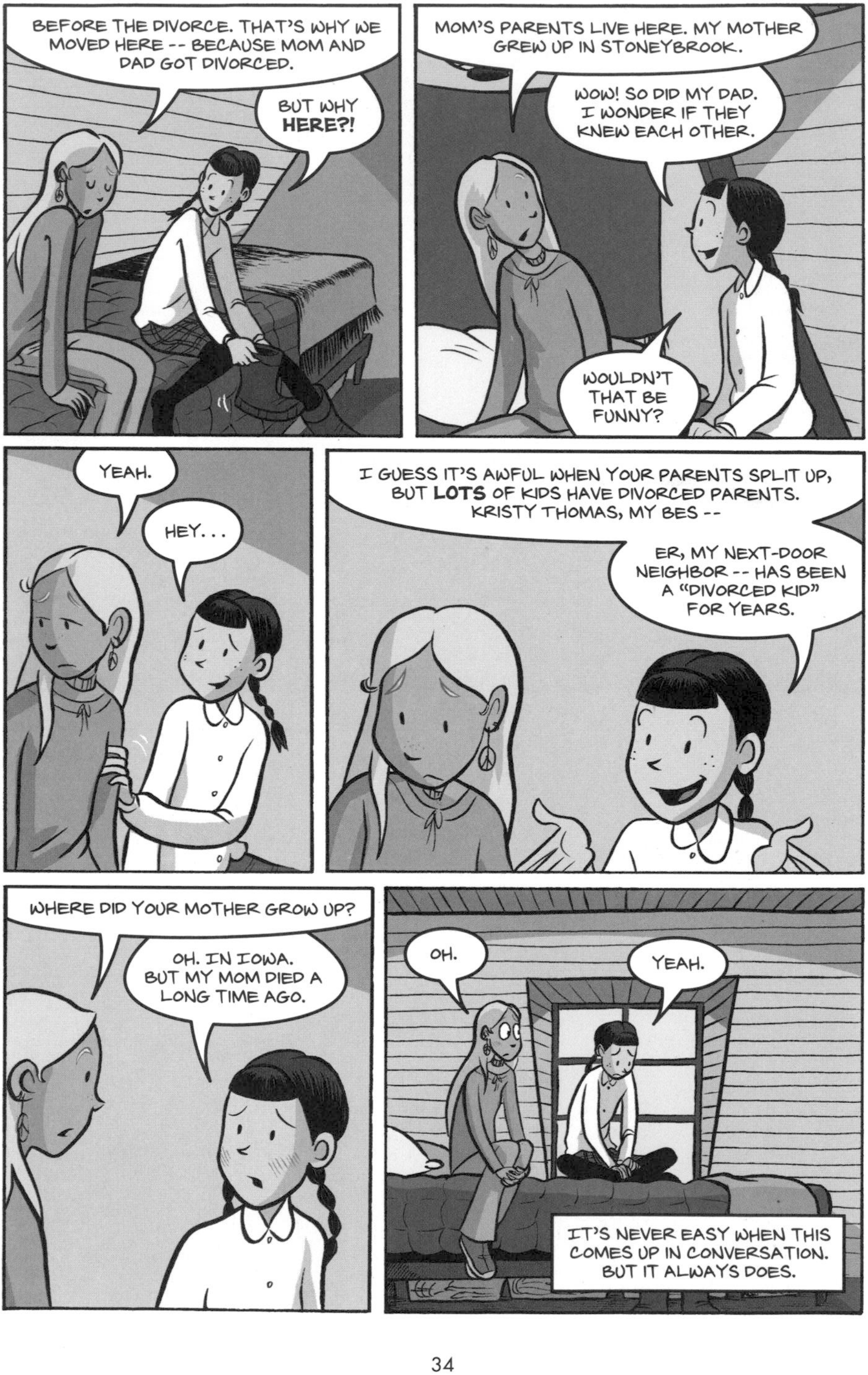
BEFORE THE DIVORCE. THAT'S WHY WE MOVED HERE -- BECAUSE MOM AND DAD GOT DIVORCED.
BUT WHY **HERE?!**
MOM'S PARENTS LIVE HERE. MY MOTHER GREW UP IN STONEYBROOK.
WOW! SO DID MY DAD. I WONDER IF THEY KNEW EACH OTHER.
WOULDN'T THAT BE FUNNY?
YEAH.
HEY. . .
I GUESS IT'S AWFUL WHEN YOUR PARENTS SPLIT UP, BUT **LOTS** OF KIDS HAVE DIVORCED PARENTS. KRISTY THOMAS, MY BES --
ER, MY NEXT-DOOR NEIGHBOR -- HAS BEEN A "DIVORCED KID" FOR YEARS.
WHERE DID YOUR MOTHER GROW UP?
OH. IN IOWA. BUT MY MOM DIED A LONG TIME AGO.
OH.
YEAH.
IT'S NEVER EASY WHEN THIS COMES UP IN CONVERSATION. BUT IT ALWAYS DOES.

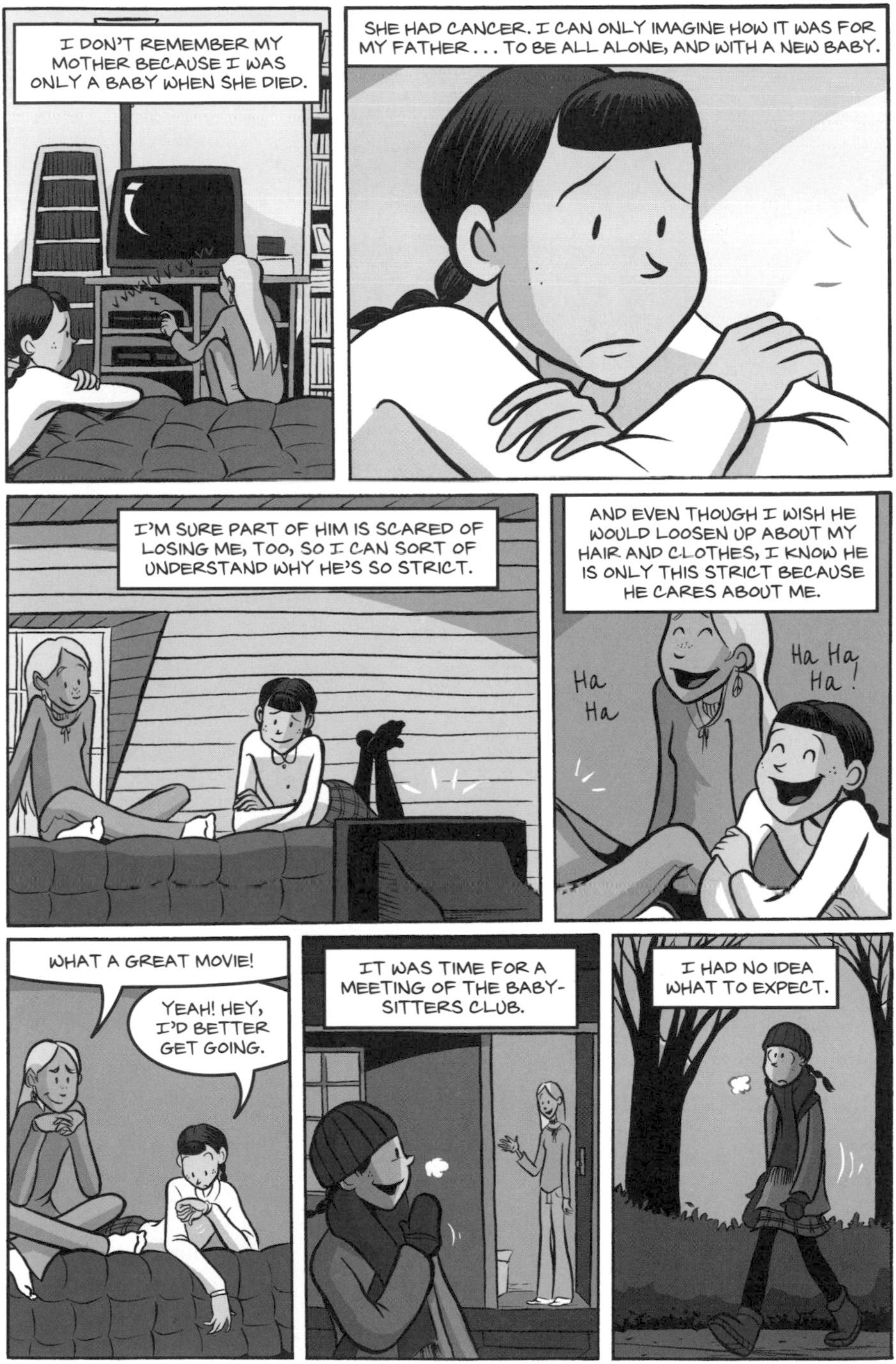
I DON'T REMEMBER MY MOTHER BECAUSE I WAS ONLY A BABY WHEN SHE DIED.
SHE HAD CANCER. I CAN ONLY IMAGINE HOW IT WAS FOR MY FATHER . . . TO BE ALL ALONE, AND WITH A NEW BABY.
I'M SURE PART OF HIM IS SCARED OF LOSING ME, TOO, SO I CAN SORT OF UNDERSTAND WHY HE'S SO STRICT.
AND EVEN THOUGH I WISH HE WOULD LOOSEN UP ABOUT MY HAIR AND CLOTHES, I KNOW HE IS ONLY THIS STRICT BECAUSE HE CARES ABOUT ME.
Ha Ha
Ha Ha Ha!
WHAT A GREAT MOVIE!
YEAH! HEY, I'D BETTER GET GOING.
IT WAS TIME FOR A MEETING OF THE BABY-SITTERS CLUB.
I HAD NO IDEA WHAT TO EXPECT.

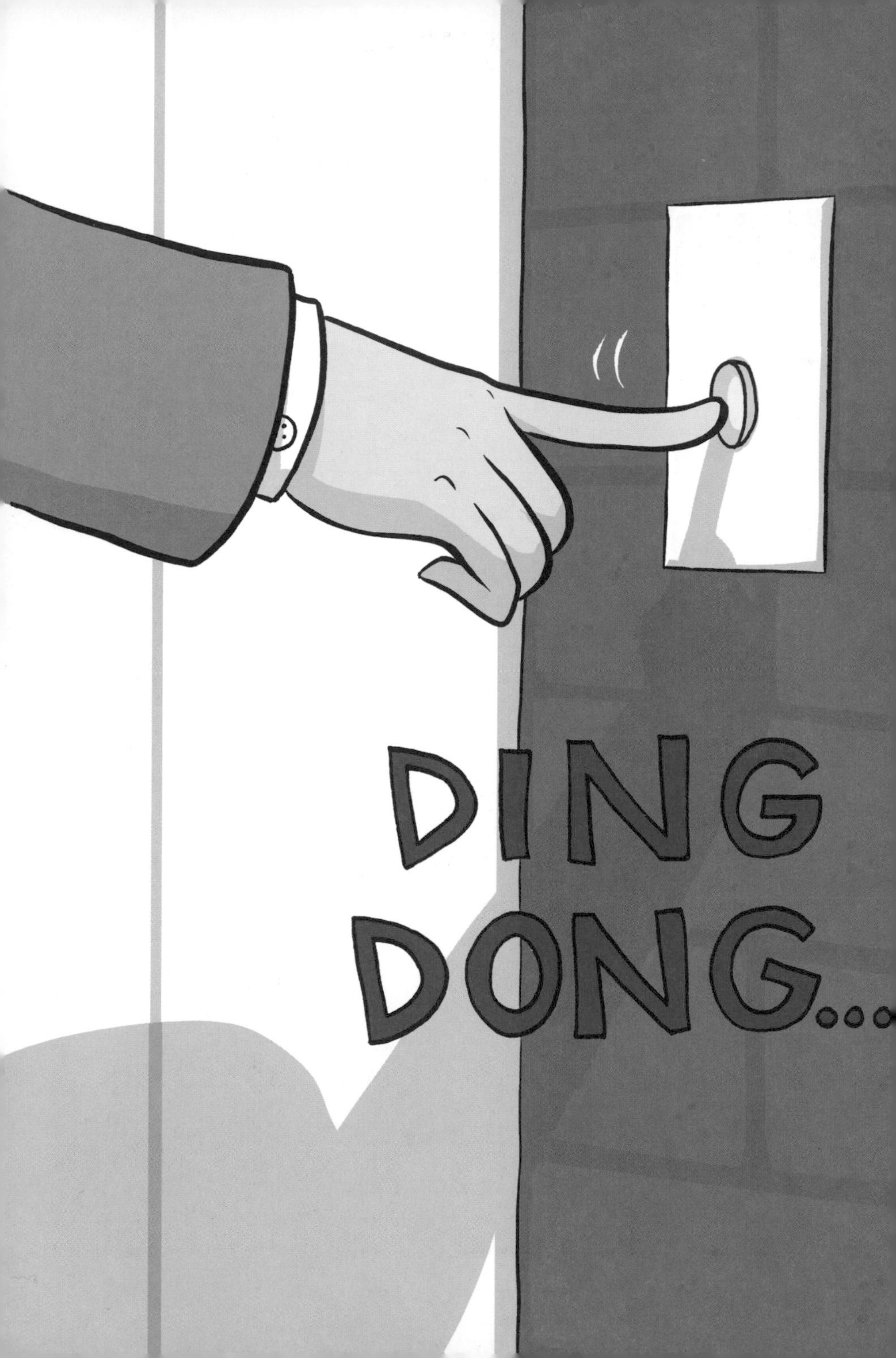
DING
DONG...

CHAPTER 5

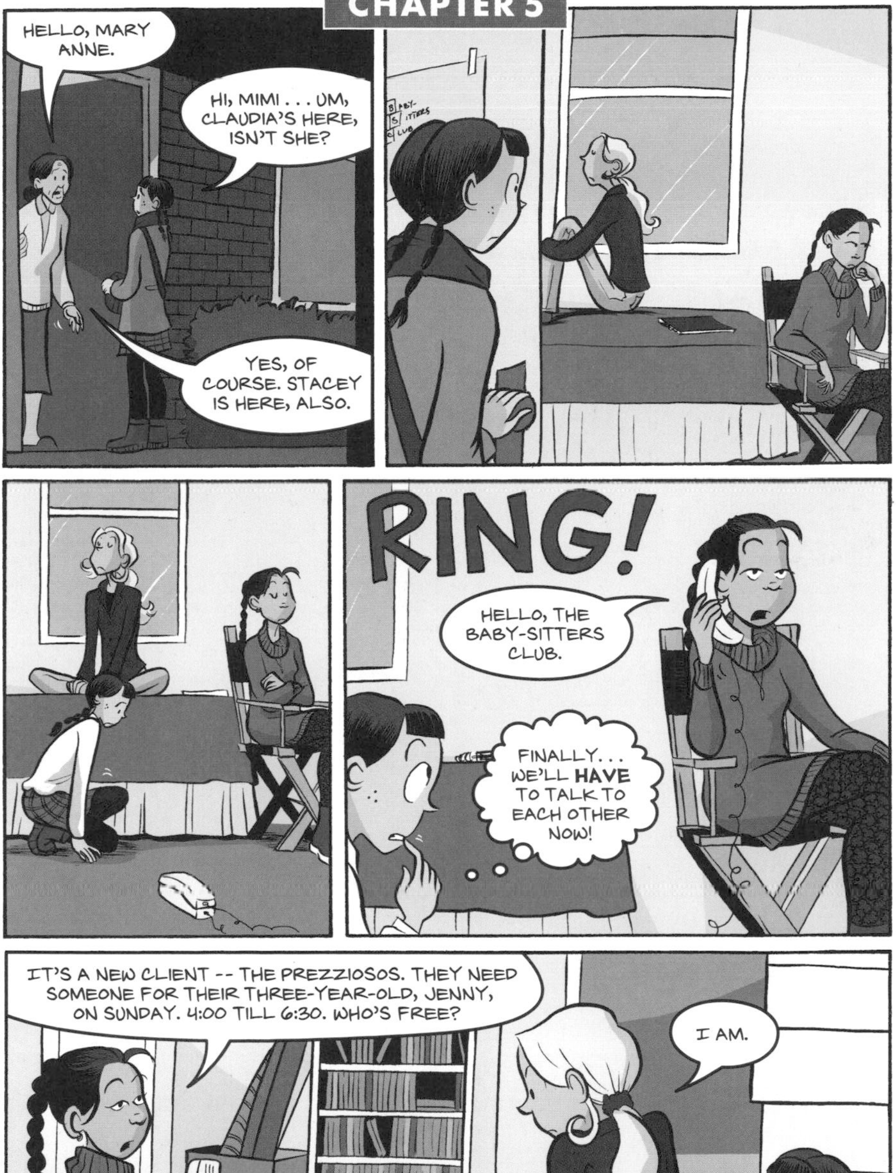
HELLO, MARY ANNE.
HI, MIMI . . . UM, CLAUDIA'S HERE, ISN'T SHE?
YES, OF COURSE. STACEY IS HERE, ALSO.
BABY-SITTERS CLUB
RING!
HELLO, THE BABY-SITTERS CLUB.
FINALLY . . . WE'LL **HAVE** TO TALK TO EACH OTHER NOW!
IT'S A NEW CLIENT -- THE PREZZIOSOS. THEY NEED SOMEONE FOR THEIR THREE-YEAR-OLD, JENNY, ON SUNDAY. 4:00 TILL 6:30. WHO'S FREE?
I AM.

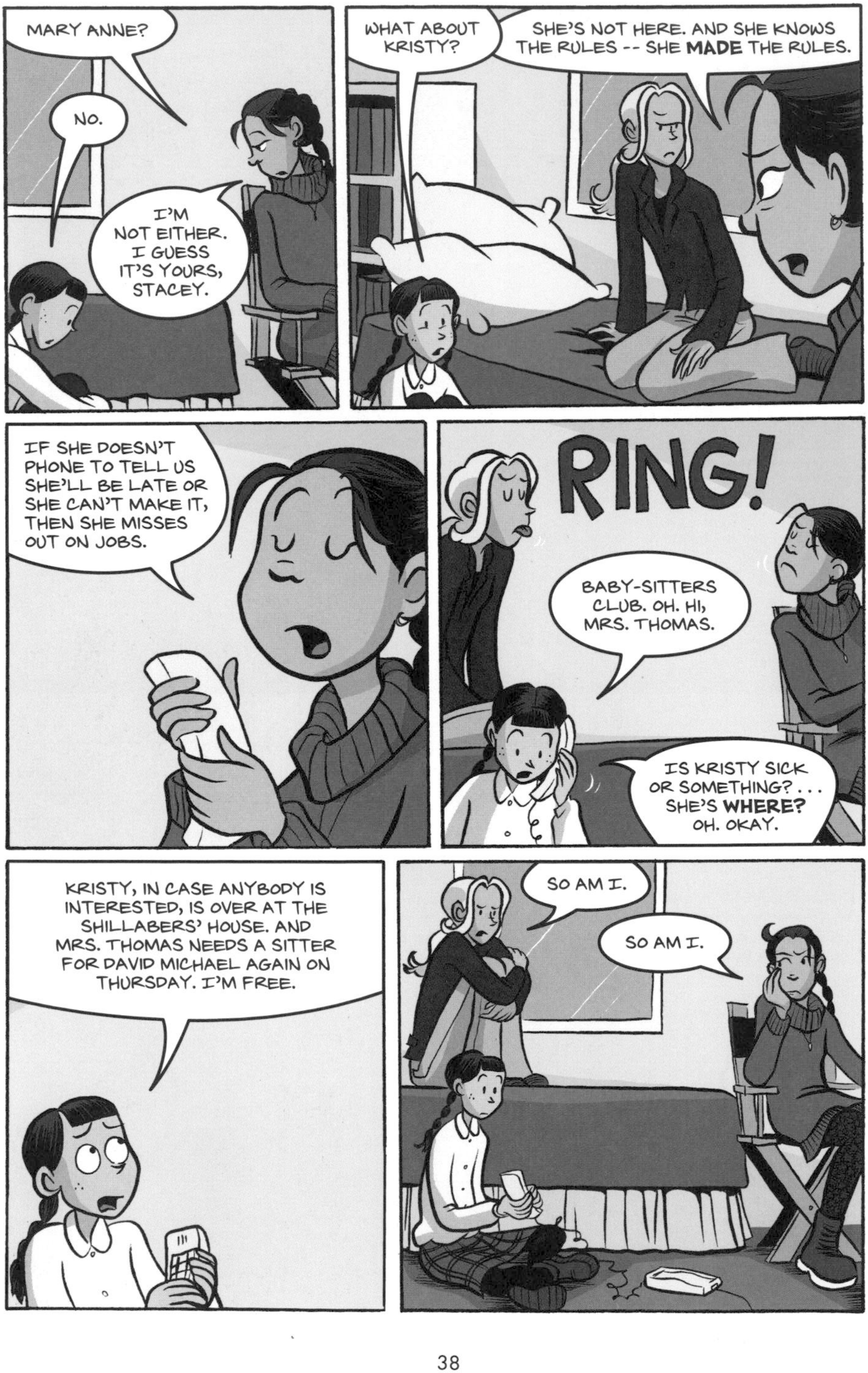
MARY ANNE?
NO.
I'M NOT EITHER. I GUESS IT'S YOURS, STACEY.
WHAT ABOUT KRISTY?
SHE'S NOT HERE. AND SHE KNOWS THE RULES -- SHE **MADE** THE RULES.
IF SHE DOESN'T PHONE TO TELL US SHE'LL BE LATE OR SHE CAN'T MAKE IT, THEN SHE MISSES OUT ON JOBS.
RING!
BABY-SITTERS CLUB. OH. HI, MRS. THOMAS.
IS KRISTY SICK OR SOMETHING? . . . SHE'S **WHERE?** OH. OKAY.
KRISTY, IN CASE ANYBODY IS INTERESTED, IS OVER AT THE SHILLABERS' HOUSE. AND MRS. THOMAS NEEDS A SITTER FOR DAVID MICHAEL AGAIN ON THURSDAY. I'M FREE.
SO AM I.
SO AM I.

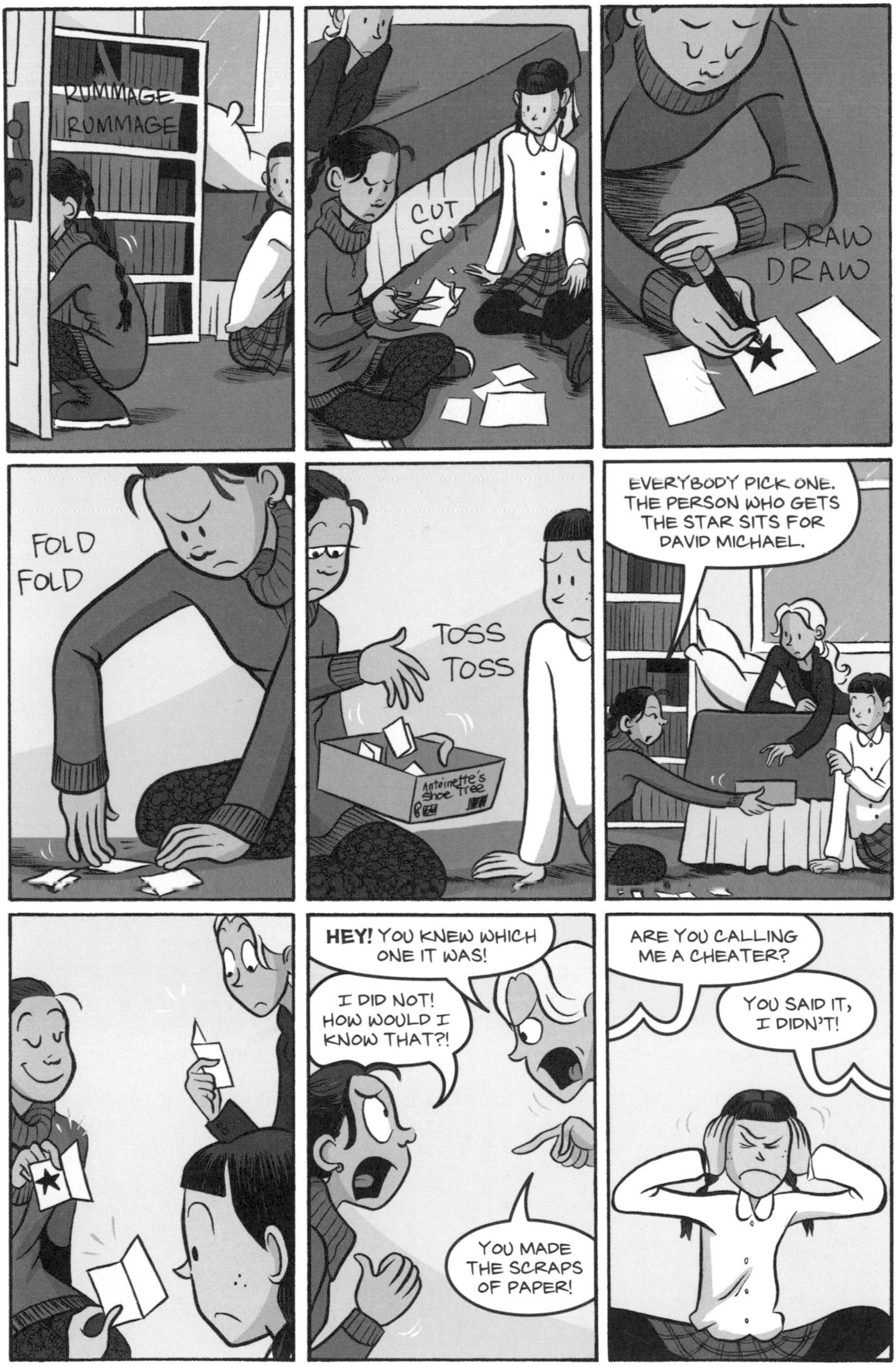
RUMMAGE
RUMMAGE
CUT
CUT
DRAW
DRAW
FOLD
FOLD
TOSS
TOSS
Antoinette's Shoe Tree
EVERYBODY PICK ONE. THE PERSON WHO GETS THE STAR SITS FOR DAVID MICHAEL.
HEY! YOU KNEW WHICH ONE IT WAS!
I DID NOT! HOW WOULD I KNOW THAT?!
YOU MADE THE SCRAPS OF PAPER!
ARE YOU CALLING ME A CHEATER?
YOU SAID IT, I DIDN'T!

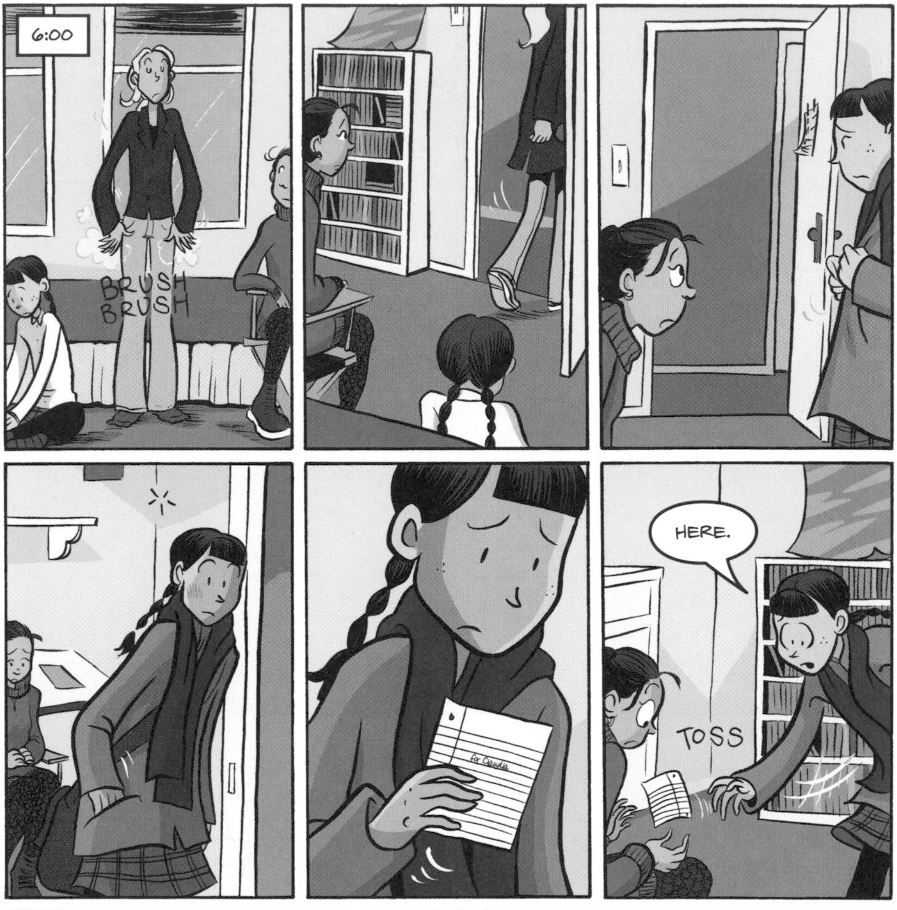
6:00
BRUSH
BRUSH
For Claudia
HERE.
TOSS
DASH

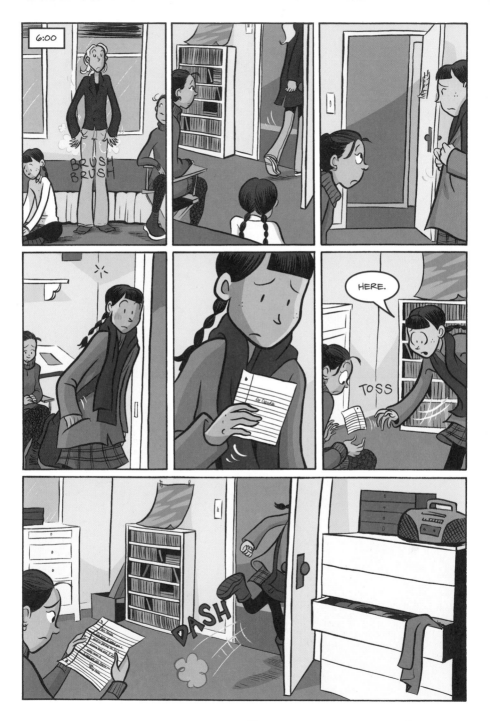

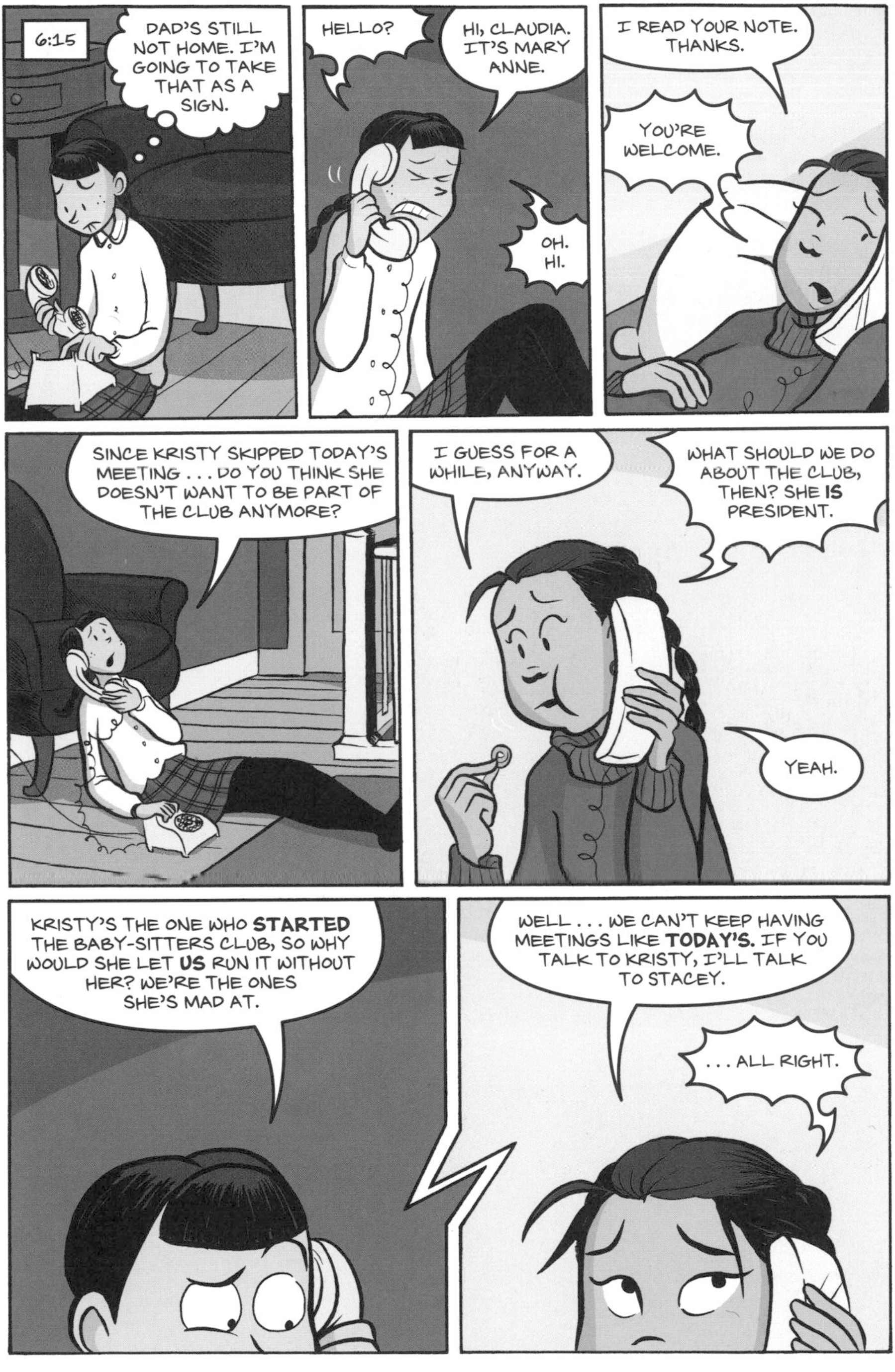
6:15
DAD'S STILL NOT HOME. I'M GOING TO TAKE THAT AS A SIGN.
HELLO?
HI, CLAUDIA. IT'S MARY ANNE.
OH. HI.
I READ YOUR NOTE. THANKS.
YOU'RE WELCOME.
SINCE KRISTY SKIPPED TODAY'S MEETING . . . DO YOU THINK SHE DOESN'T WANT TO BE PART OF THE CLUB ANYMORE?
I GUESS FOR A WHILE, ANYWAY.
WHAT SHOULD WE DO ABOUT THE CLUB, THEN? SHE **IS** PRESIDENT.
YEAH.
KRISTY'S THE ONE WHO **STARTED** THE BABY-SITTERS CLUB, SO WHY WOULD SHE LET **US** RUN IT WITHOUT HER? WE'RE THE ONES SHE'S MAD AT.
WELL . . . WE CAN'T KEEP HAVING MEETINGS LIKE **TODAY'S.** IF YOU TALK TO KRISTY, I'LL TALK TO STACEY.
. . . ALL RIGHT.

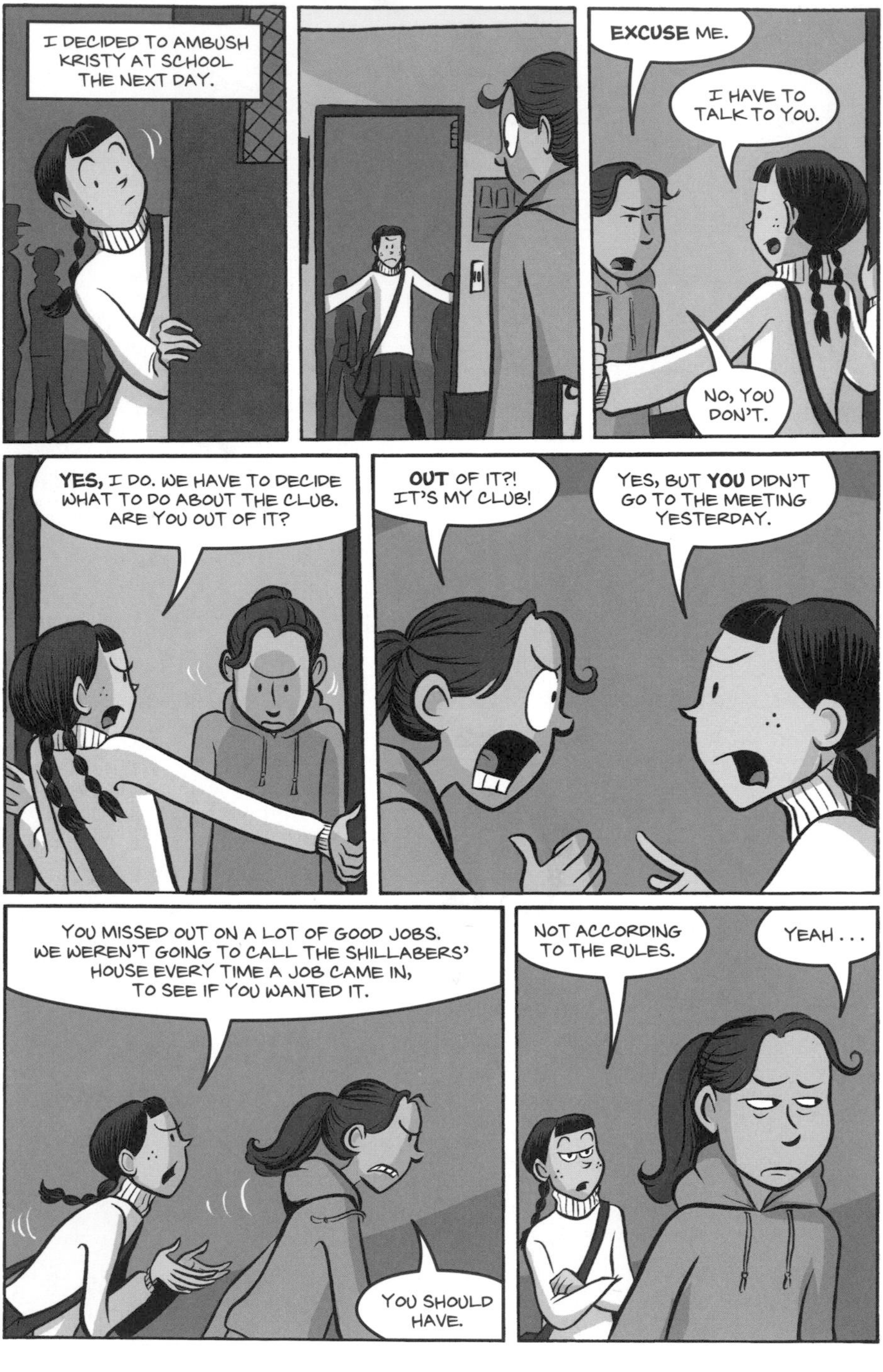

I DECIDED TO AMBUSH KRISTY AT SCHOOL THE NEXT DAY.
EXCUSE ME.
I HAVE TO TALK TO YOU.
NO, YOU DON'T.
YES, I DO. WE HAVE TO DECIDE WHAT TO DO ABOUT THE CLUB. ARE YOU OUT OF IT?
OUT OF IT?! IT'S MY CLUB!
YES, BUT YOU DIDN'T GO TO THE MEETING YESTERDAY.
YOU MISSED OUT ON A LOT OF GOOD JOBS. WE WEREN'T GOING TO CALL THE SHILLABERS' HOUSE EVERY TIME A JOB CAME IN, TO SEE IF YOU WANTED IT.
YOU SHOULD HAVE.
NOT ACCORDING TO THE RULES.
YEAH . . .

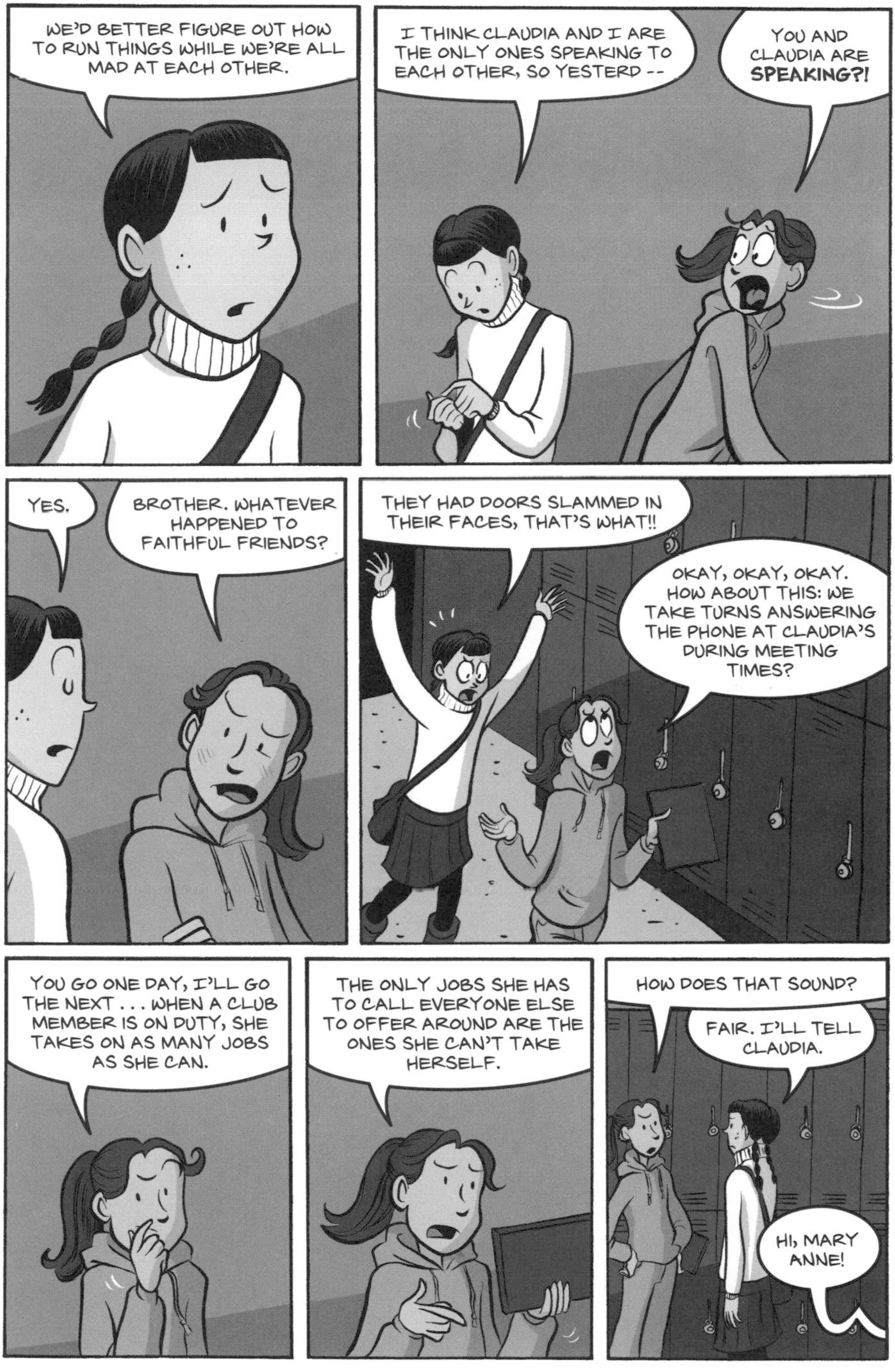
WE'D BETTER FIGURE OUT HOW TO RUN THINGS WHILE WE'RE ALL MAD AT EACH OTHER.
I THINK CLAUDIA AND I ARE THE ONLY ONES SPEAKING TO EACH OTHER, SO YESTERD --
YOU AND CLAUDIA ARE **SPEAKING?!**
YES.
BROTHER. WHATEVER HAPPENED TO FAITHFUL FRIENDS?
THEY HAD DOORS SLAMMED IN THEIR FACES, THAT'S WHAT!!
OKAY, OKAY, OKAY. HOW ABOUT THIS: WE TAKE TURNS ANSWERING THE PHONE AT CLAUDIA'S DURING MEETING TIMES?
YOU GO ONE DAY, I'LL GO THE NEXT . . . WHEN A CLUB MEMBER IS ON DUTY, SHE TAKES ON AS MANY JOBS AS SHE CAN.
THE ONLY JOBS SHE HAS TO CALL EVERYONE ELSE TO OFFER AROUND ARE THE ONES SHE CAN'T TAKE HERSELF.
HOW DOES THAT SOUND?
FAIR. I'LL TELL CLAUDIA.
HI, MARY ANNE!

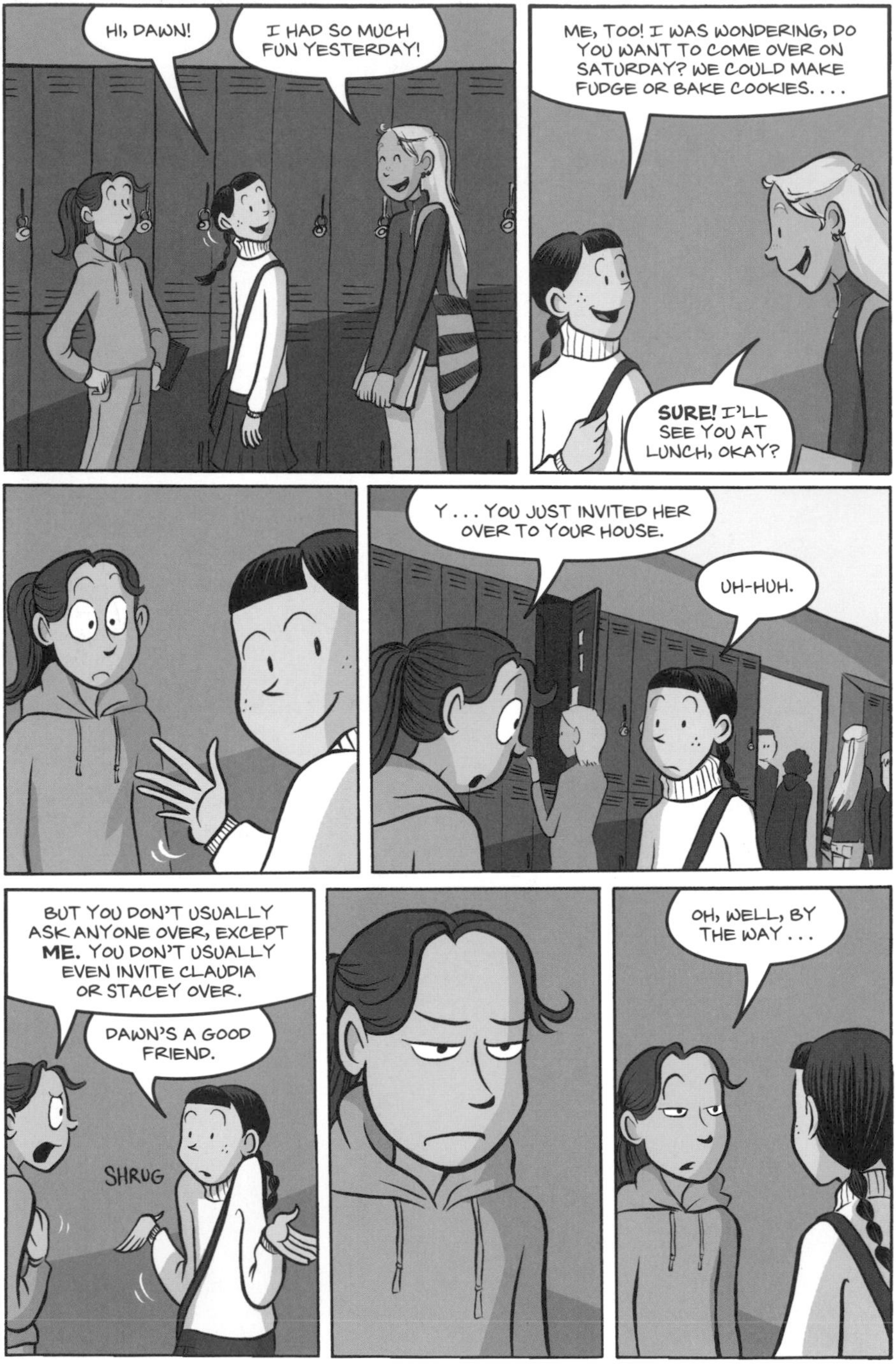
HI, DAWN!
I HAD SO MUCH FUN YESTERDAY!
ME, TOO! I WAS WONDERING, DO YOU WANT TO COME OVER ON SATURDAY? WE COULD MAKE FUDGE OR BAKE COOKIES. . . .
SURE! I'LL SEE YOU AT LUNCH, OKAY?
Y . . . YOU JUST INVITED HER OVER TO YOUR HOUSE.
UH-HUH.
BUT YOU DON'T USUALLY ASK ANYONE OVER, EXCEPT ME. YOU DON'T USUALLY EVEN INVITE CLAUDIA OR STACEY OVER.
DAWN'S A GOOD FRIEND.
SHRUG
OH, WELL, BY THE WAY . . .

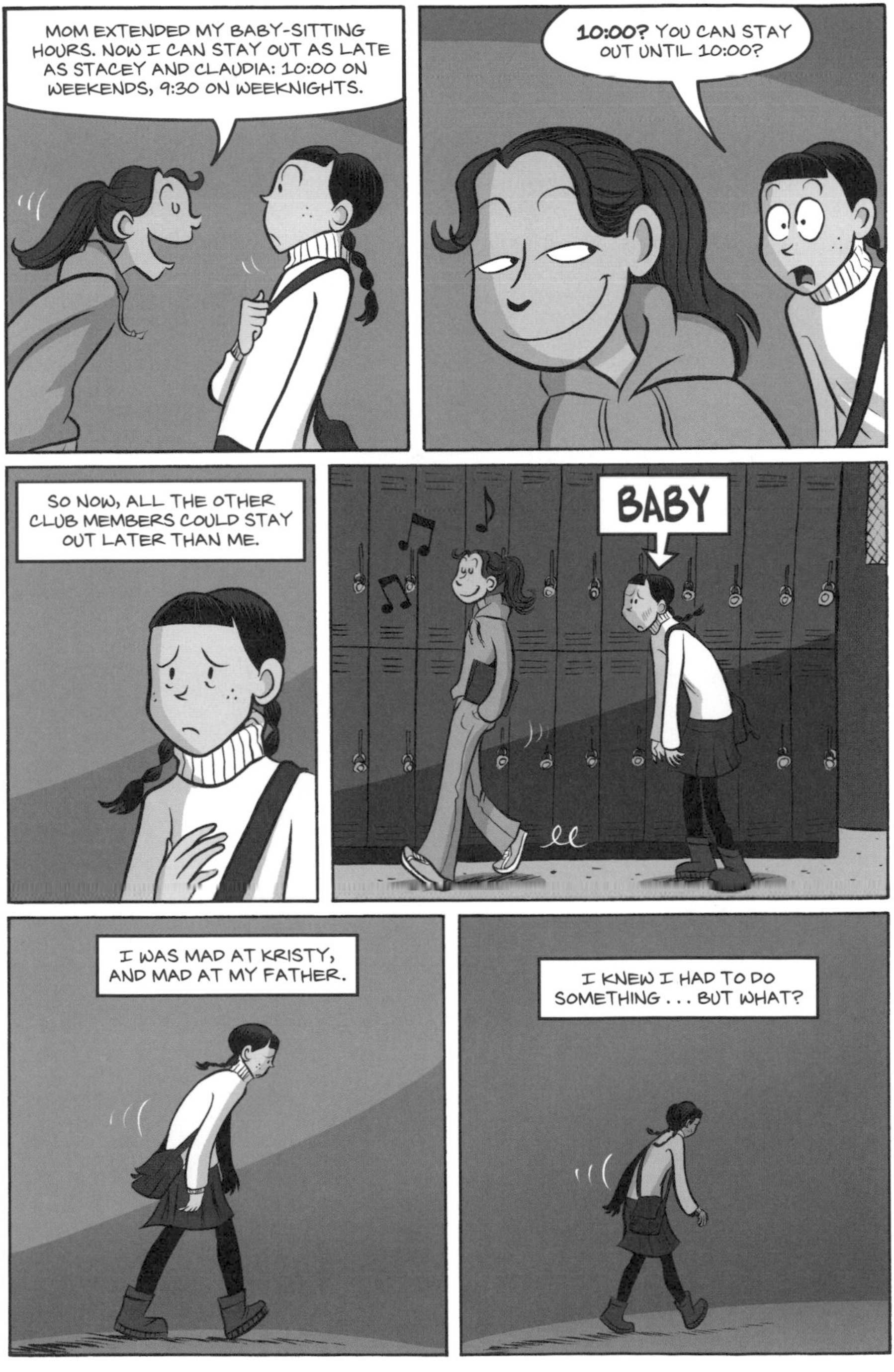
MOM EXTENDED MY BABY-SITTING HOURS. NOW I CAN STAY OUT AS LATE AS STACEY AND CLAUDIA: 10:00 ON WEEKENDS, 9:30 ON WEEKNIGHTS.
10:00? YOU CAN STAY OUT UNTIL 10:00?
SO NOW, ALL THE OTHER CLUB MEMBERS COULD STAY OUT LATER THAN ME.
BABY
I WAS MAD AT KRISTY, AND MAD AT MY FATHER.
I KNEW I HAD TO DO SOMETHING . . . BUT WHAT?

Sunday, January 11

This afternoon, I sat for Jenny Prezzioso. Jenny
is three. She's the Pikes' neighbor, so I had met
her a few times before today. She and her parents
both look very prim and proper but Mrs. Prezzioso
is the only one who acts that way. She looks like
she just stepped out of the pages of a magazine.
And she dresses Jenny as if every day were Easter
Sunday: frilly dresses, lacy socks, and ribbons
in her hair. Mrs. P probably thinks "jeans" is
a dirty word.

Mr. P, on the other hand, looks like he'd rather be
dozing in front of the TV in sweats, a T-shirt, and
mismatched socks. And Jenny tries hard, but she just
isn't what her mother wants her to be. . . .

Stacey

CHAPTER 6

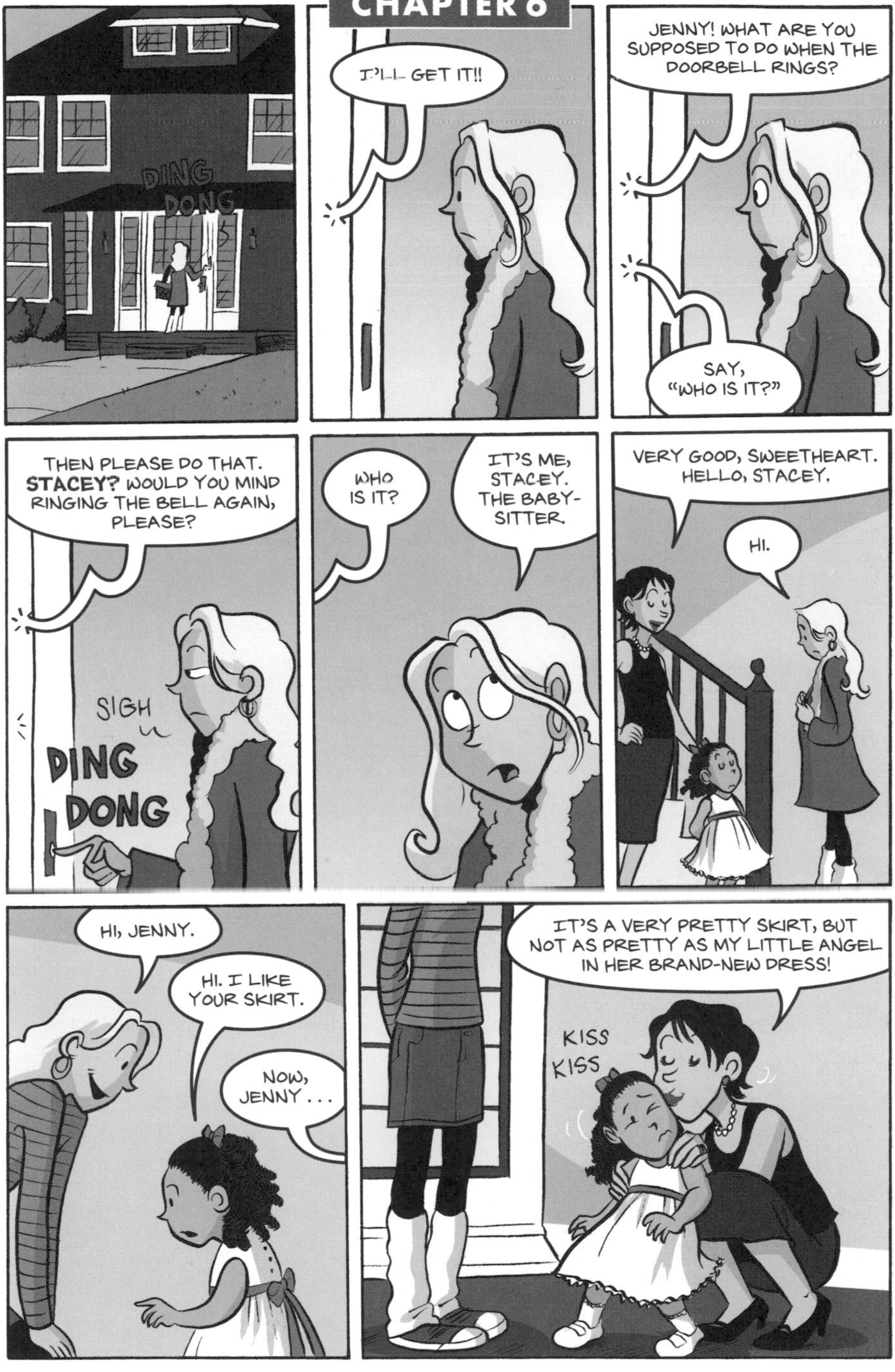
DING
DONG
I'LL GET IT!!
JENNY! WHAT ARE YOU SUPPOSED TO DO WHEN THE DOORBELL RINGS?
SAY, "WHO IS IT?"
THEN PLEASE DO THAT. STACEY? WOULD YOU MIND RINGING THE BELL AGAIN, PLEASE?
SIGH
DING
DONG
WHO IS IT?
IT'S ME, STACEY. THE BABY-SITTER.
VERY GOOD, SWEETHEART. HELLO, STACEY.
HI.
HI, JENNY.
HI. I LIKE YOUR SKIRT.
NOW, JENNY . . .
IT'S A VERY PRETTY SKIRT, BUT NOT AS PRETTY AS MY LITTLE ANGEL IN HER BRAND-NEW DRESS!
KISS
KISS

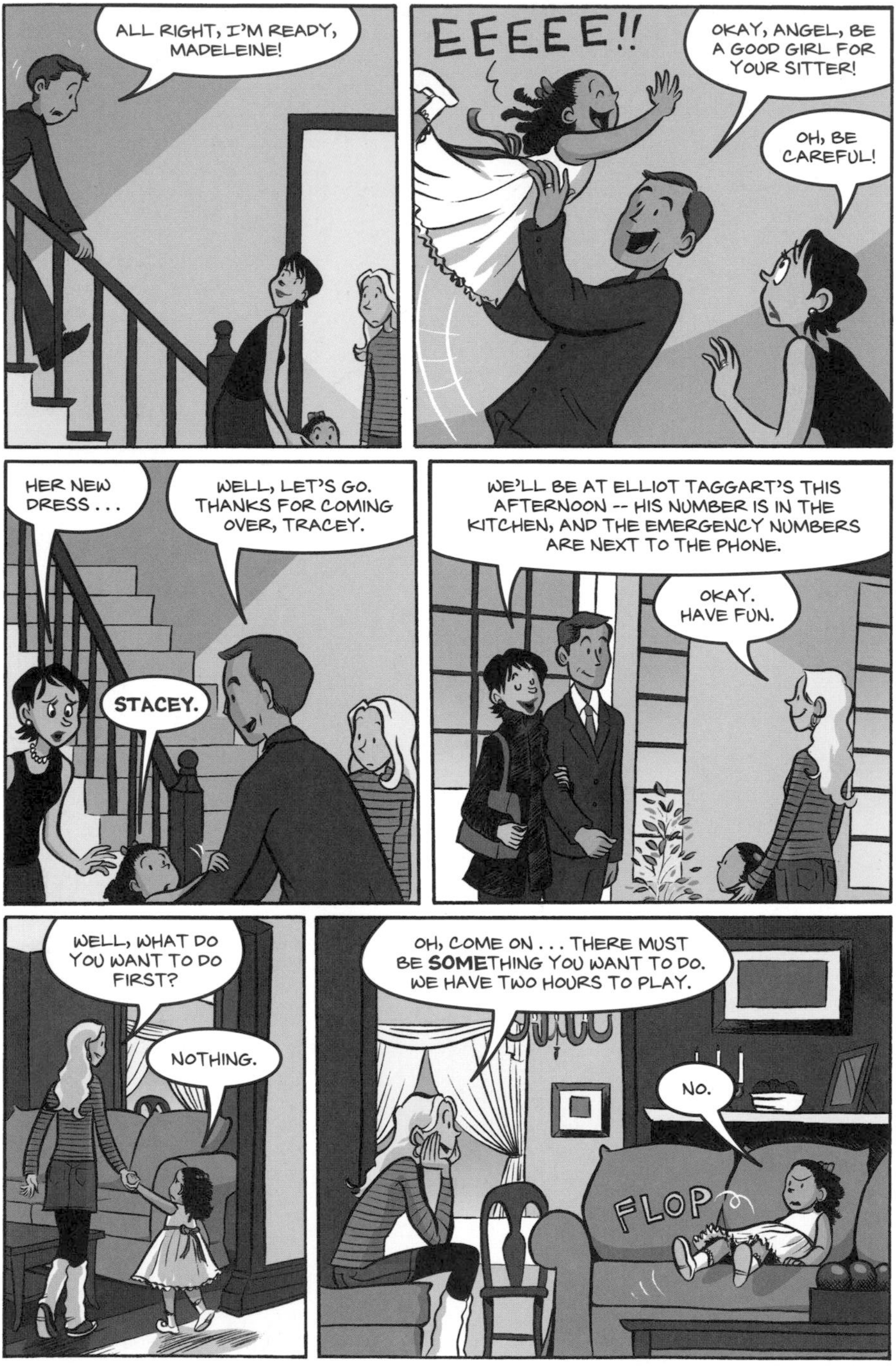
ALL RIGHT, I'M READY, MADELEINE!
EEEEE!!
OKAY, ANGEL, BE A GOOD GIRL FOR YOUR SITTER!
OH, BE CAREFUL!
HER NEW DRESS . . .
WELL, LET'S GO. THANKS FOR COMING OVER, TRACEY.
STACEY.
WE'LL BE AT ELLIOT TAGGART'S THIS AFTERNOON -- HIS NUMBER IS IN THE KITCHEN, AND THE EMERGENCY NUMBERS ARE NEXT TO THE PHONE.
OKAY. HAVE FUN.
WELL, WHAT DO YOU WANT TO DO FIRST?
NOTHING.
OH, COME ON . . . THERE MUST BE **SOME**THING YOU WANT TO DO. WE HAVE TWO HOURS TO PLAY.
NO.
FLOP

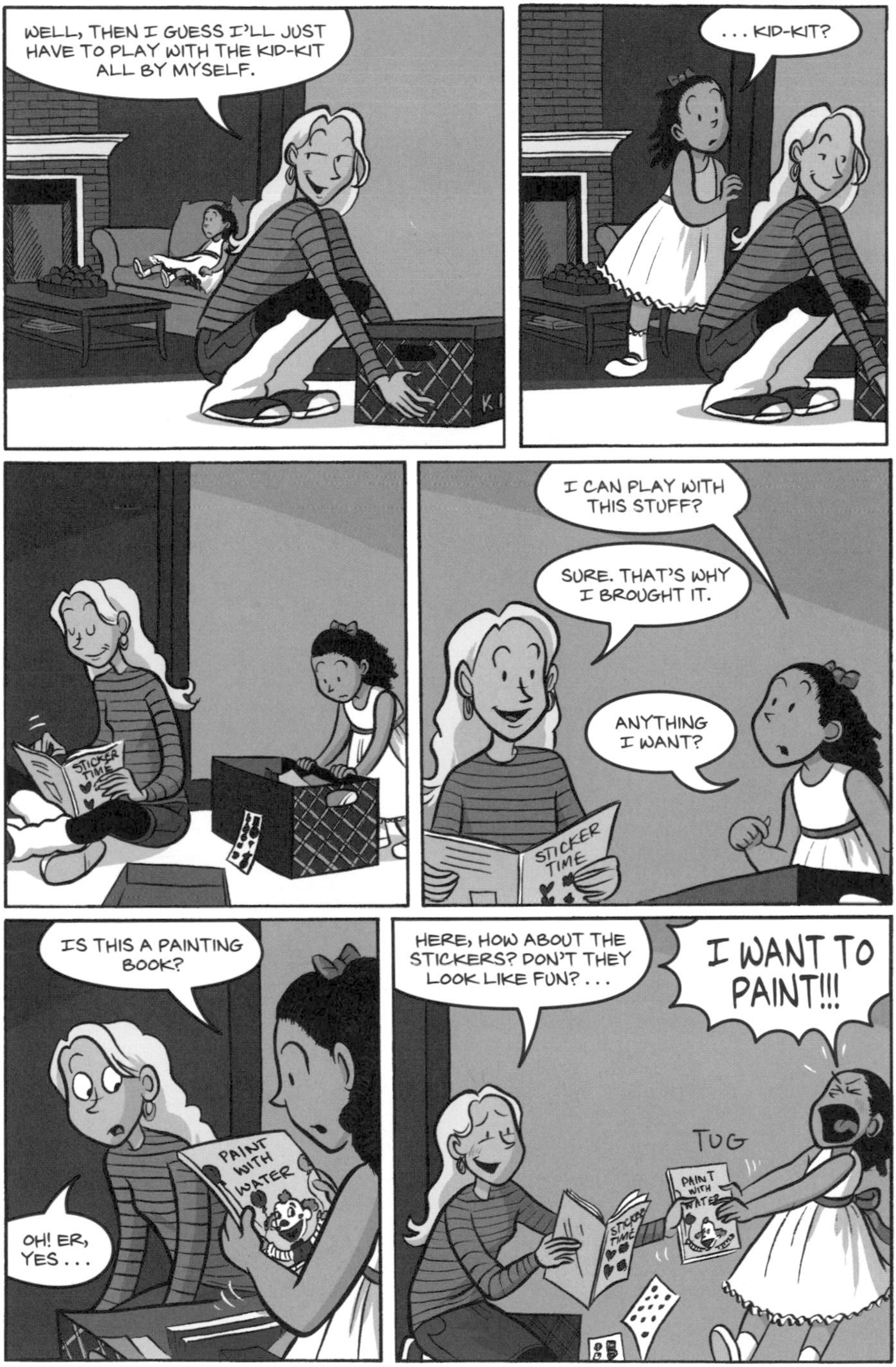
WELL, THEN I GUESS I'LL JUST HAVE TO PLAY WITH THE KID-KIT ALL BY MYSELF.
. . . KID-KIT?
I CAN PLAY WITH THIS STUFF?
SURE. THAT'S WHY I BROUGHT IT.
ANYTHING I WANT?
STICKER TIME
IS THIS A PAINTING BOOK?
PAINT WITH WATER
OH! ER, YES . . .
HERE, HOW ABOUT THE STICKERS? DON'T THEY LOOK LIKE FUN? . . .
I WANT TO PAINT!!!
TUG

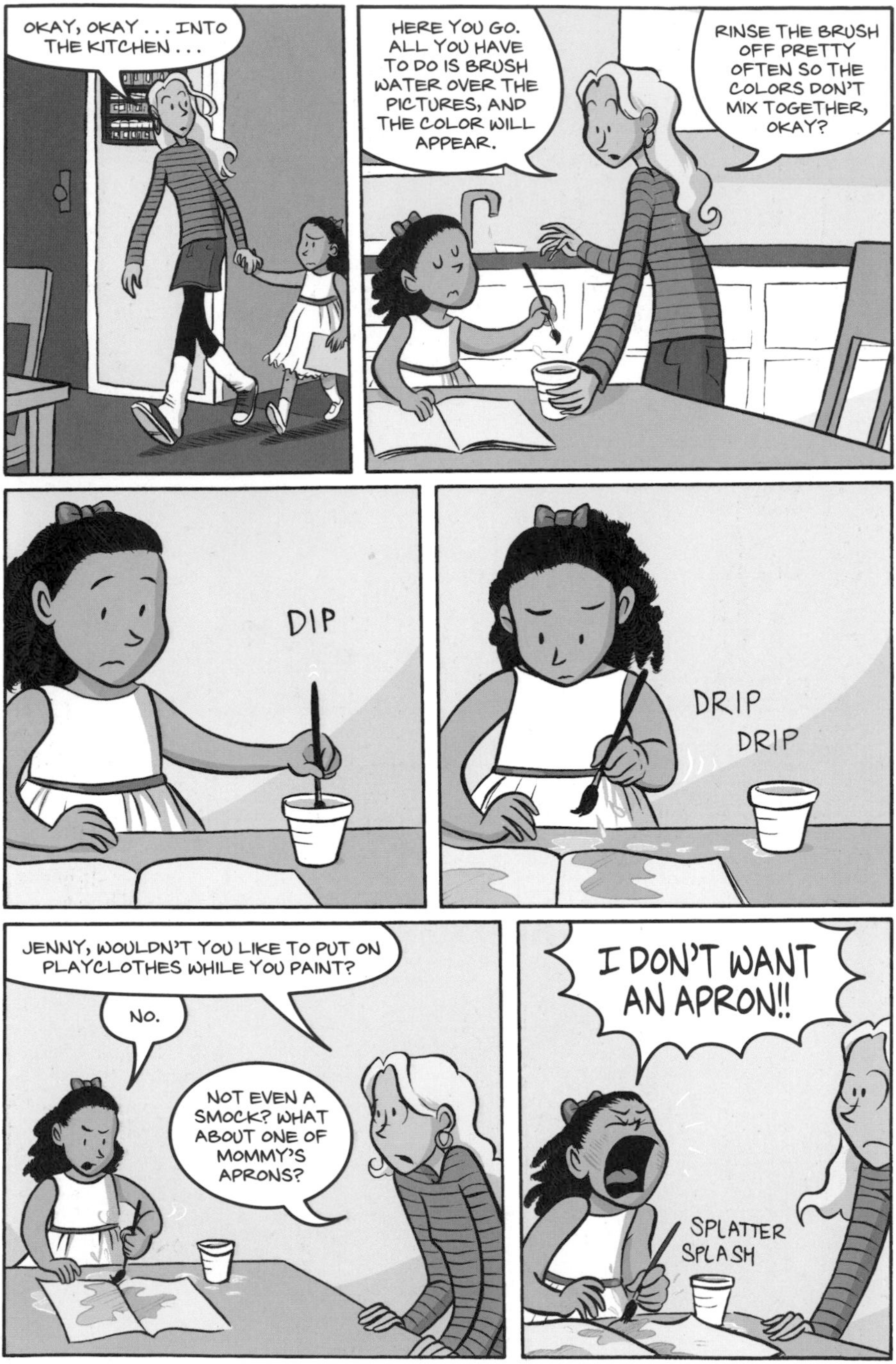
OKAY, OKAY . . . INTO THE KITCHEN . . .
HERE YOU GO. ALL YOU HAVE TO DO IS BRUSH WATER OVER THE PICTURES, AND THE COLOR WILL APPEAR.
RINSE THE BRUSH OFF PRETTY OFTEN SO THE COLORS DON'T MIX TOGETHER, OKAY?
DIP
DRIP
DRIP
JENNY, WOULDN'T YOU LIKE TO PUT ON PLAYCLOTHES WHILE YOU PAINT?
NO.
NOT EVEN A SMOCK? WHAT ABOUT ONE OF MOMMY'S APRONS?
I DON'T WANT AN APRON!!
SPLATTER
SPLASH

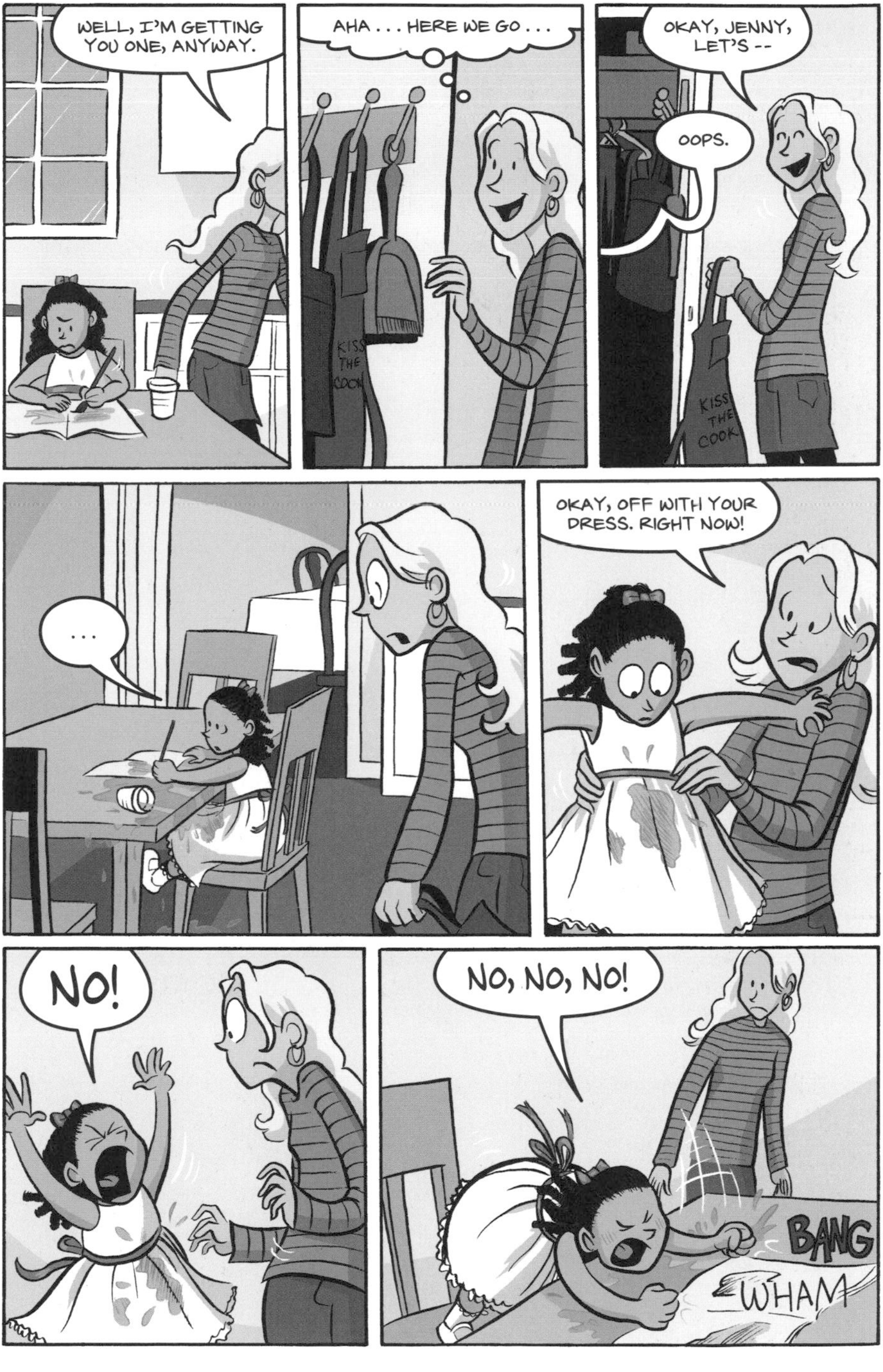
WELL, I'M GETTING YOU ONE, ANYWAY.
AHA . . . HERE WE GO . . .
KISS THE COOK
OKAY, JENNY, LET'S --
OOPS.
KISS THE COOK
. . .
OKAY, OFF WITH YOUR DRESS. RIGHT NOW!
NO!
NO, NO, NO!
BANG
WHAM

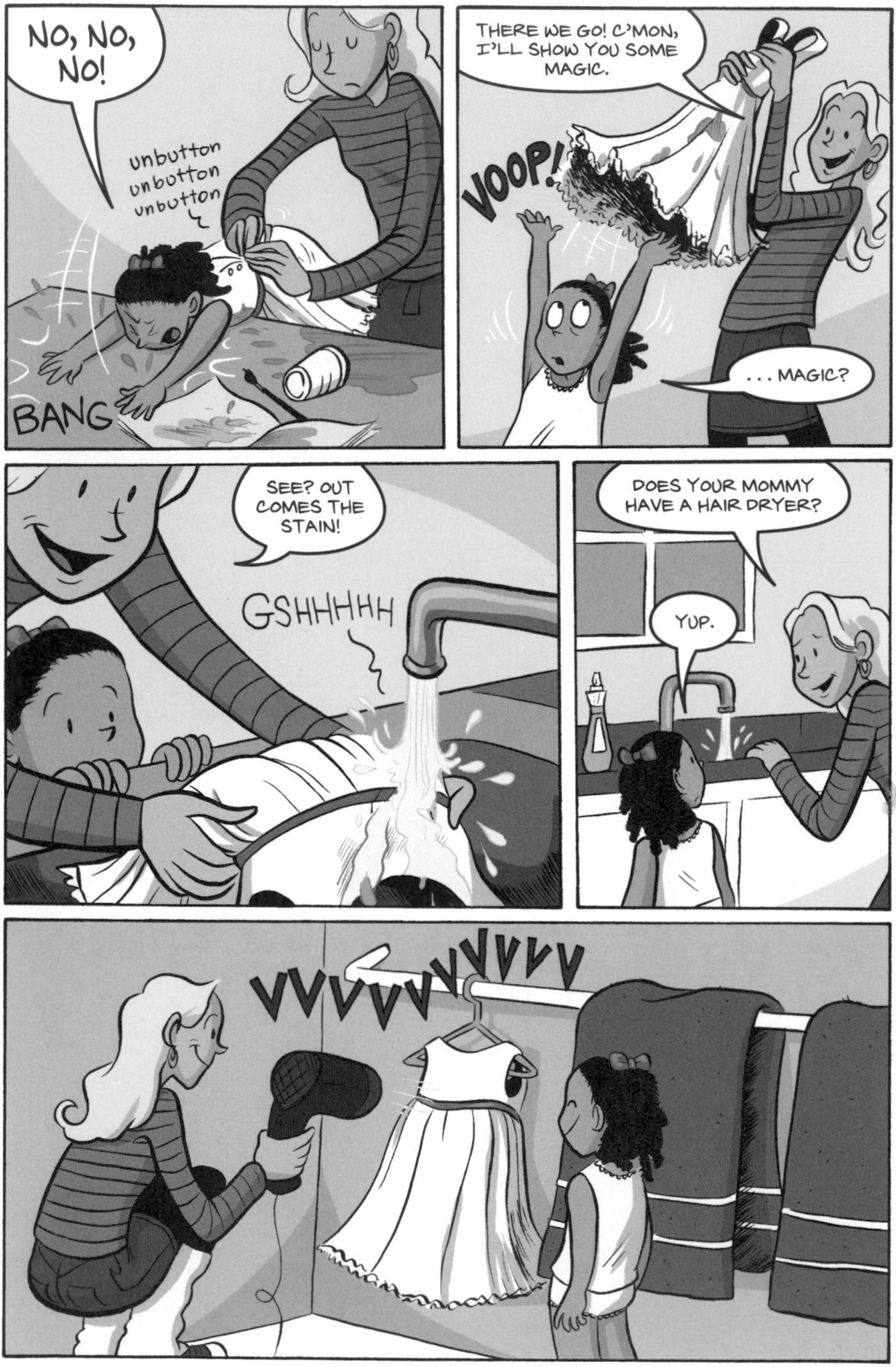
NO, NO, NO!
unbutton unbutton unbutton
BANG
THERE WE GO! C'MON, I'LL SHOW YOU SOME MAGIC.
VOOP!
. . . MAGIC?
SEE? OUT COMES THE STAIN!
GSHHHHH
DOES YOUR MOMMY HAVE A HAIR DRYER?
YUP.
VVVVVVVVVVV

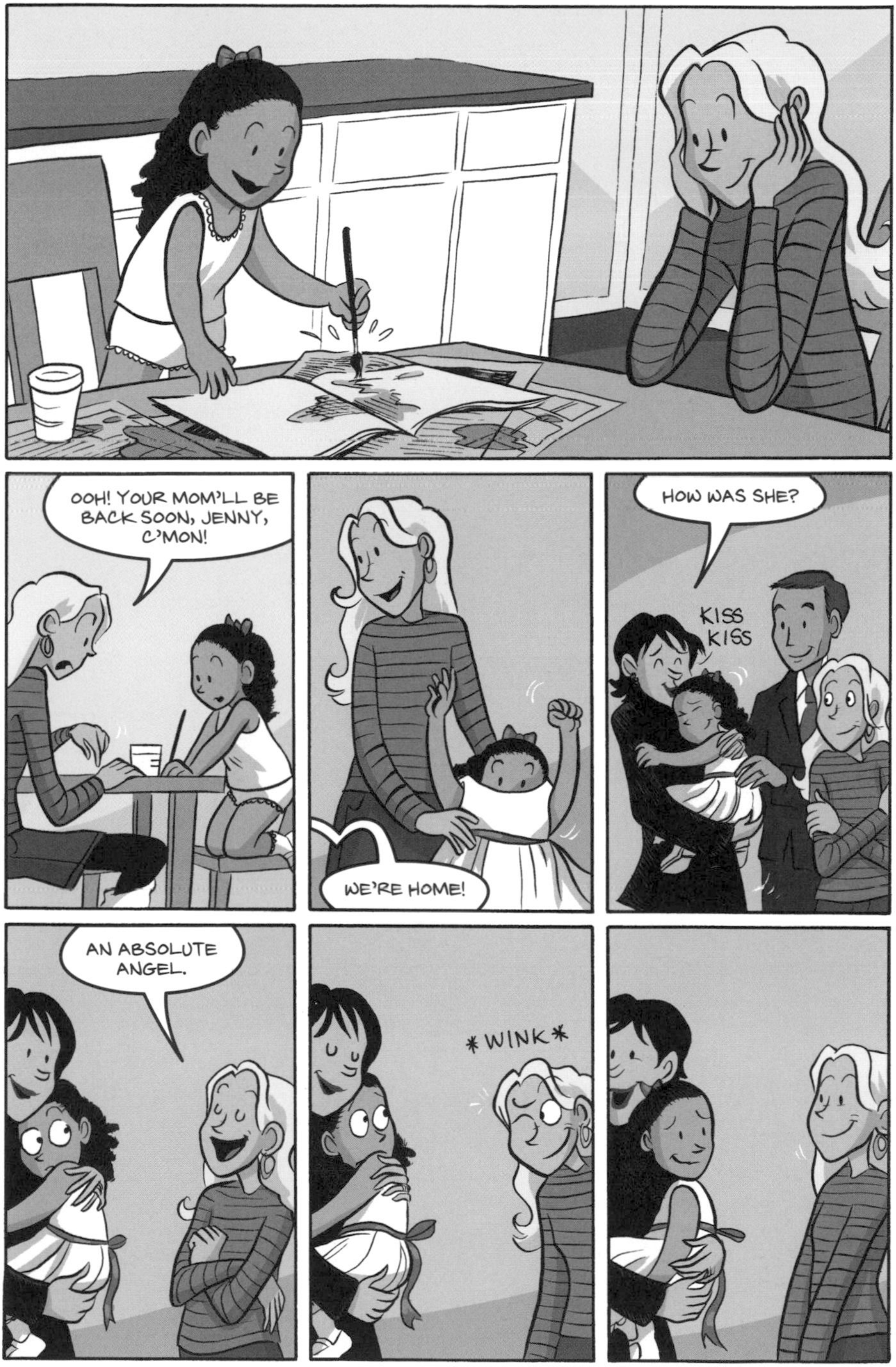
OOH! YOUR MOM'LL BE BACK SOON, JENNY, C'MON!
WE'RE HOME!
HOW WAS SHE?
KISS KISS
AN ABSOLUTE ANGEL.
WINK

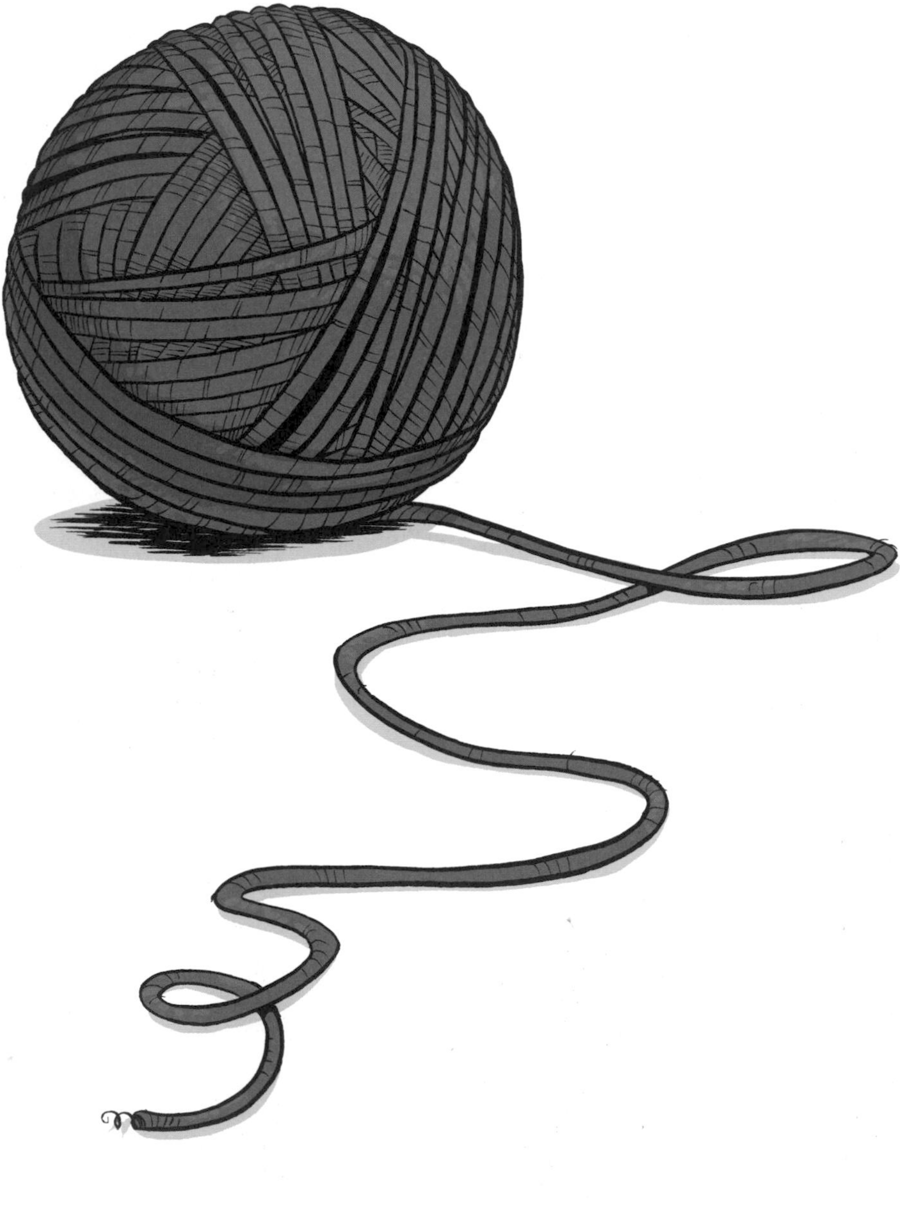

CHAPTER 7

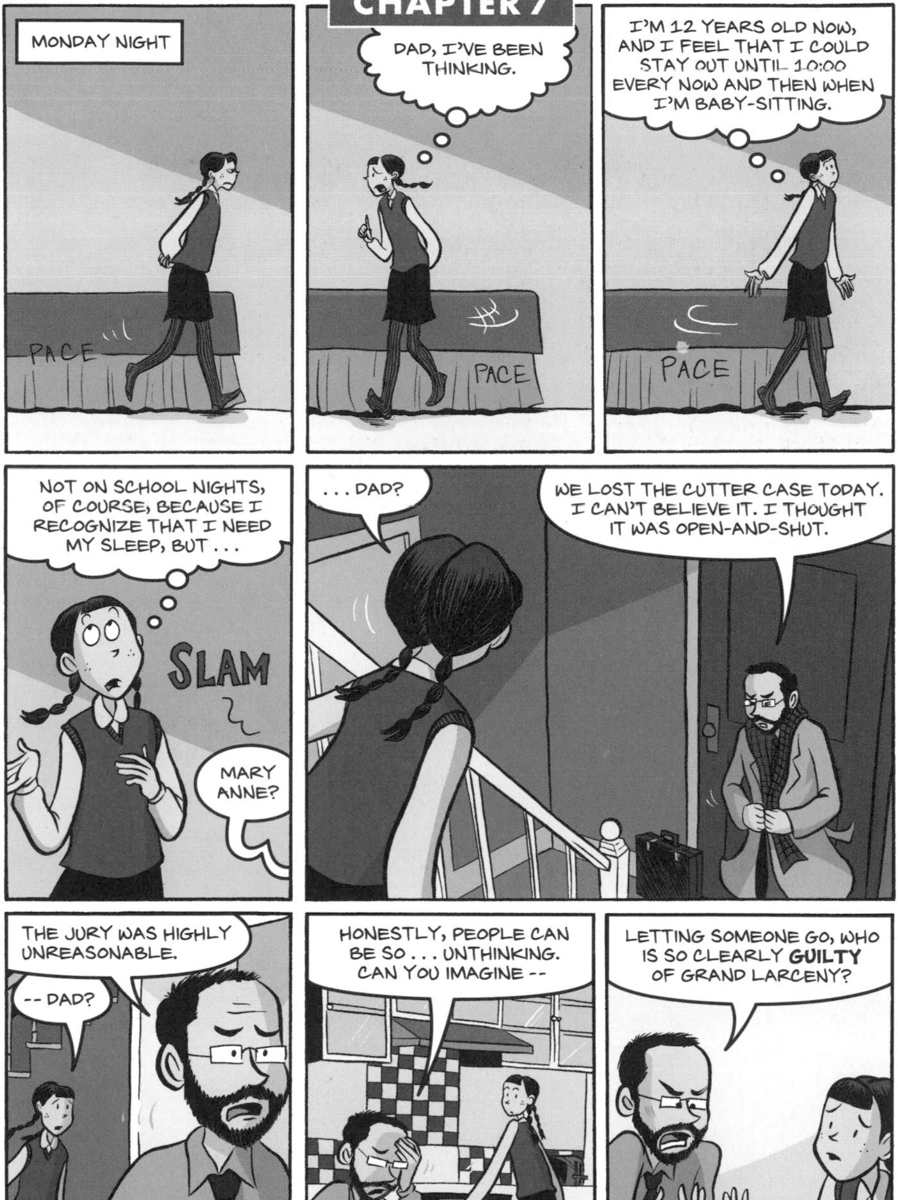
MONDAY NIGHT
PACE
DAD, I'VE BEEN THINKING.
PACE
I'M 12 YEARS OLD NOW, AND I FEEL THAT I COULD STAY OUT UNTIL 10:00 EVERY NOW AND THEN WHEN I'M BABY-SITTING.
PACE
NOT ON SCHOOL NIGHTS, OF COURSE, BECAUSE I RECOGNIZE THAT I NEED MY SLEEP, BUT . . .
SLAM
MARY ANNE?
. . . DAD?
WE LOST THE CUTTER CASE TODAY. I CAN'T BELIEVE IT. I THOUGHT IT WAS OPEN-AND-SHUT.
THE JURY WAS HIGHLY UNREASONABLE.
-- DAD?
HONESTLY, PEOPLE CAN BE SO . . . UNTHINKING. CAN YOU IMAGINE --
LETTING SOMEONE GO, WHO IS SO CLEARLY **GUILTY** OF GRAND LARCENY?
I GUESS NOT . . . DAD?

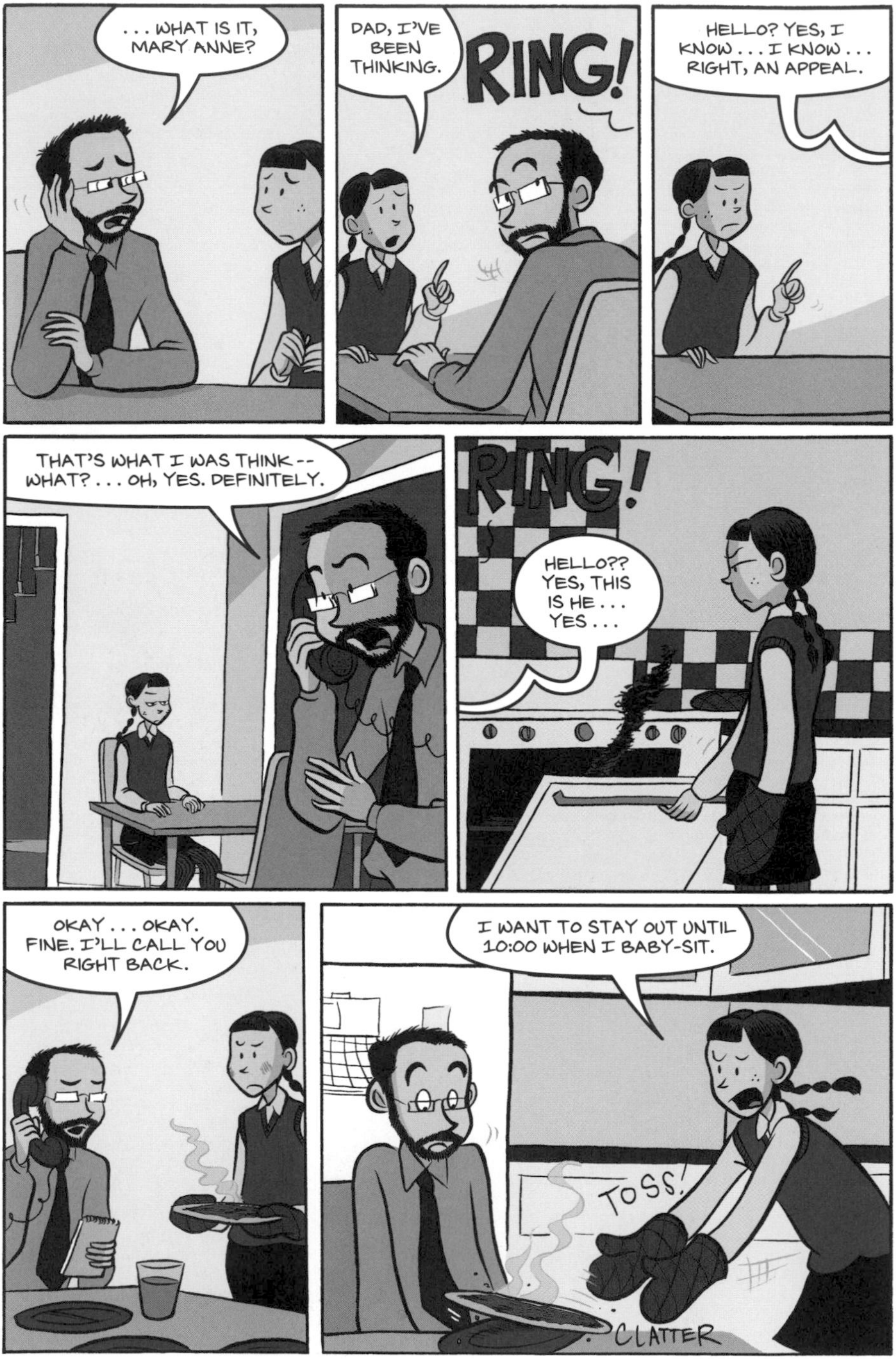
. . . WHAT IS IT, MARY ANNE?
DAD, I'VE BEEN THINKING.
RING!
HELLO? YES, I KNOW . . . I KNOW . . . RIGHT, AN APPEAL.
THAT'S WHAT I WAS THINK -- WHAT? . . . OH, YES. DEFINITELY.
RING!
HELLO?? YES, THIS IS HE . . . YES . . .
OKAY . . . OKAY. FINE. I'LL CALL YOU RIGHT BACK.
I WANT TO STAY OUT UNTIL 10:00 WHEN I BABY-SIT.
TOSS!
CLATTER

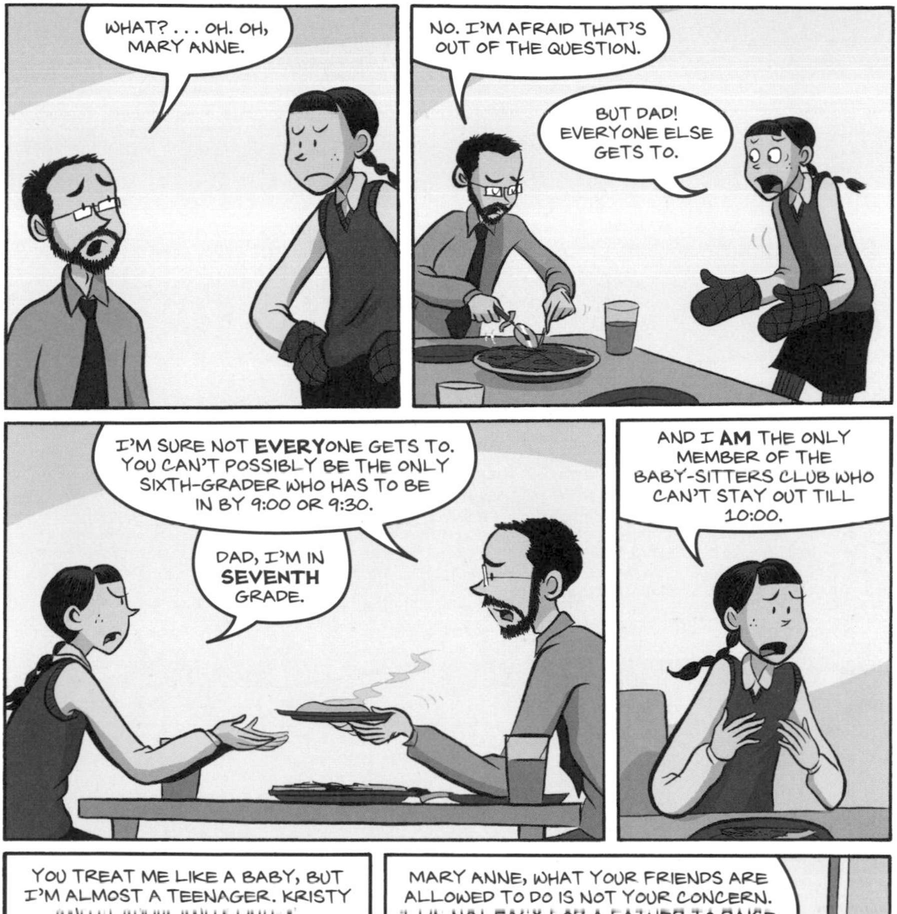
WHAT? . . . OH. OH, MARY ANNE.
NO. I'M AFRAID THAT'S OUT OF THE QUESTION.
BUT DAD! EVERYONE ELSE GETS TO.
I'M SURE NOT **EVERY**ONE GETS TO. YOU CAN'T POSSIBLY BE THE ONLY SIXTH-GRADER WHO HAS TO BE IN BY 9:00 OR 9:30.
DAD, I'M IN **SEVENTH** GRADE.
AND I **AM** THE ONLY MEMBER OF THE BABY-SITTERS CLUB WHO CAN'T STAY OUT TILL 10:00.
YOU TREAT ME LIKE A BABY, BUT I'M ALMOST A TEENAGER. KRISTY AND CLAUDIA AND STACEY --
MARY ANNE, WHAT YOUR FRIENDS ARE ALLOWED TO DO IS NOT YOUR CONCERN. IT'S NOT EASY FOR A FATHER TO RAISE A DAUGHTER ALONE. PLUS, I'M NOT HOME MUCH. I'M DOING THE BEST I CAN.

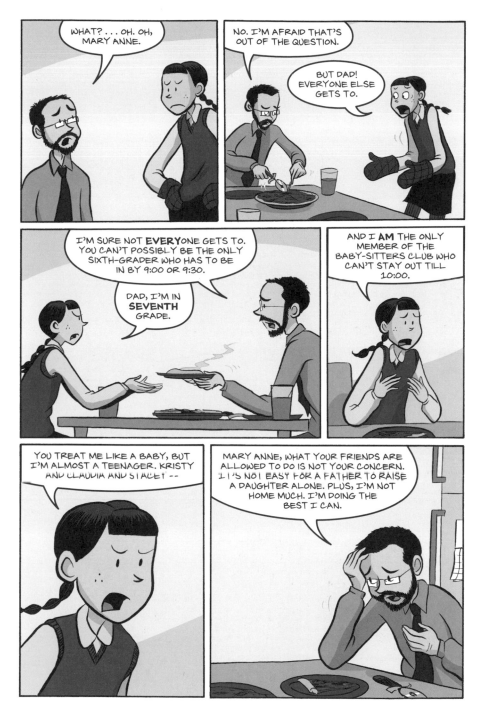

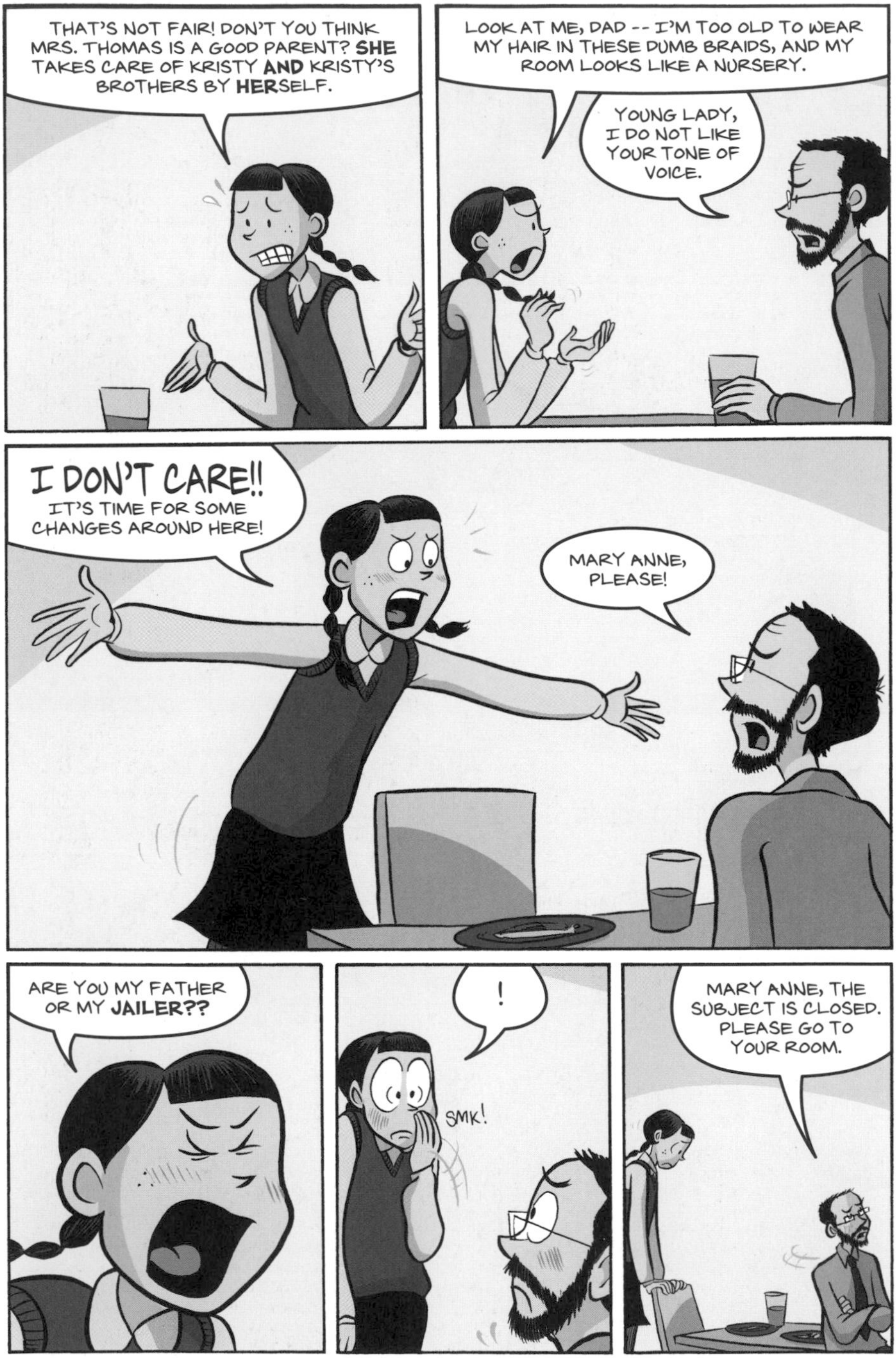
THAT'S NOT FAIR! DON'T YOU THINK MRS. THOMAS IS A GOOD PARENT? **SHE** TAKES CARE OF KRISTY **AND** KRISTY'S BROTHERS BY **HER**SELF.
LOOK AT ME, DAD -- I'M TOO OLD TO WEAR MY HAIR IN THESE DUMB BRAIDS, AND MY ROOM LOOKS LIKE A NURSERY.
YOUNG LADY, I DO NOT LIKE YOUR TONE OF VOICE.
I DON'T CARE!! IT'S TIME FOR SOME CHANGES AROUND HERE!
MARY ANNE, PLEASE!
ARE YOU MY FATHER OR MY **JAILER??**
!
SMK!
MARY ANNE, THE SUBJECT IS CLOSED. PLEASE GO TO YOUR ROOM.

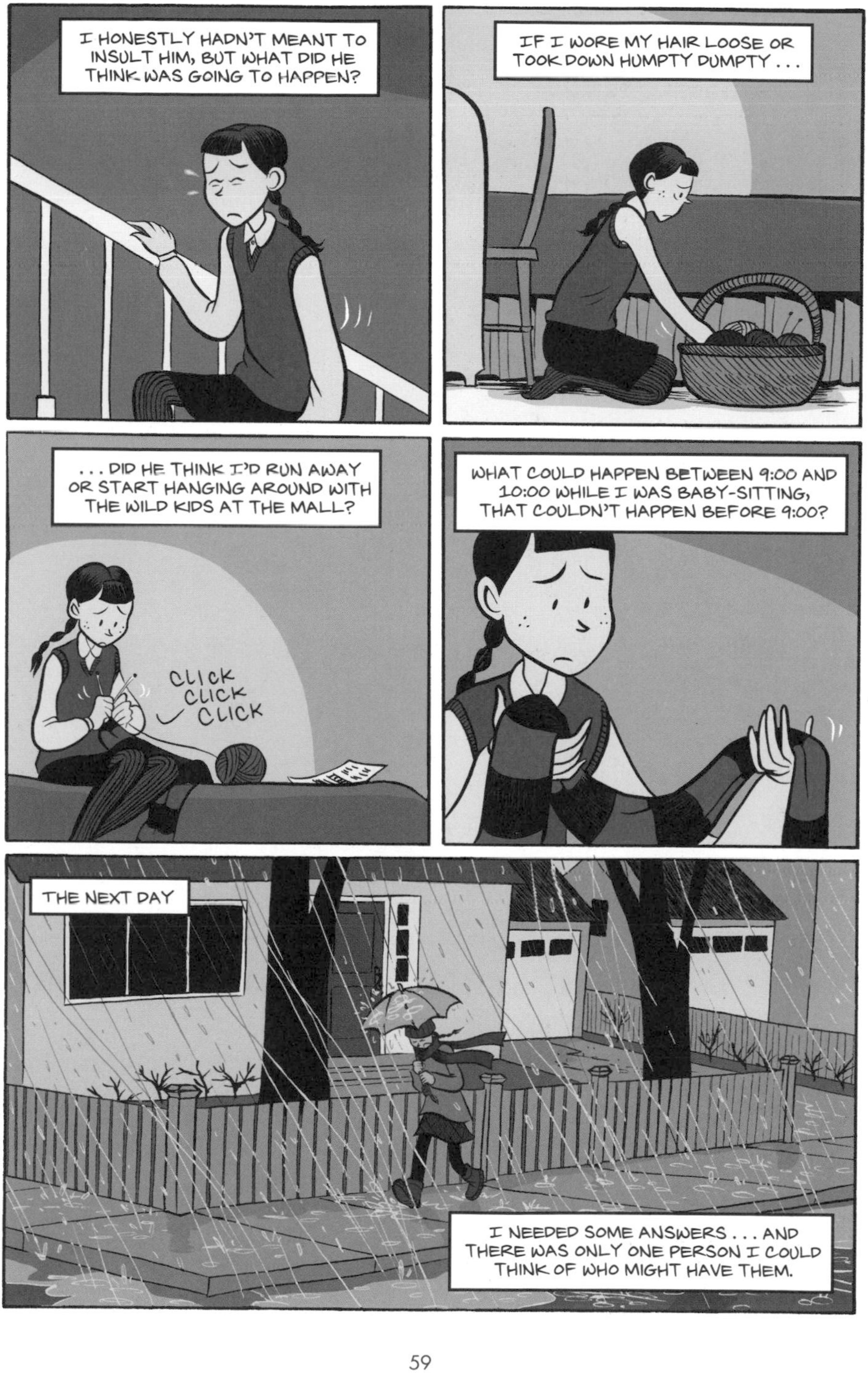
I HONESTLY HADN'T MEANT TO INSULT HIM, BUT WHAT DID HE THINK WAS GOING TO HAPPEN?
IF I WORE MY HAIR LOOSE OR TOOK DOWN HUMPTY DUMPTY . . .
. . . DID HE THINK I'D RUN AWAY OR START HANGING AROUND WITH THE WILD KIDS AT THE MALL?
CLICK CLICK CLICK
WHAT COULD HAPPEN BETWEEN 9:00 AND 10:00 WHILE I WAS BABY-SITTING, THAT COULDN'T HAPPEN BEFORE 9:00?
THE NEXT DAY
I NEEDED SOME ANSWERS . . . AND THERE WAS ONLY ONE PERSON I COULD THINK OF WHO MIGHT HAVE THEM.

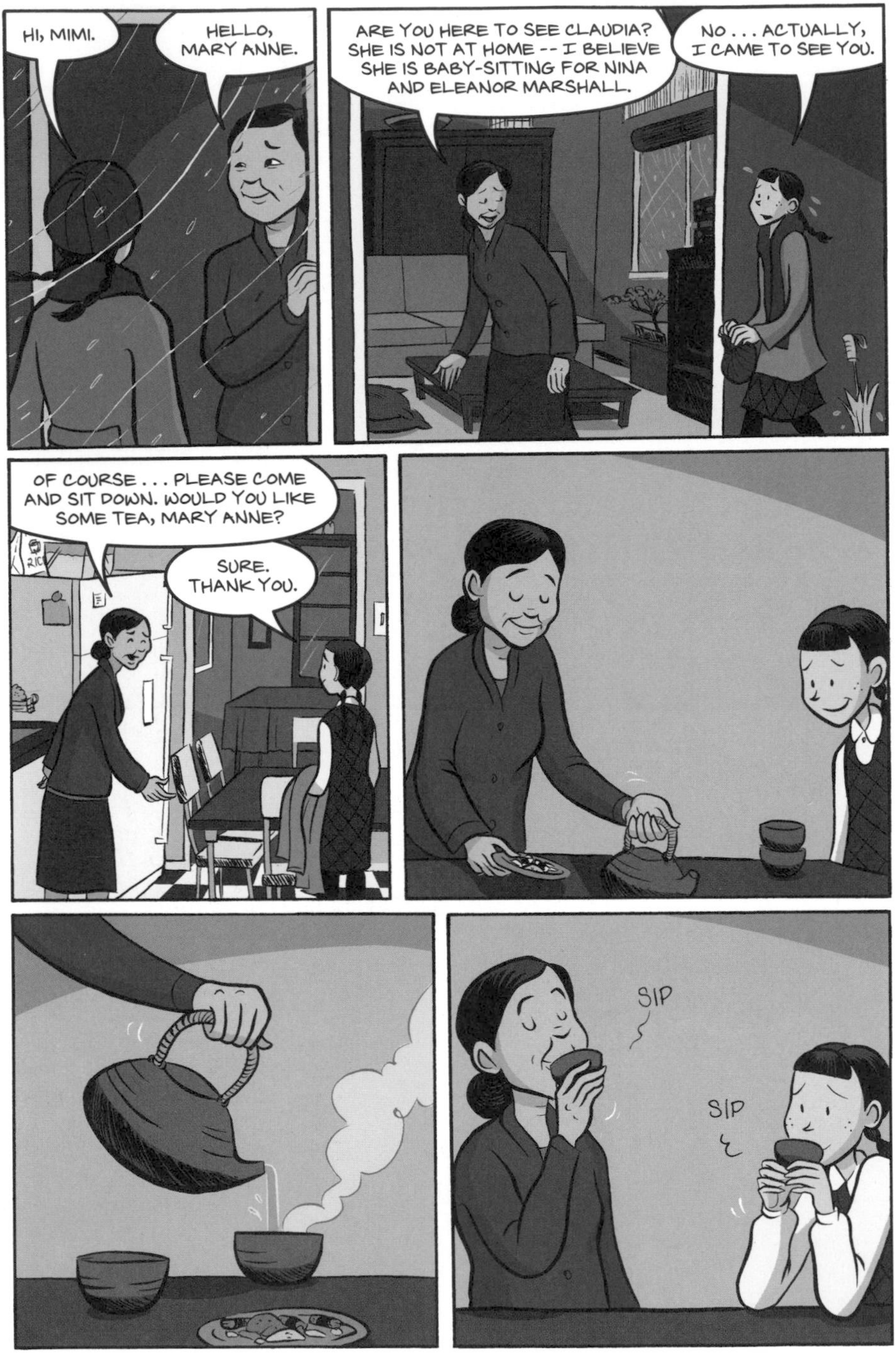
HI, MIMI.
HELLO, MARY ANNE.
ARE YOU HERE TO SEE CLAUDIA? SHE IS NOT AT HOME -- I BELIEVE SHE IS BABY-SITTING FOR NINA AND ELEANOR MARSHALL.
NO . . . ACTUALLY, I CAME TO SEE YOU.
OF COURSE . . . PLEASE COME AND SIT DOWN. WOULD YOU LIKE SOME TEA, MARY ANNE?
SURE. THANK YOU.
SIP
SIP

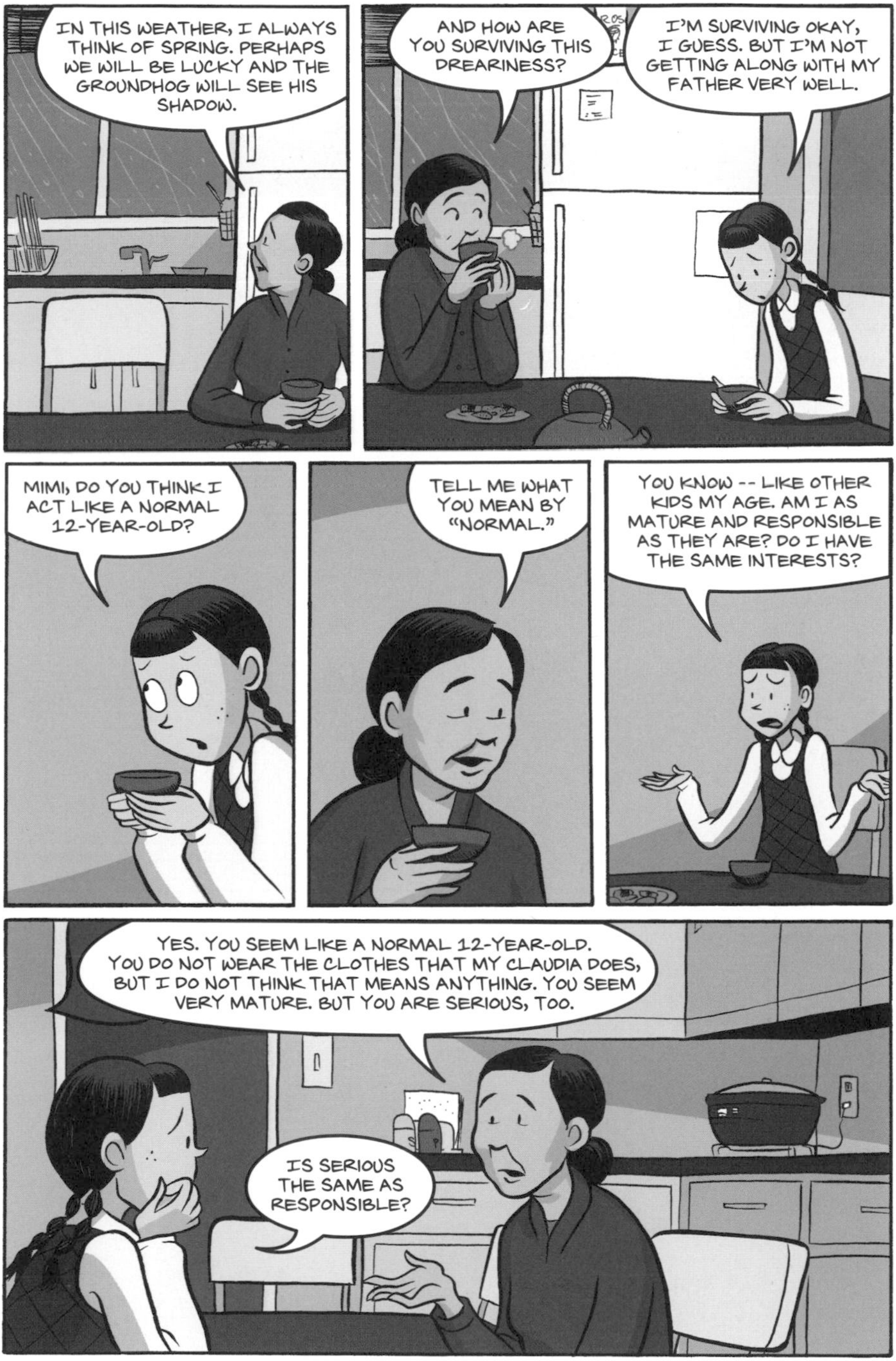
IN THIS WEATHER, I ALWAYS THINK OF SPRING. PERHAPS WE WILL BE LUCKY AND THE GROUNDHOG WILL SEE HIS SHADOW.
AND HOW ARE YOU SURVIVING THIS DREARINESS?
I'M SURVIVING OKAY, I GUESS. BUT I'M NOT GETTING ALONG WITH MY FATHER VERY WELL.
MIMI, DO YOU THINK I ACT LIKE A NORMAL 12-YEAR-OLD?
TELL ME WHAT YOU MEAN BY "NORMAL."
YOU KNOW -- LIKE OTHER KIDS MY AGE. AM I AS MATURE AND RESPONSIBLE AS THEY ARE? DO I HAVE THE SAME INTERESTS?
YES. YOU SEEM LIKE A NORMAL 12-YEAR-OLD. YOU DO NOT WEAR THE CLOTHES THAT MY CLAUDIA DOES, BUT I DO NOT THINK THAT MEANS ANYTHING. YOU SEEM VERY MATURE. BUT YOU ARE SERIOUS, TOO.
IS SERIOUS THE SAME AS RESPONSIBLE?

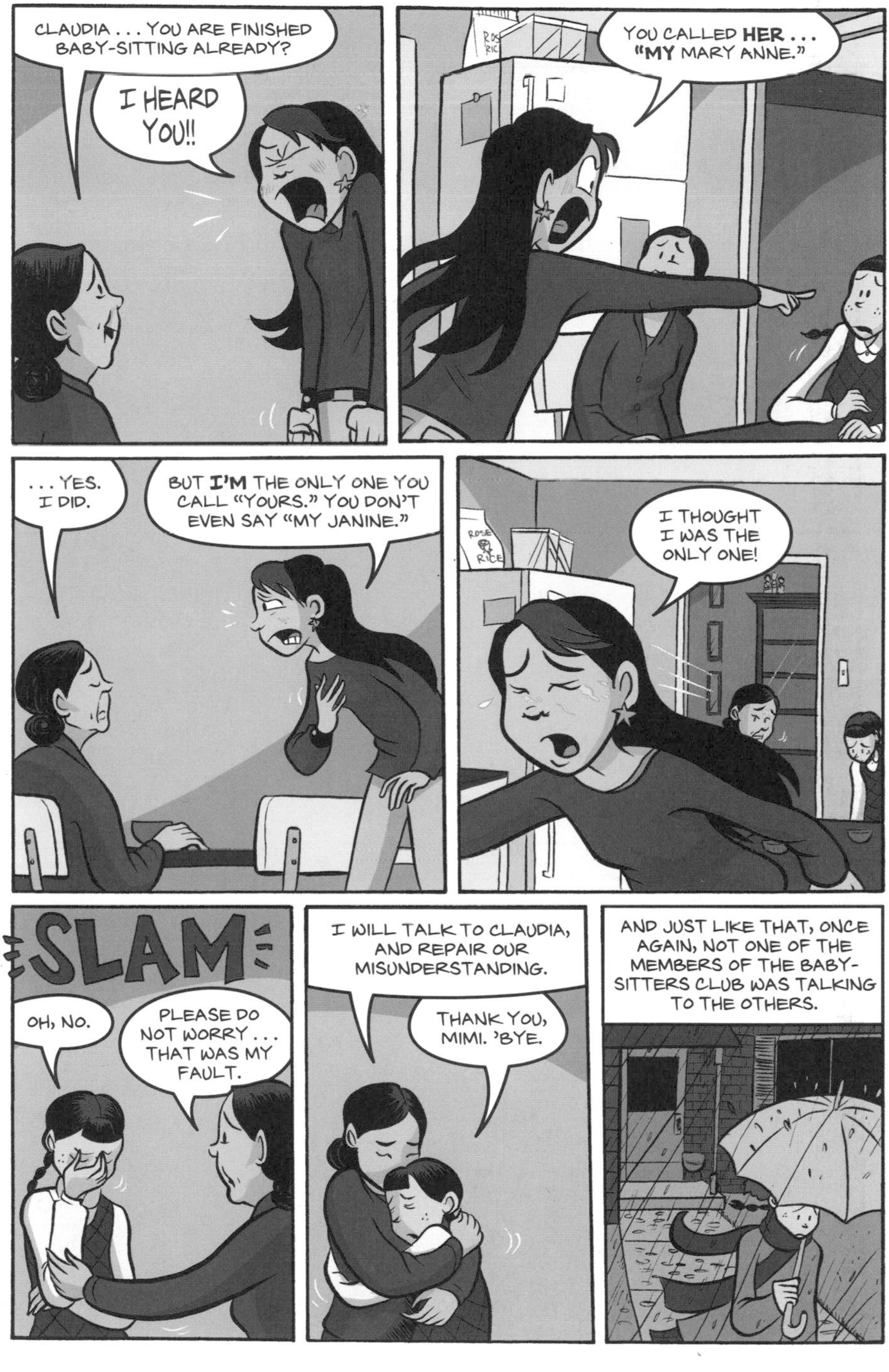
CLAUDIA . . . YOU ARE FINISHED BABY-SITTING ALREADY?
I HEARD YOU!!
YOU CALLED **HER . . . "MY** MARY ANNE."
. . . YES. I DID.
BUT **I'M** THE ONLY ONE YOU CALL "YOURS." YOU DON'T EVEN SAY "MY JANINE."
ROSE RICE
I THOUGHT I WAS THE ONLY ONE!
SLAM
OH, NO.
PLEASE DO NOT WORRY . . . THAT WAS MY FAULT.
I WILL TALK TO CLAUDIA, AND REPAIR OUR MISUNDERSTANDING.
THANK YOU, MIMI. 'BYE.
AND JUST LIKE THAT, ONCE AGAIN, NOT ONE OF THE MEMBERS OF THE BABY-SITTERS CLUB WAS TALKING TO THE OTHERS.

Teusday, January 20

I am so made! I know this notebook is
for writing our siting jobs so we can keep
track of club problems. Well, this is not
a sitting job, but I have a club probleme.
Her name is Mary Anne Spier or as she
is otherwise known **MY MARY ANNE**. Where
does Mary Anne get off being so chummy
with Mimi? It isn't fair. It's one thing
for Mimi to help her with her ~~niting~~ knitting
but today they were sharing tea in the
special cups and Mimi called her
My Mary Anne. <u>NO FAIR.</u> So there.

      * Claudia *

CHAPTER 8

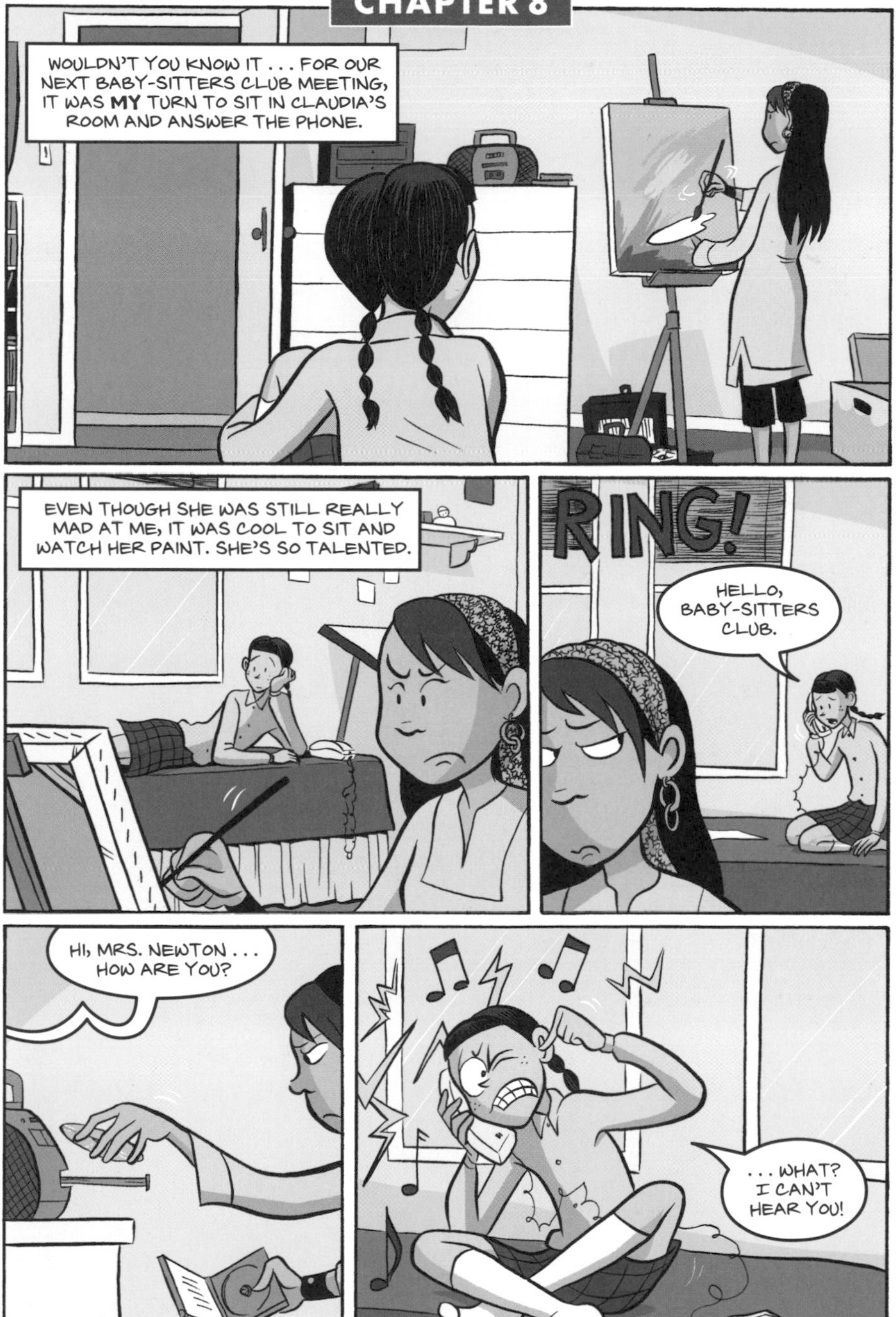
WOULDN'T YOU KNOW IT . . . FOR OUR NEXT BABY-SITTERS CLUB MEETING, IT WAS **MY** TURN TO SIT IN CLAUDIA'S ROOM AND ANSWER THE PHONE.
EVEN THOUGH SHE WAS STILL REALLY MAD AT ME, IT WAS COOL TO SIT AND WATCH HER PAINT. SHE'S SO TALENTED.
RING!
HELLO, BABY-SITTERS CLUB.
HI, MRS. NEWTON . . . HOW ARE YOU?
. . . WHAT? I CAN'T HEAR YOU!

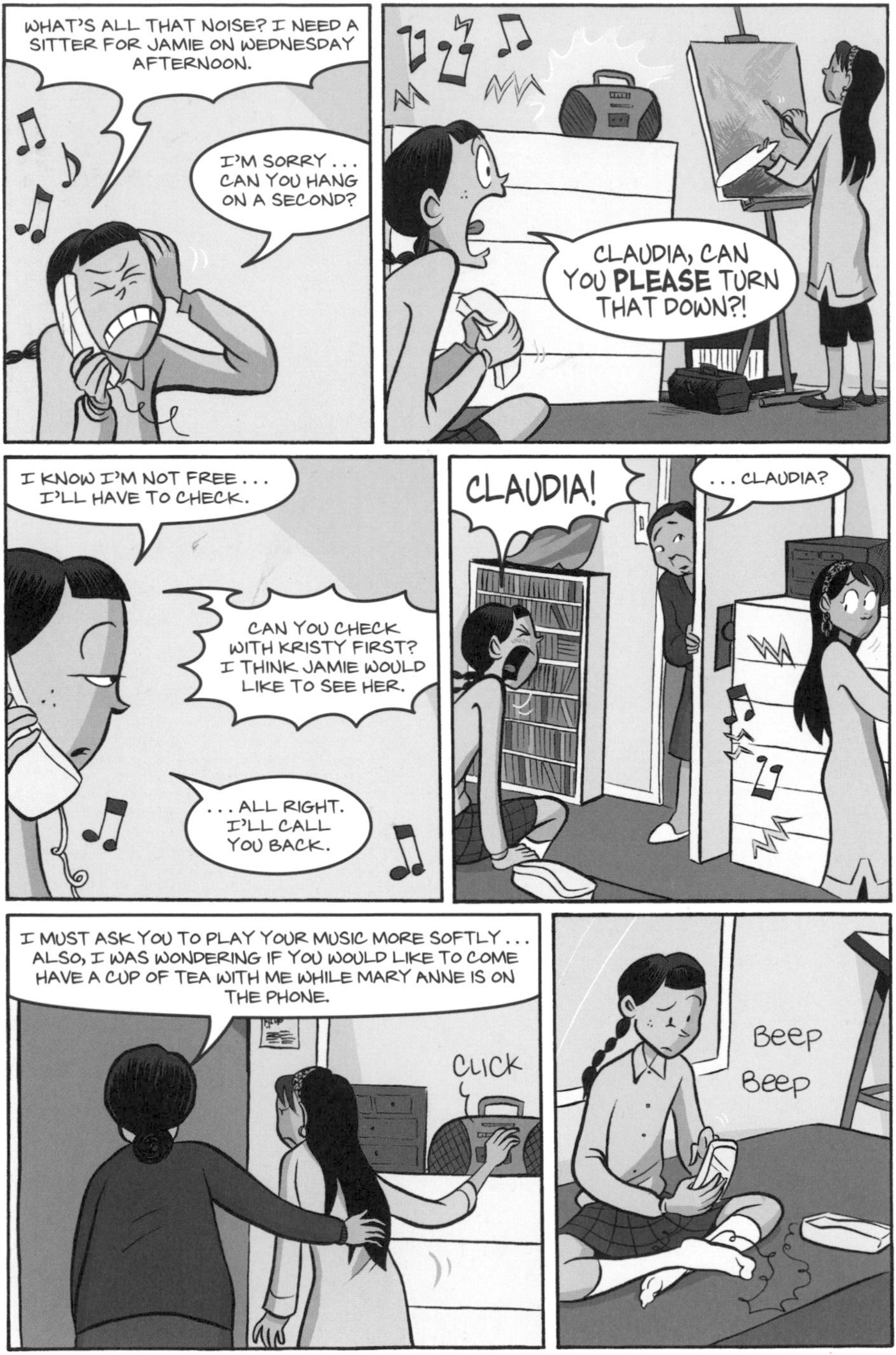
WHAT'S ALL THAT NOISE? I NEED A SITTER FOR JAMIE ON WEDNESDAY AFTERNOON.
I'M SORRY . . . CAN YOU HANG ON A SECOND?
CLAUDIA, CAN YOU **PLEASE** TURN THAT DOWN?!
I KNOW I'M NOT FREE . . . I'LL HAVE TO CHECK.
CAN YOU CHECK WITH KRISTY FIRST? I THINK JAMIE WOULD LIKE TO SEE HER.
. . . ALL RIGHT. I'LL CALL YOU BACK.
CLAUDIA!
. . . CLAUDIA?
I MUST ASK YOU TO PLAY YOUR MUSIC MORE SOFTLY . . . ALSO, I WAS WONDERING IF YOU WOULD LIKE TO COME HAVE A CUP OF TEA WITH ME WHILE MARY ANNE IS ON THE PHONE.
CLICK
Beep
Beep

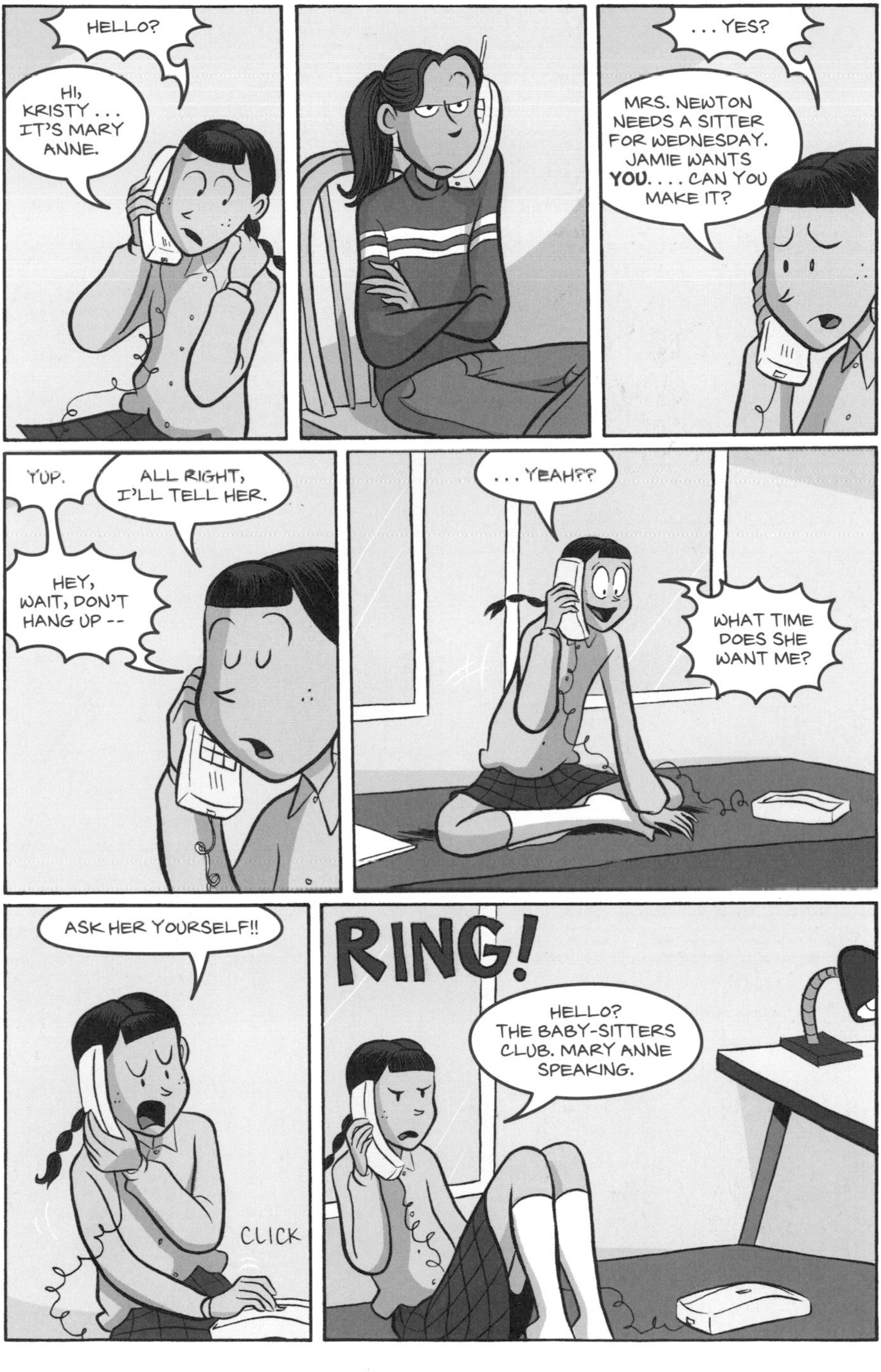
HELLO?
HI, KRISTY . . . IT'S MARY ANNE.
. . . YES?
MRS. NEWTON NEEDS A SITTER FOR WEDNESDAY. JAMIE WANTS **YOU**. . . . CAN YOU MAKE IT?
YUP.
ALL RIGHT, I'LL TELL HER.
HEY, WAIT, DON'T HANG UP --
. . . YEAH??
WHAT TIME DOES SHE WANT ME?
ASK HER YOURSELF!!
CLICK
RING!
HELLO? THE BABY-SITTERS CLUB. MARY ANNE SPEAKING.

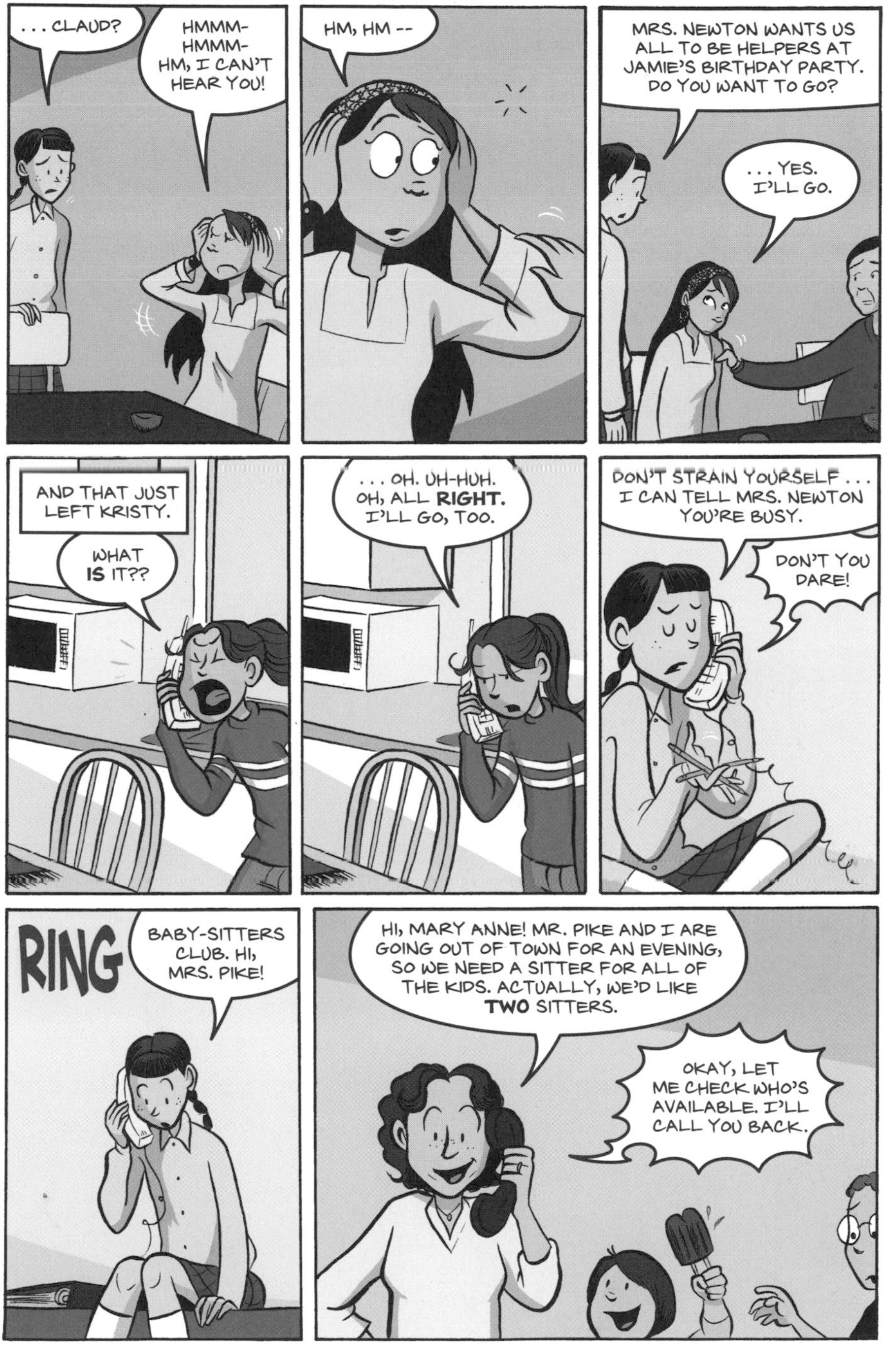
. . . CLAUD?
HMMM-HMMM-HM, I CAN'T HEAR YOU!
HM, HM --
MRS. NEWTON WANTS US ALL TO BE HELPERS AT JAMIE'S BIRTHDAY PARTY. DO YOU WANT TO GO?
. . . YES. I'LL GO.
AND THAT JUST LEFT KRISTY.
WHAT **IS** IT??
. . . OH. UH-HUH. OH, ALL **RIGHT.** I'LL GO, TOO.
DON'T STRAIN YOURSELF . . . I CAN TELL MRS. NEWTON YOU'RE BUSY.
DON'T YOU DARE!
RING
BABY-SITTERS CLUB. HI, MRS. PIKE!
HI, MARY ANNE! MR. PIKE AND I ARE GOING OUT OF TOWN FOR AN EVENING, SO WE NEED A SITTER FOR ALL OF THE KIDS. ACTUALLY, WE'D LIKE **TWO** SITTERS.
OKAY, LET ME CHECK WHO'S AVAILABLE. I'LL CALL YOU BACK.

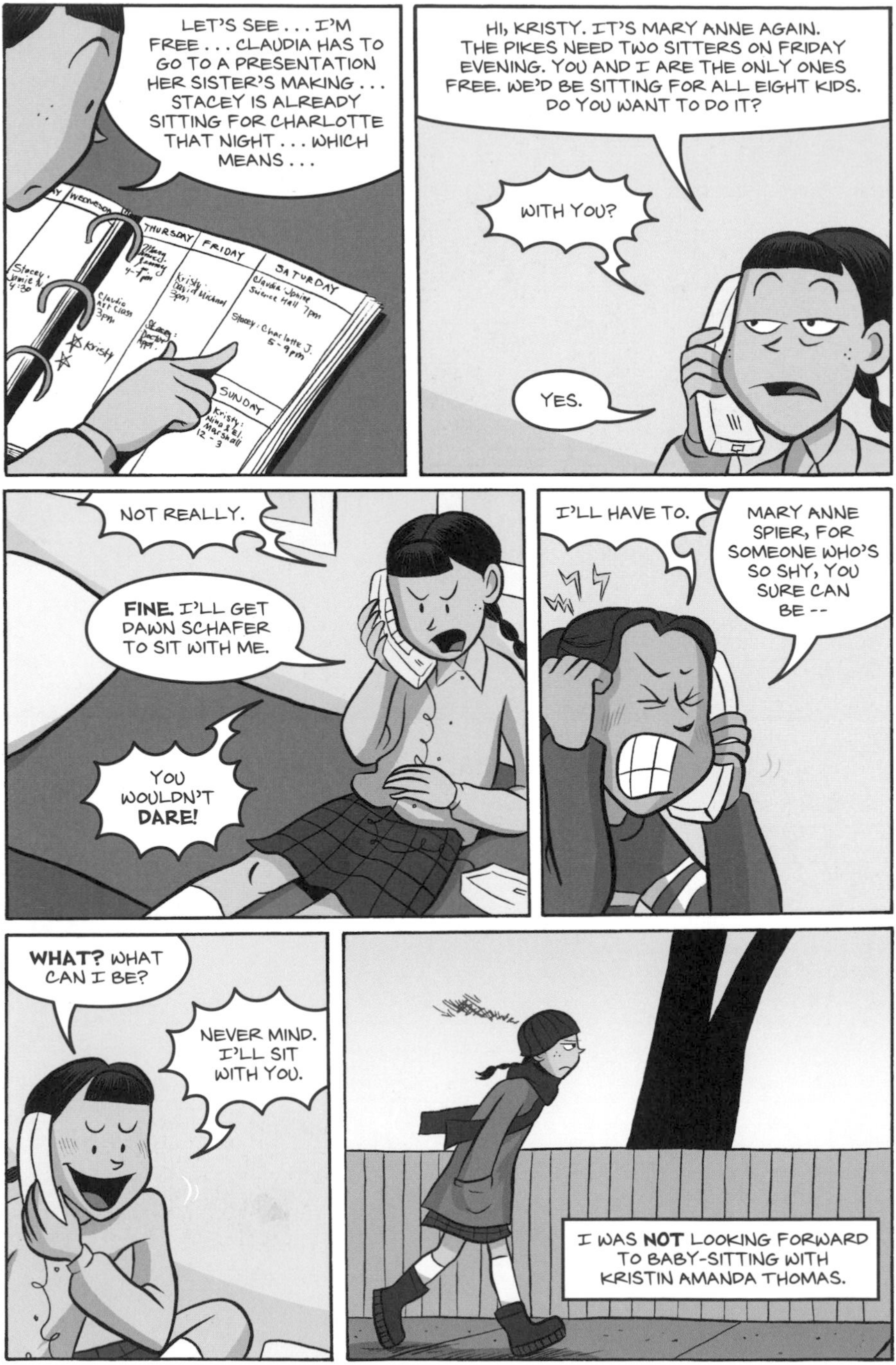
LET'S SEE . . . I'M FREE . . . CLAUDIA HAS TO GO TO A PRESENTATION HER SISTER'S MAKING . . . STACEY IS ALREADY SITTING FOR CHARLOTTE THAT NIGHT . . . WHICH MEANS . . .
THURSDAY
FRIDAY
SATURDAY
SUNDAY
Claudia: Janine Science Hall 7pm
Stacey: Charlotte J. 5-9pm
HI, KRISTY. IT'S MARY ANNE AGAIN. THE PIKES NEED TWO SITTERS ON FRIDAY EVENING. YOU AND I ARE THE ONLY ONES FREE. WE'D BE SITTING FOR ALL EIGHT KIDS. DO YOU WANT TO DO IT?
WITH YOU?
YES.
NOT REALLY.
FINE. I'LL GET DAWN SCHAFER TO SIT WITH ME.
YOU WOULDN'T **DARE!**
I'LL HAVE TO.
MARY ANNE SPIER, FOR SOMEONE WHO'S SO SHY, YOU SURE CAN BE --
WHAT? WHAT CAN I BE?
NEVER MIND. I'LL SIT WITH YOU.
I WAS **NOT** LOOKING FORWARD TO BABY-SITTING WITH KRISTIN AMANDA THOMAS.

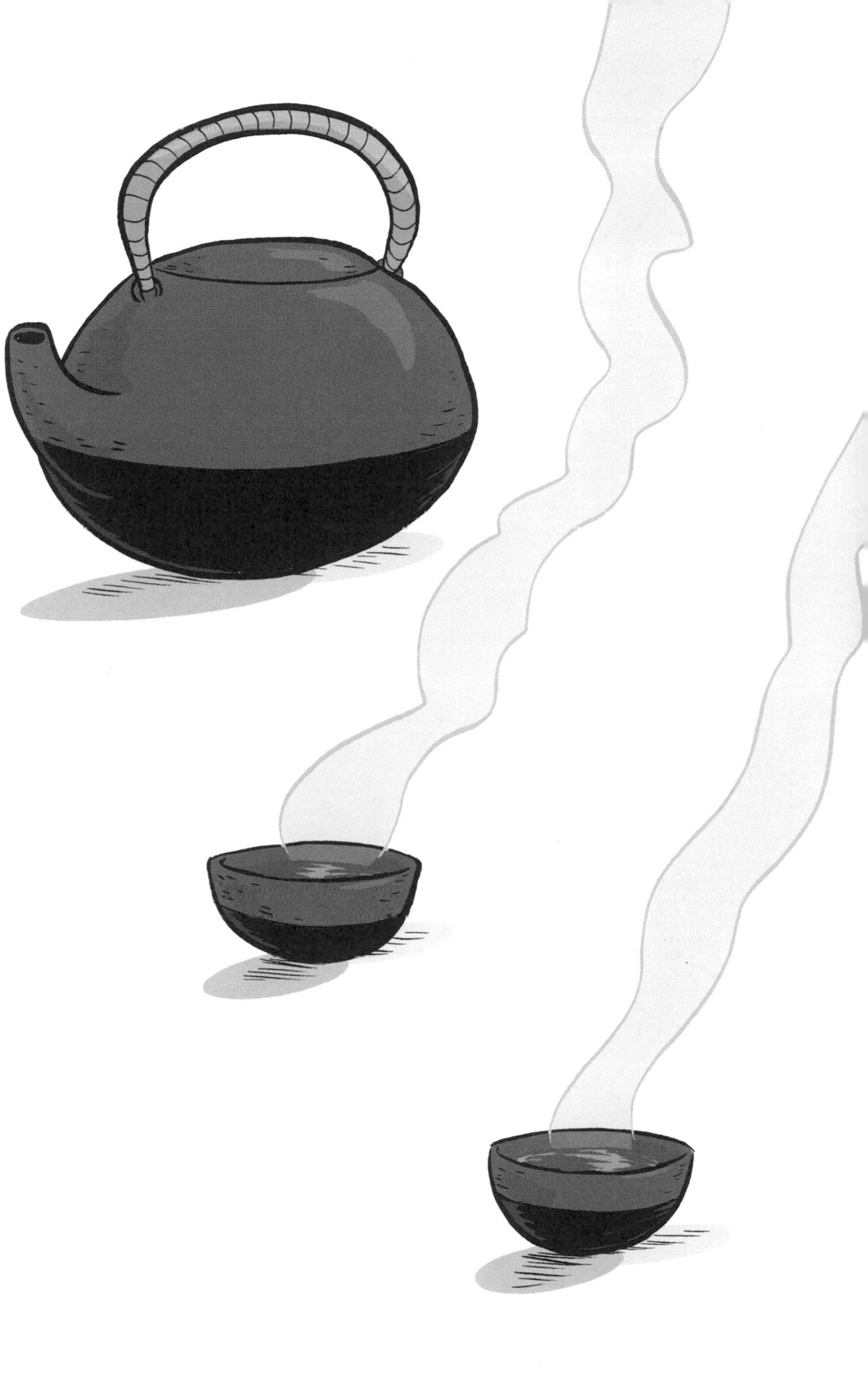

Saturday, January 31

Yesterday, Mary Anne and I baby-sat for the Pikes. I'm really surprised that we were able to pull it off. Hereby let it be known that it is possible:

1. For two people to baby-sit for eight kids without losing their sanity (the sitters' OR the kids'), and

2. for the baby-sitters to accomplish this without ever speaking to each other.

There should be a Baby-sitters' Hall of Fame where experiences like ours could be recorded and preserved for all to read about. To do what we did takes a lot of imagination.

. . . And a really good fight, I guess.

— Kristy

CHAPTER 9

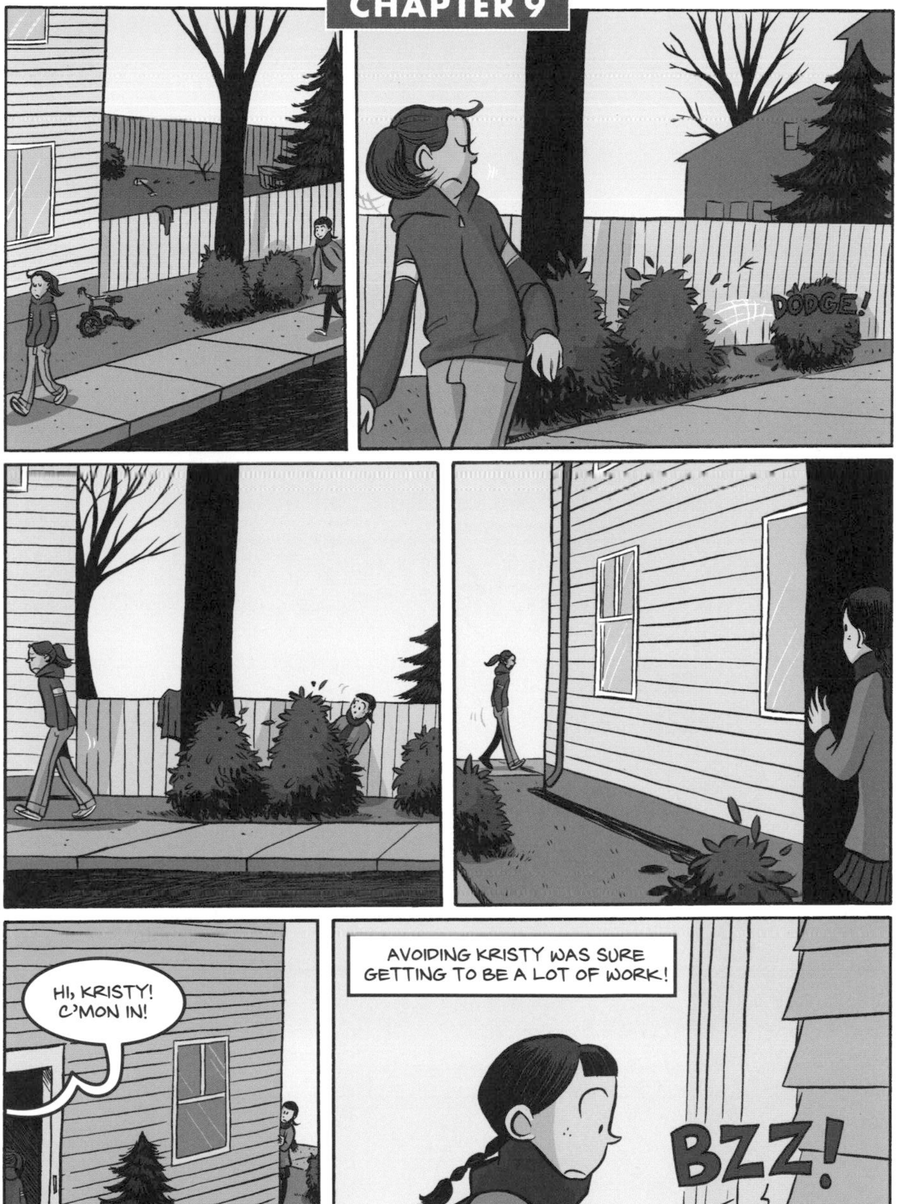
DODGE!
HI, KRISTY! C'MON IN!
AVOIDING KRISTY WAS SURE GETTING TO BE A LOT OF WORK!
BZZ!

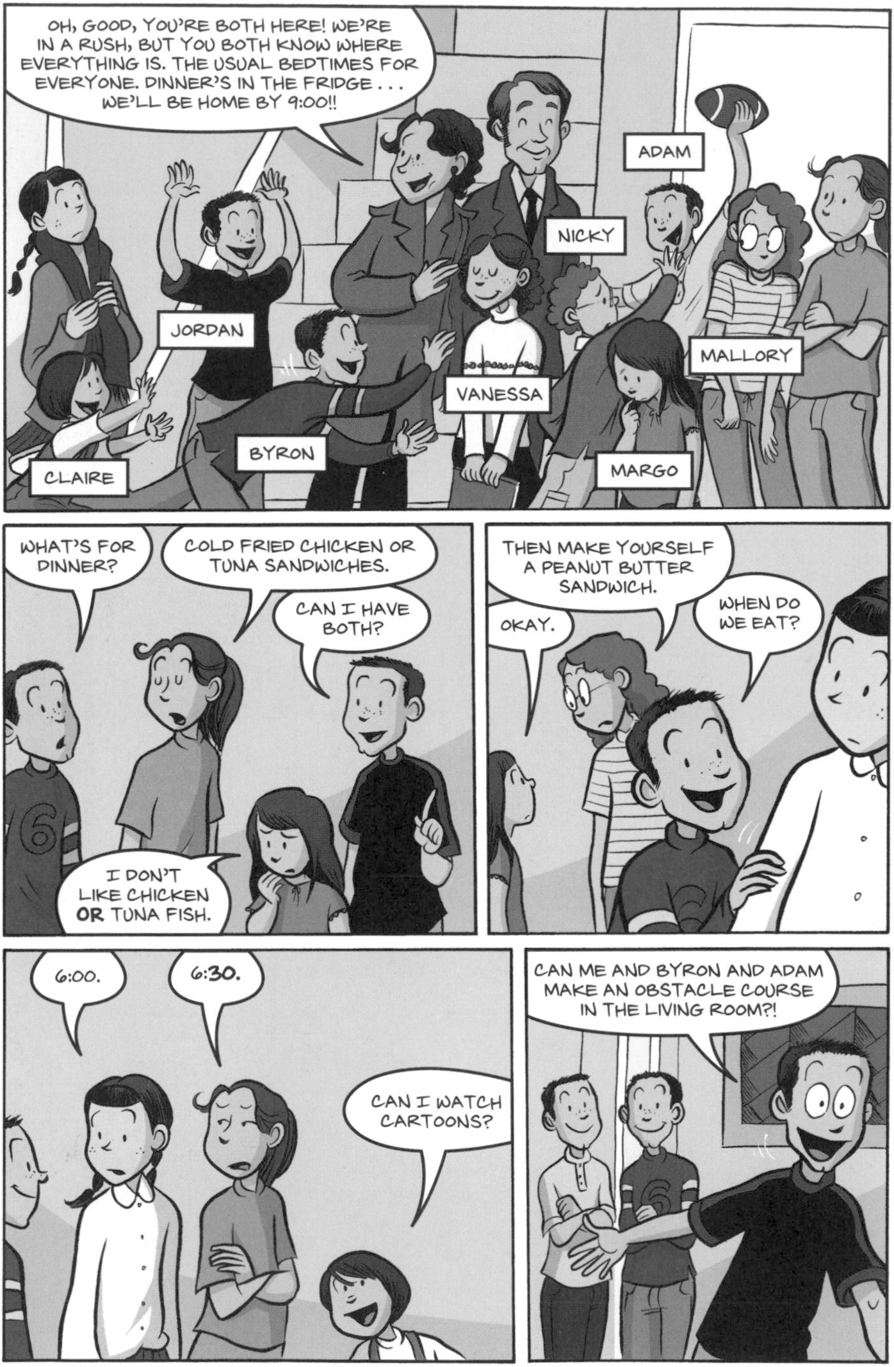
OH, GOOD, YOU'RE BOTH HERE! WE'RE IN A RUSH, BUT YOU BOTH KNOW WHERE EVERYTHING IS. THE USUAL BEDTIMES FOR EVERYONE. DINNER'S IN THE FRIDGE . . . WE'LL BE HOME BY 9:00!!
ADAM
NICKY
JORDAN
MALLORY
VANESSA
BYRON
MARGO
CLAIRE
WHAT'S FOR DINNER?
COLD FRIED CHICKEN OR TUNA SANDWICHES.
CAN I HAVE BOTH?
I DON'T LIKE CHICKEN **OR** TUNA FISH.
THEN MAKE YOURSELF A PEANUT BUTTER SANDWICH.
OKAY.
WHEN DO WE EAT?
6:00.
6:**30.**
CAN I WATCH CARTOONS?
CAN ME AND BYRON AND ADAM MAKE AN OBSTACLE COURSE IN THE LIVING ROOM?!

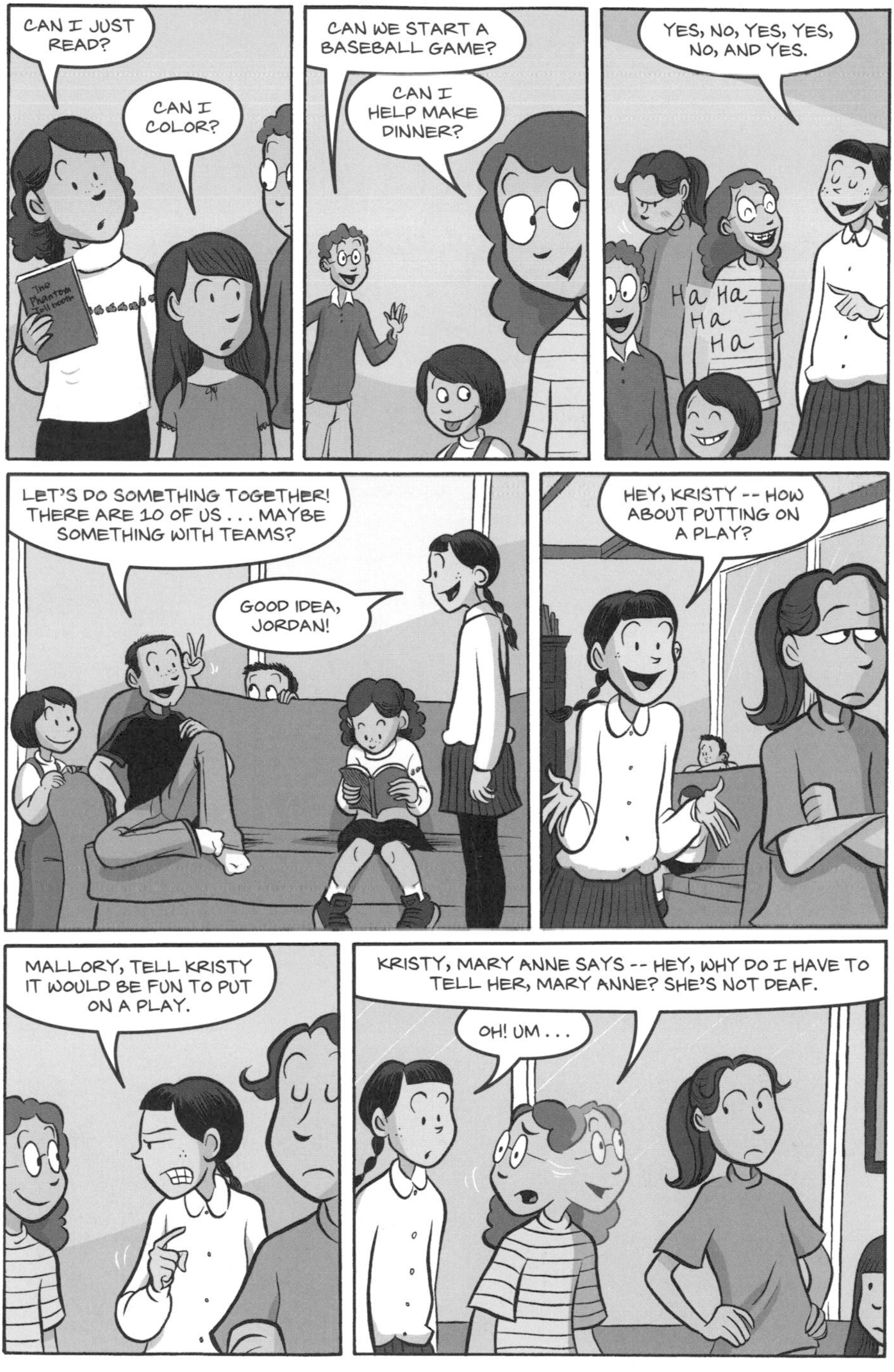
CAN I JUST READ?
CAN I COLOR?
The Phantom Tollbooth
CAN WE START A BASEBALL GAME?
CAN I HELP MAKE DINNER?
YES, NO, YES, YES, NO, AND YES.
Ha Ha Ha Ha
LET'S DO SOMETHING TOGETHER! THERE ARE 10 OF US . . . MAYBE SOMETHING WITH TEAMS?
GOOD IDEA, JORDAN!
HEY, KRISTY -- HOW ABOUT PUTTING ON A PLAY?
MALLORY, TELL KRISTY IT WOULD BE FUN TO PUT ON A PLAY.
KRISTY, MARY ANNE SAYS -- HEY, WHY DO I HAVE TO TELL HER, MARY ANNE? SHE'S NOT DEAF.
OH! UM . . .

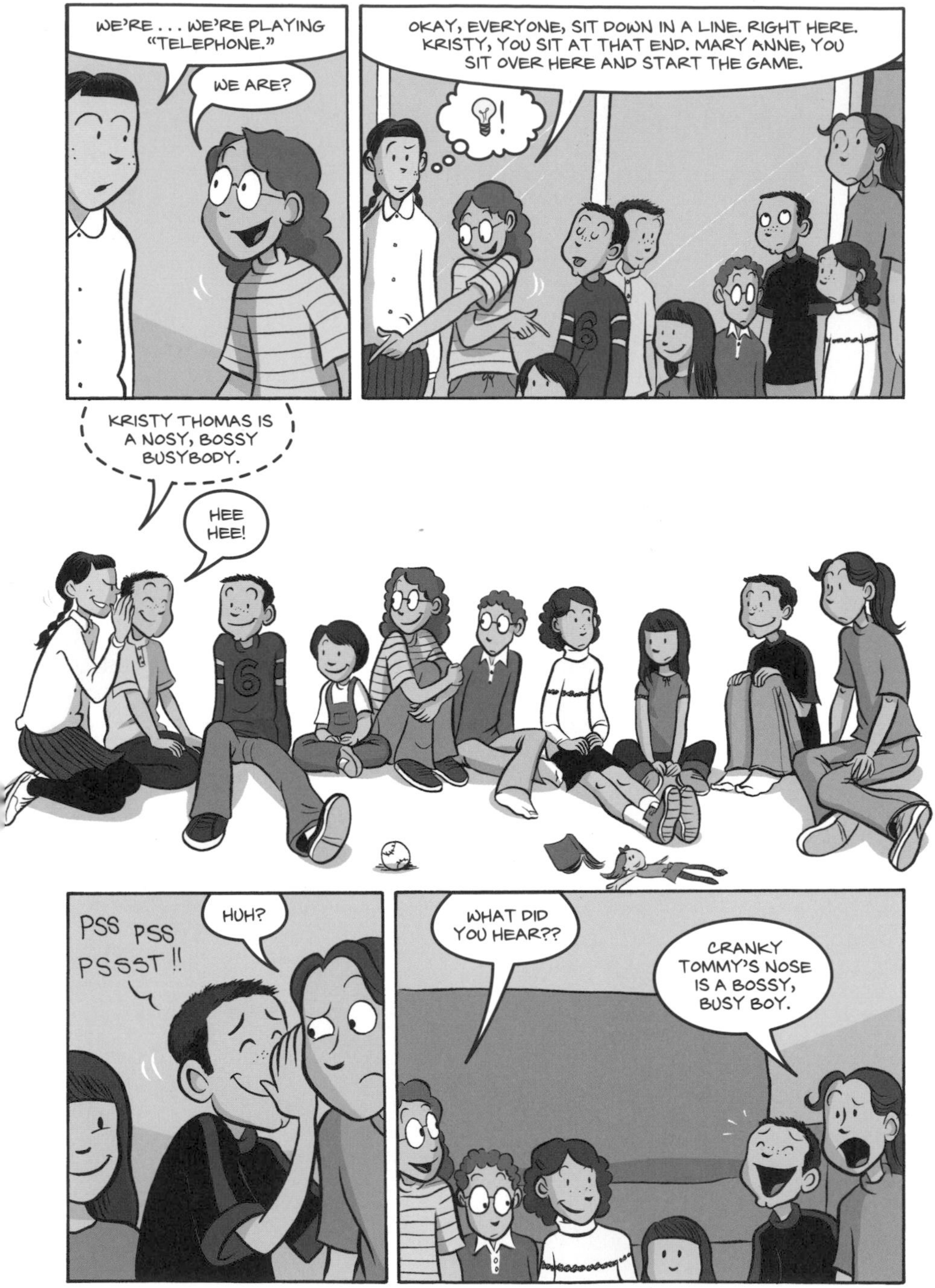
WE'RE . . . WE'RE PLAYING "TELEPHONE."
WE ARE?
OKAY, EVERYONE, SIT DOWN IN A LINE. RIGHT HERE. KRISTY, YOU SIT AT THAT END. MARY ANNE, YOU SIT OVER HERE AND START THE GAME.
!
KRISTY THOMAS IS A NOSY, BOSSY BUSYBODY.
HEE HEE!
PSS PSS PSSST!!
HUH?
WHAT DID YOU HEAR??
CRANKY TOMMY'S NOSE IS A BOSSY, BUSY BOY.

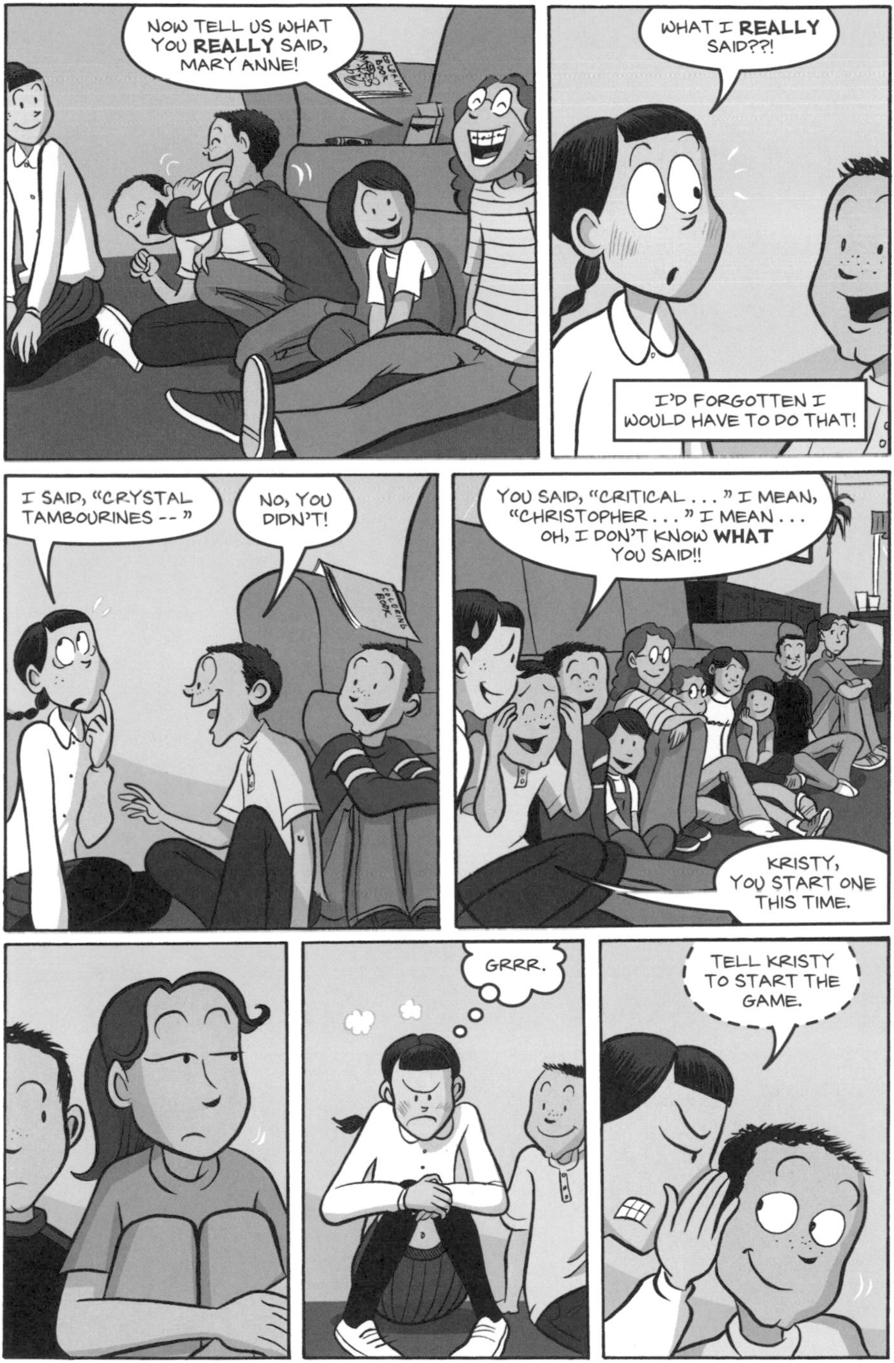
NOW TELL US WHAT YOU **REALLY** SAID, MARY ANNE!
WHAT I **REALLY** SAID??!
I'D FORGOTTEN I WOULD HAVE TO DO THAT!
I SAID, "CRYSTAL TAMBOURINES --"
NO, YOU DIDN'T!
COLORING BOOK
YOU SAID, "CRITICAL . . ." I MEAN, "CHRISTOPHER . . ." I MEAN . . . OH, I DON'T KNOW **WHAT** YOU SAID!!
KRISTY, YOU START ONE THIS TIME.
GRRR.
TELL KRISTY TO START THE GAME.

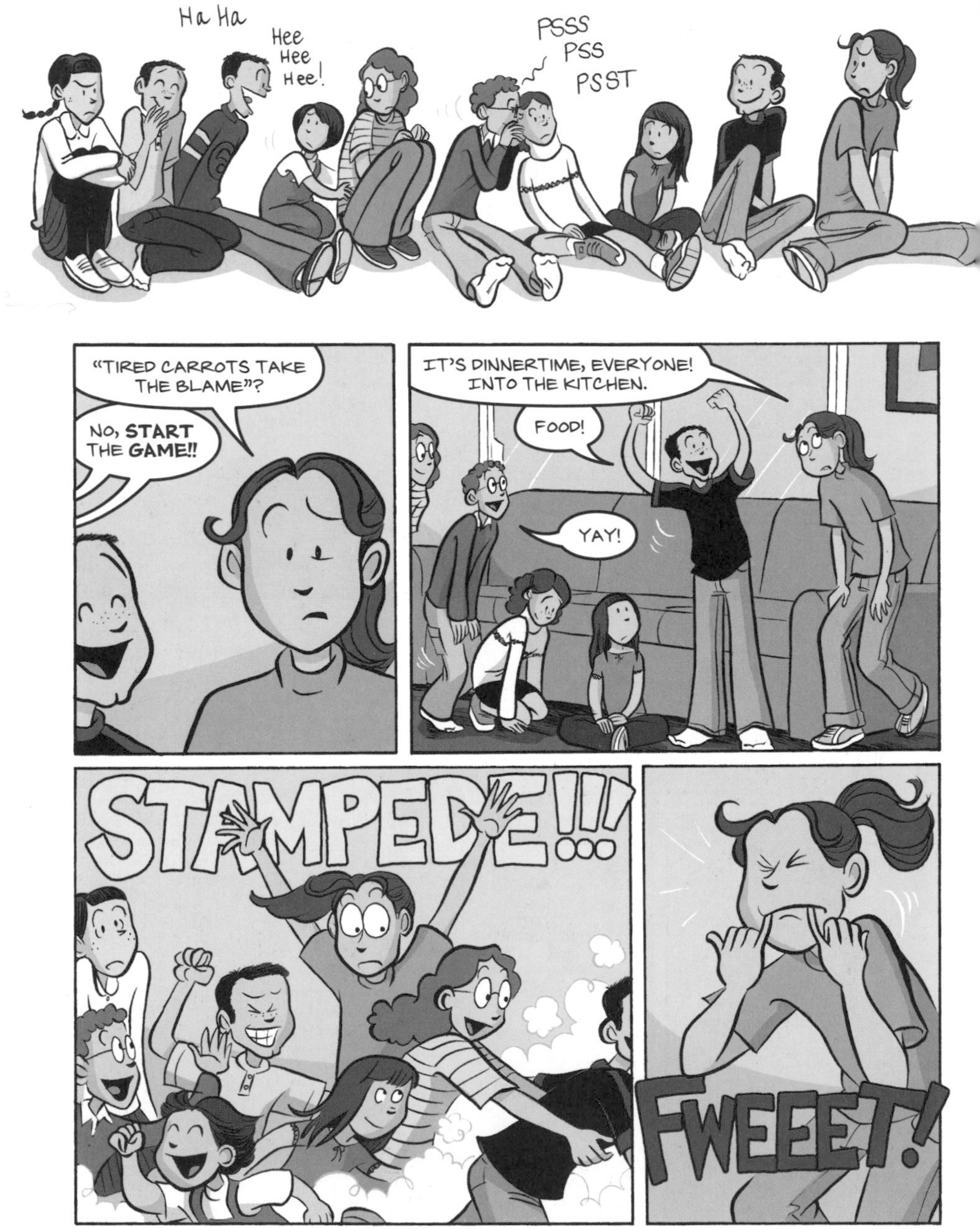

Ha Ha
Hee Hee Hee!
PSSS PSS PSST
"TIRED CARROTS TAKE THE BLAME"?
NO, **START** THE **GAME**!!
IT'S DINNERTIME, EVERYONE! INTO THE KITCHEN.
FOOD!
YAY!
STAMPEDE!!!
FWEEET!

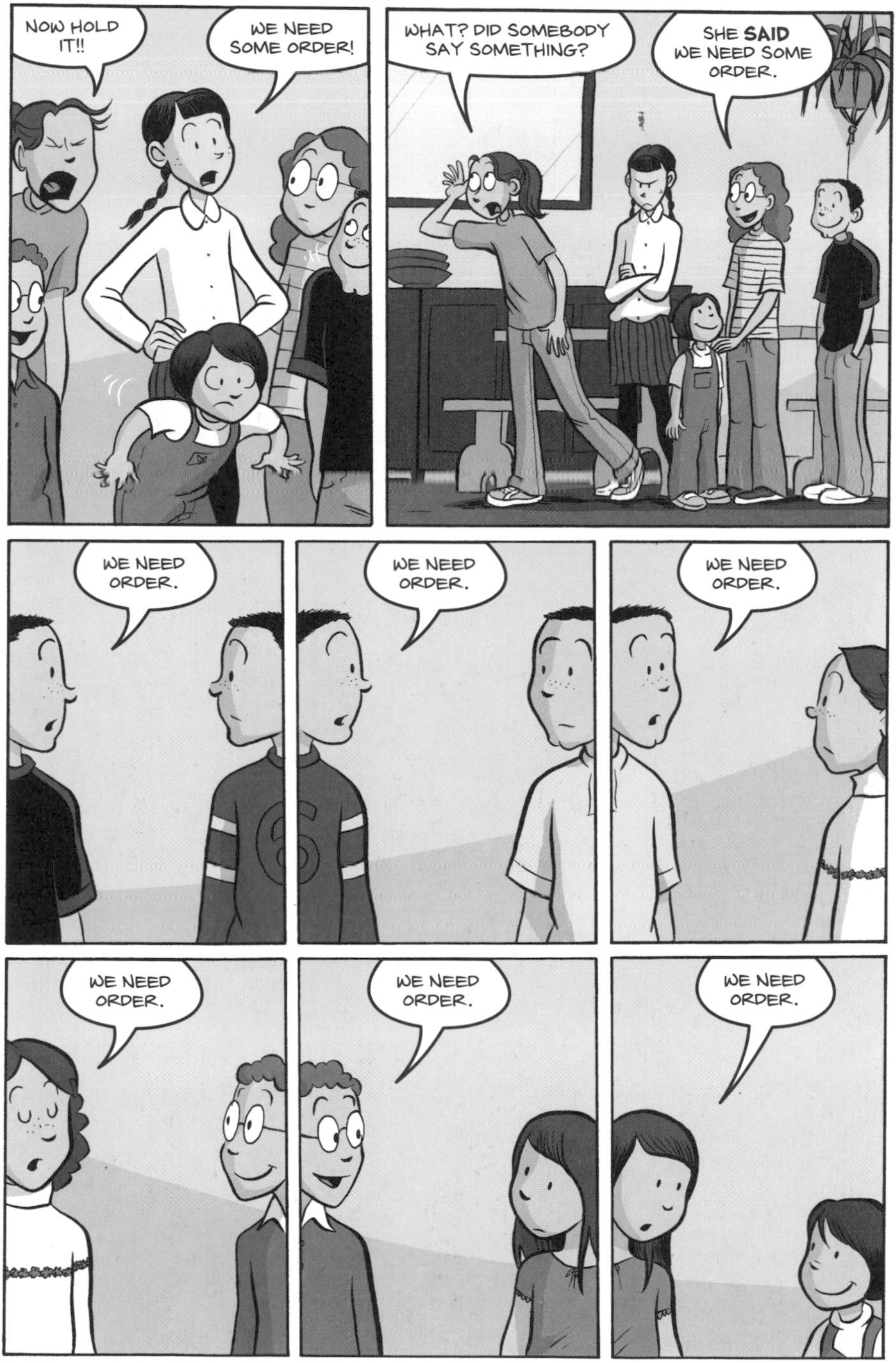
NOW HOLD IT!!
WE NEED SOME ORDER!
WHAT? DID SOMEBODY SAY SOMETHING?
SHE **SAID** WE NEED SOME ORDER.
WE NEED ORDER.
WE NEED ORDER.
WE NEED ORDER.
WE NEED ORDER.
WE NEED ORDER.
WE NEED ORDER.

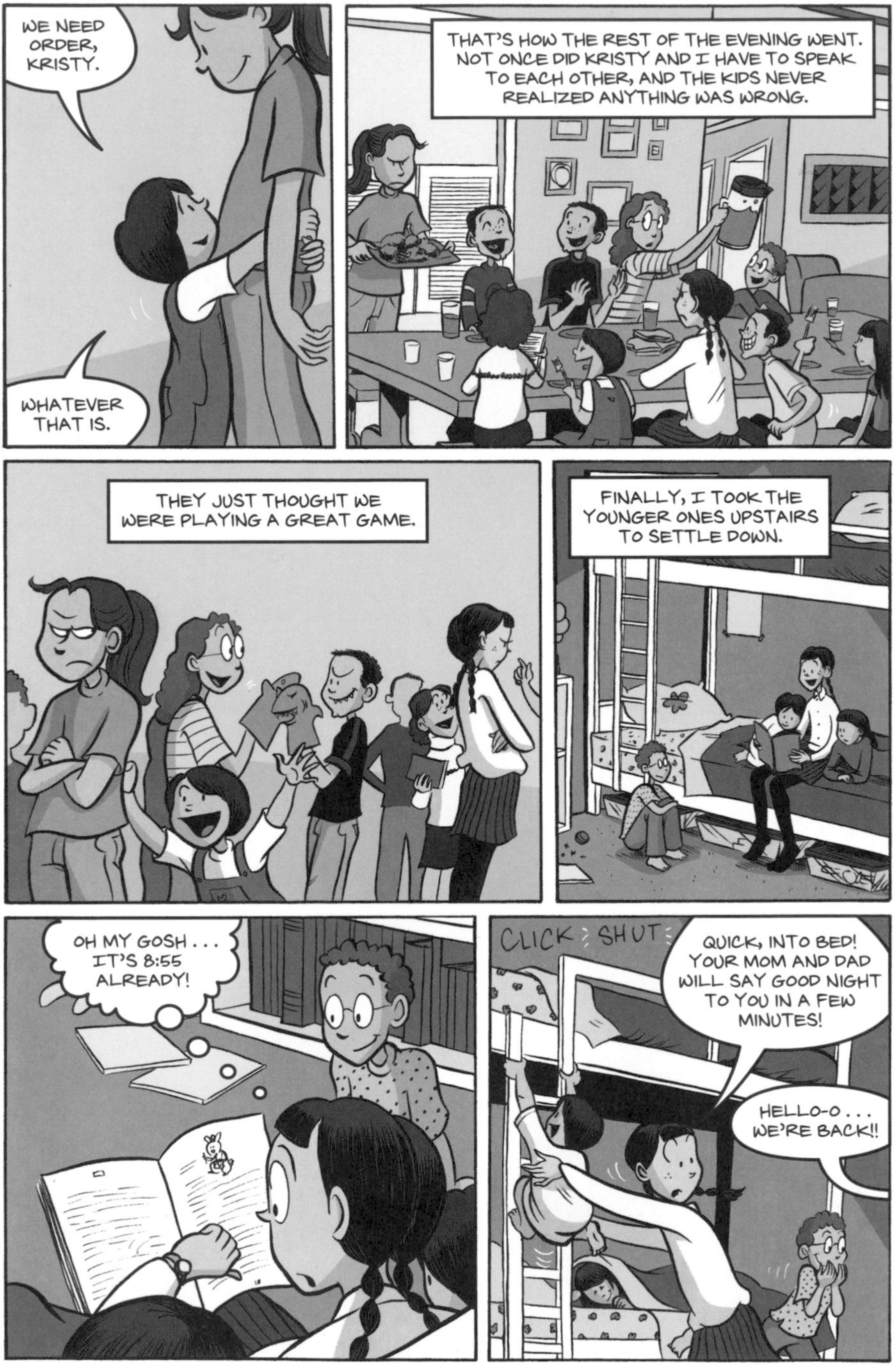
WE NEED ORDER, KRISTY.
WHATEVER THAT IS.
THAT'S HOW THE REST OF THE EVENING WENT. NOT ONCE DID KRISTY AND I HAVE TO SPEAK TO EACH OTHER, AND THE KIDS NEVER REALIZED ANYTHING WAS WRONG.
THEY JUST THOUGHT WE WERE PLAYING A GREAT GAME.
FINALLY, I TOOK THE YOUNGER ONES UPSTAIRS TO SETTLE DOWN.
OH MY GOSH . . . IT'S 8:55 ALREADY!
CLICK
SHUT
QUICK, INTO BED! YOUR MOM AND DAD WILL SAY GOOD NIGHT TO YOU IN A FEW MINUTES!
HELLO-O . . . WE'RE BACK!!

FIVE MINUTES AFTER NINE!!

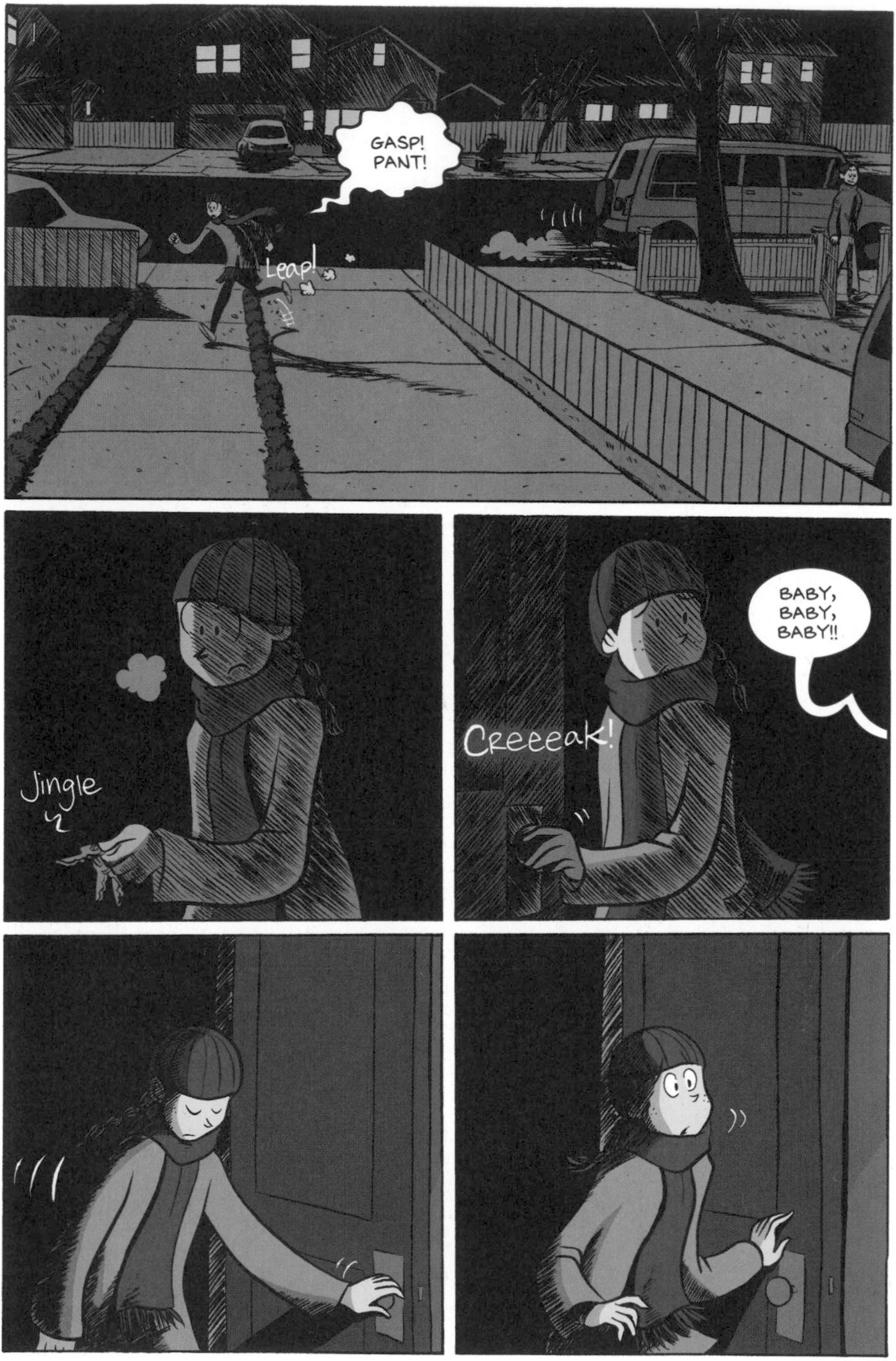
GASP! PANT!
Leap!
Jingle
Creeeak!
BABY, BABY, BABY!!

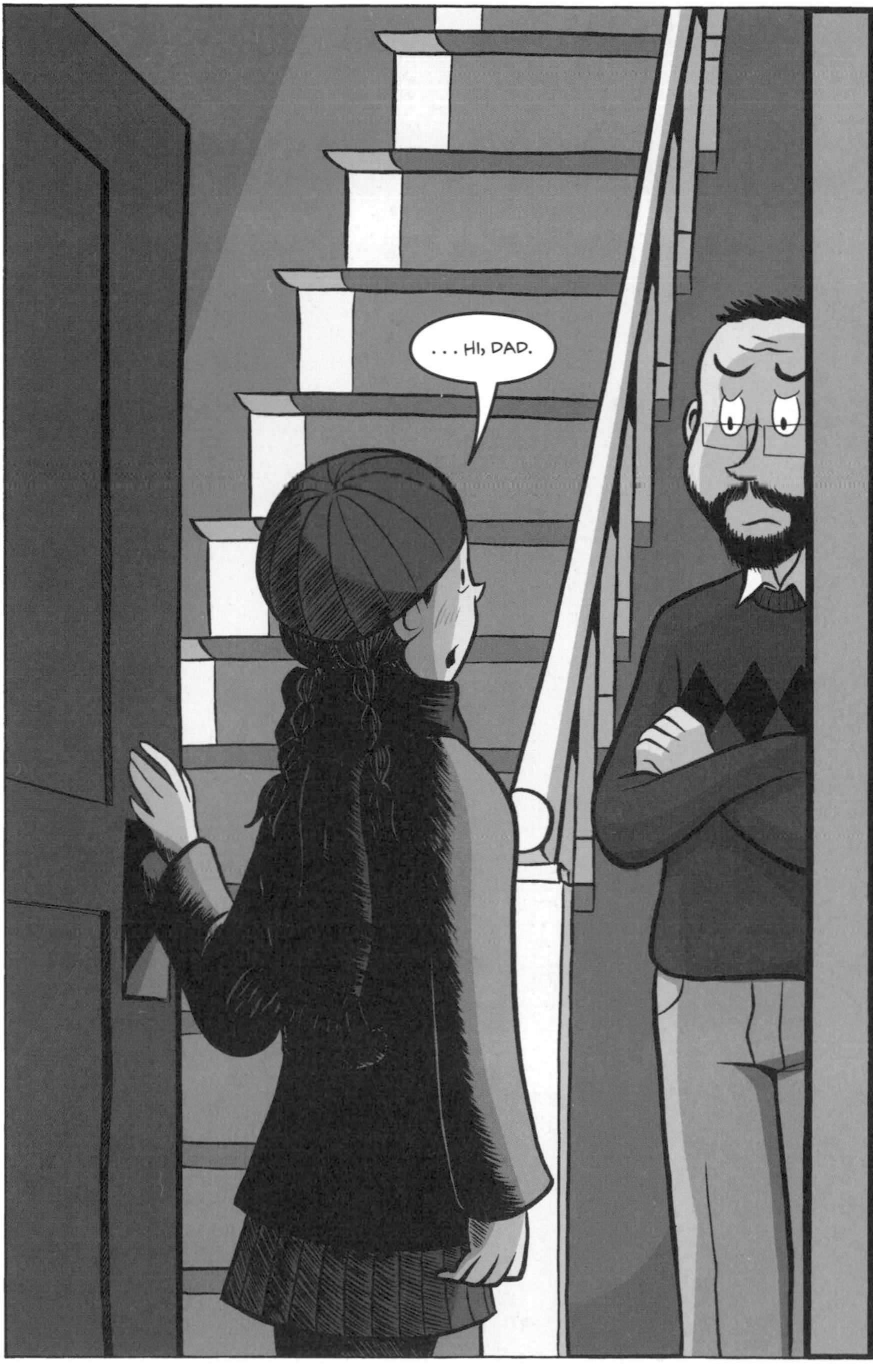
. . . HI, DAD.

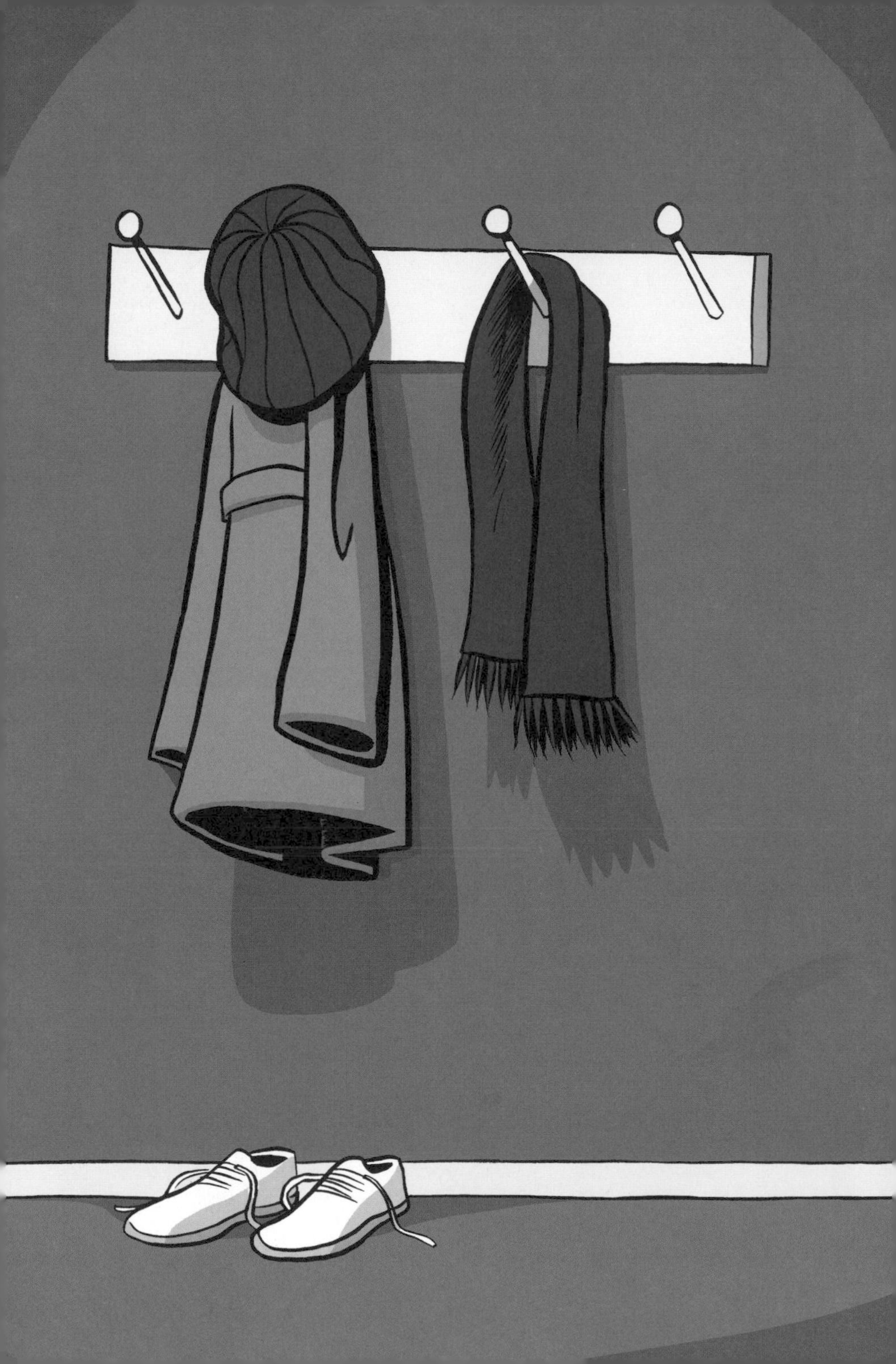

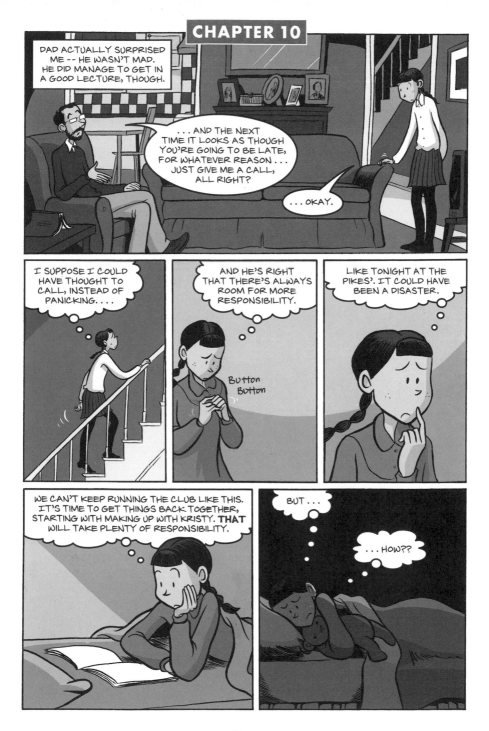

CHAPTER 10

DAD ACTUALLY SURPRISED ME -- HE WASN'T MAD. HE DID MANAGE TO GET IN A GOOD LECTURE, THOUGH.

... AND THE NEXT TIME IT LOOKS AS THOUGH YOU'RE GOING TO BE LATE, FOR WHATEVER REASON ... JUST GIVE ME A CALL, ALL RIGHT?

... OKAY.

I SUPPOSE I COULD HAVE THOUGHT TO CALL, INSTEAD OF PANICKING. . . .

AND HE'S RIGHT THAT THERE'S ALWAYS ROOM FOR MORE RESPONSIBILITY.

Button Button

LIKE TONIGHT AT THE PIKES'. IT COULD HAVE BEEN A DISASTER.

WE CAN'T KEEP RUNNING THE CLUB LIKE THIS. IT'S TIME TO GET THINGS BACK TOGETHER, STARTING WITH MAKING UP WITH KRISTY. **THAT** WILL TAKE PLENTY OF RESPONSIBILITY.

BUT . . .

... HOW??

CHAPTER 11

BUT THEN ON SATURDAY, SOMETHING HAPPENED TO KEEP MY MIND OFF OF OUR PARENTS, **AND** THE CLUB.

I HAD A SITTING JOB FOR JENNY PREZZIOSO. I GOT TO HER HOUSE AT 11:30.

DING DONG!

WHO IS IT?

IT'S MARY ANNE SPIER, YOUR BABY-SITTER.

ARE YOU A STRANGER?

NO, I'M MARY ANNE. MAYBE YOU SHOULD GO GET YOUR MOTHER.

THIS COULD BE A **VERY** LONG AFTERNOON.

STACEY HAD WARNED US ALL ABOUT JENNY IN THE CLUB NOTEBOOK, SO I WAS PREPARED.

HI, MARY ANNE. I'M MRS. PREZZIOSO, AND THIS IS MY LITTLE ANGEL, JENNY.

MY HUSBAND AND I ARE GOING UP TO CHATHAM FOR A BASKETBALL GAME.

HIS COLLEGE IS PLAYING THEIR BIGGEST RIVAL, SO HE'S VERY EXCITED.

READY, HONEY?

93

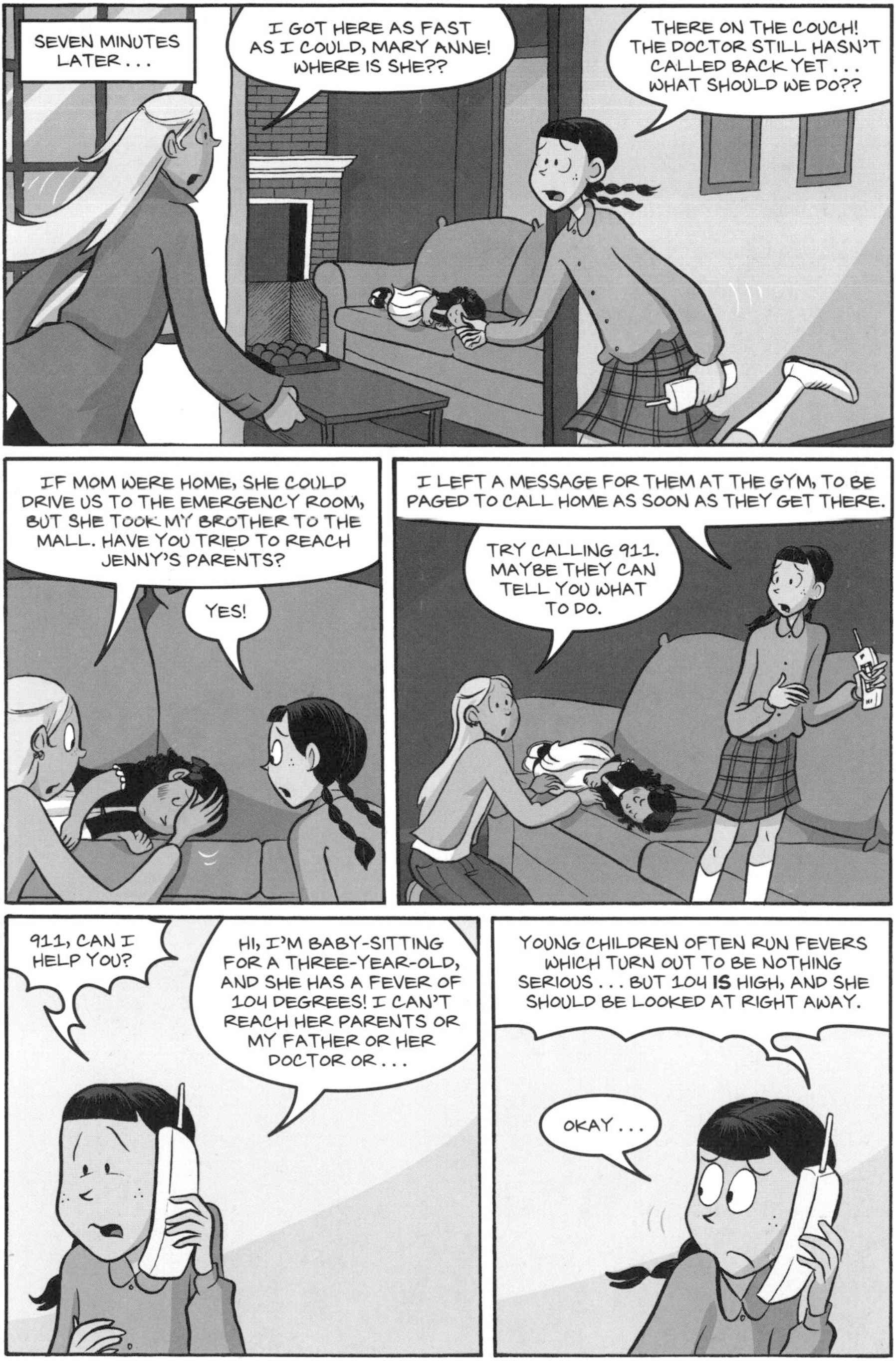
SEVEN MINUTES LATER . . .
I GOT HERE AS FAST AS I COULD, MARY ANNE! WHERE IS SHE??
THERE ON THE COUCH! THE DOCTOR STILL HASN'T CALLED BACK YET . . . WHAT SHOULD WE DO??
IF MOM WERE HOME, SHE COULD DRIVE US TO THE EMERGENCY ROOM, BUT SHE TOOK MY BROTHER TO THE MALL. HAVE YOU TRIED TO REACH JENNY'S PARENTS?
YES!
I LEFT A MESSAGE FOR THEM AT THE GYM, TO BE PAGED TO CALL HOME AS SOON AS THEY GET THERE.
TRY CALLING 911. MAYBE THEY CAN TELL YOU WHAT TO DO.
911, CAN I HELP YOU?
HI, I'M BABY-SITTING FOR A THREE-YEAR-OLD, AND SHE HAS A FEVER OF 104 DEGREES! I CAN'T REACH HER PARENTS OR MY FATHER OR HER DOCTOR OR . . .
YOUNG CHILDREN OFTEN RUN FEVERS WHICH TURN OUT TO BE NOTHING SERIOUS . . . BUT 104 **IS** HIGH, AND SHE SHOULD BE LOOKED AT RIGHT AWAY.
OKAY . . .

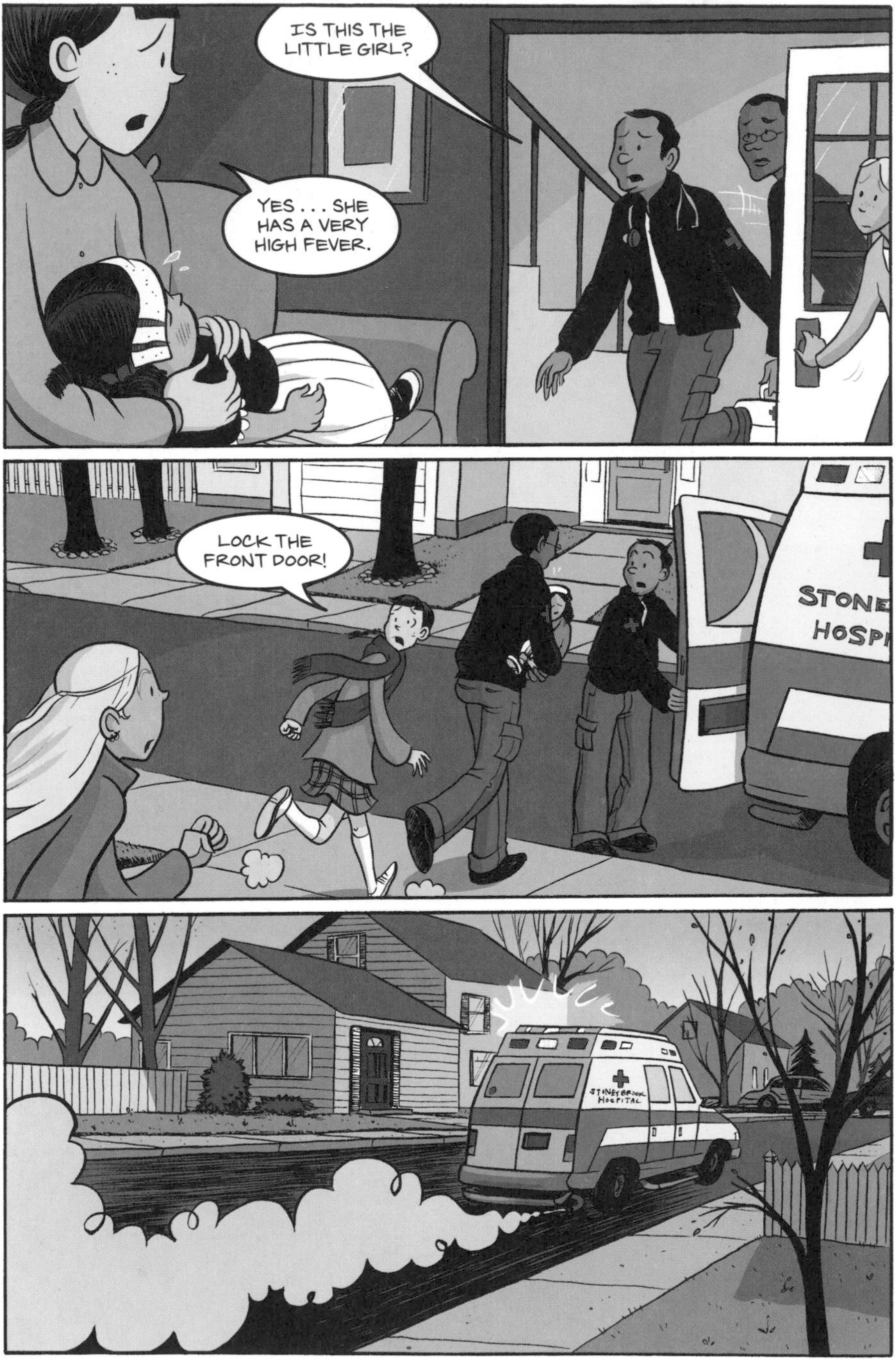
IS THIS THE LITTLE GIRL?
YES . . . SHE HAS A VERY HIGH FEVER.
LOCK THE FRONT DOOR!
STONEYBROOK HOSPITAL

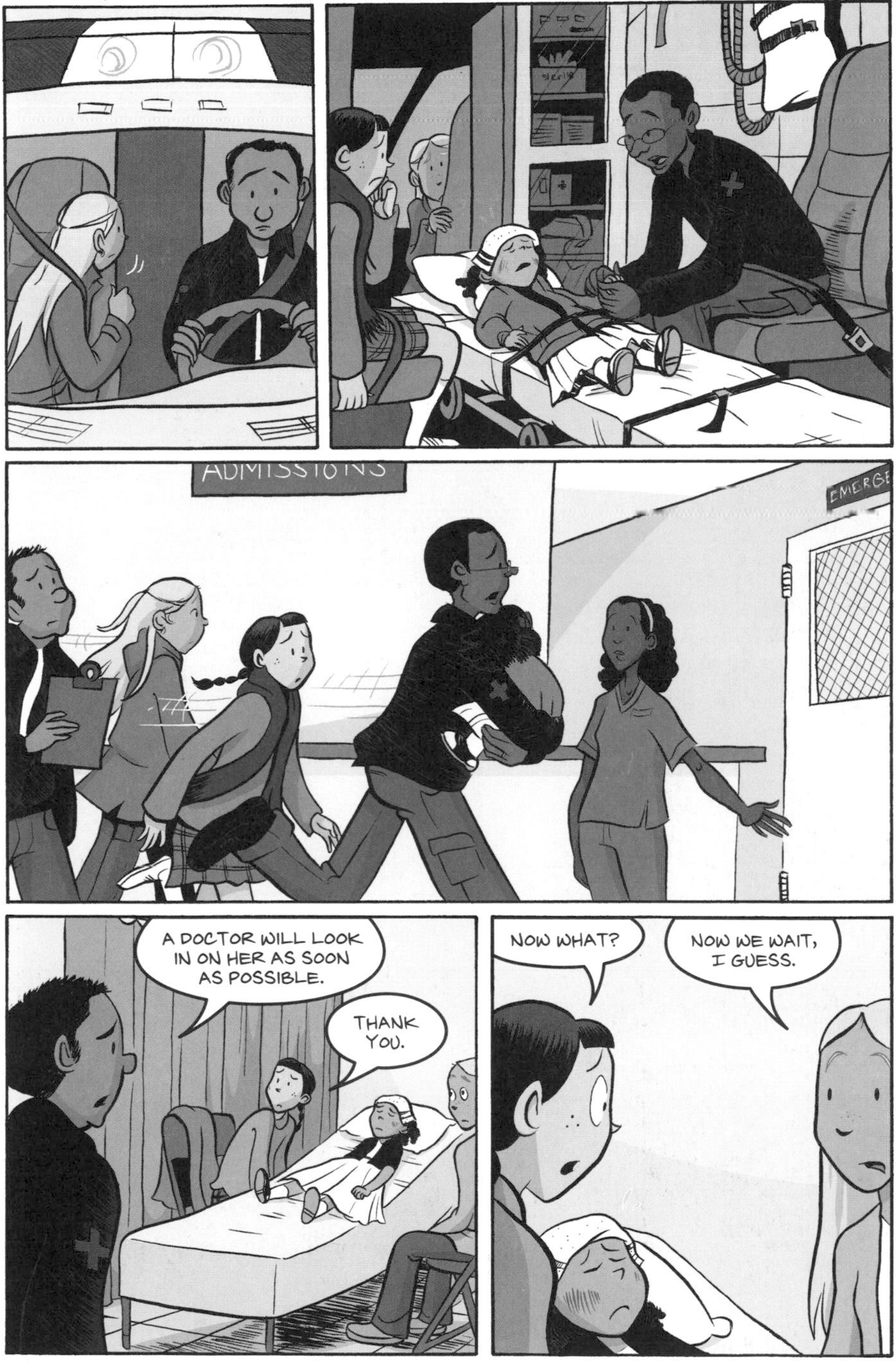
ADMISSIONS
EMERGE
A DOCTOR WILL LOOK IN ON HER AS SOON AS POSSIBLE.
THANK YOU.
NOW WHAT?
NOW WE WAIT, I GUESS.

105

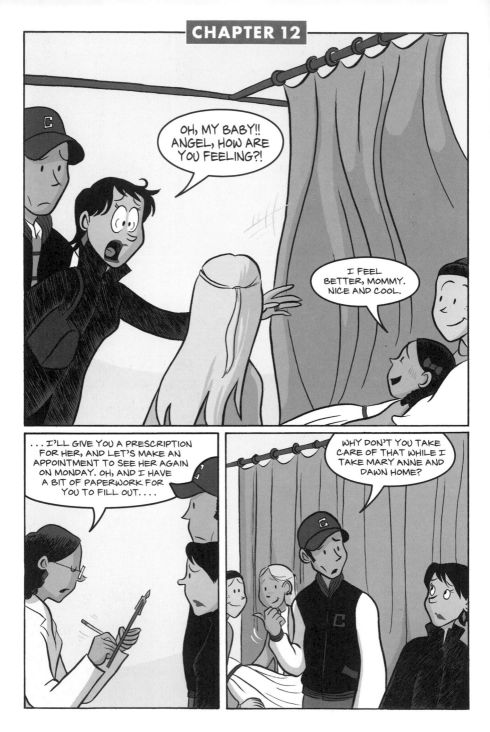

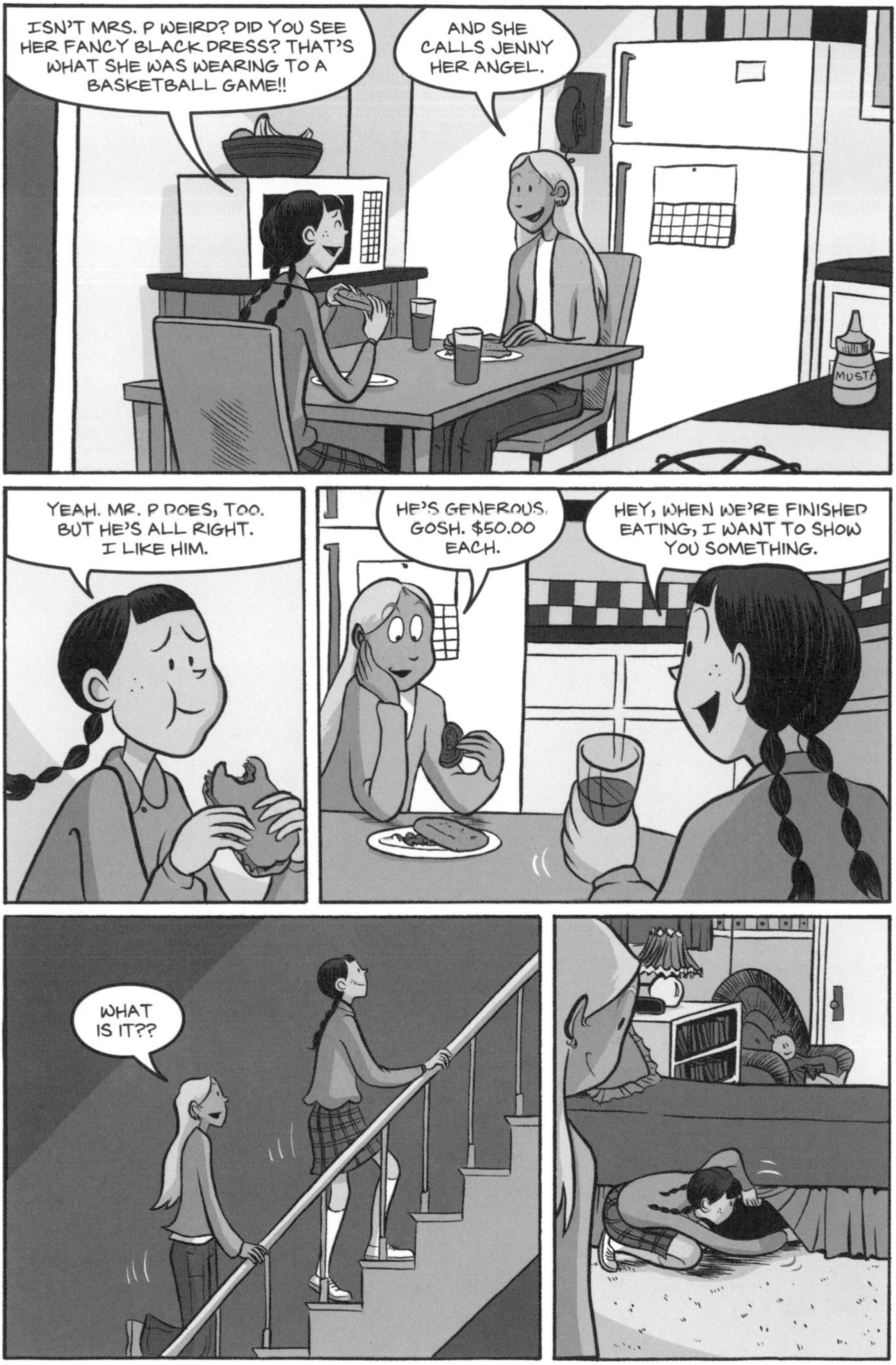
ISN'T MRS. P WEIRD? DID YOU SEE HER FANCY BLACK DRESS? THAT'S WHAT SHE WAS WEARING TO A BASKETBALL GAME!!
AND SHE CALLS JENNY HER ANGEL.
MUSTA
YEAH. MR. P DOES, TOO. BUT HE'S ALL RIGHT. I LIKE HIM.
HE'S GENEROUS. GOSH. $50.00 EACH.
HEY, WHEN WE'RE FINISHED EATING, I WANT TO SHOW YOU SOMETHING.
WHAT IS IT??

110

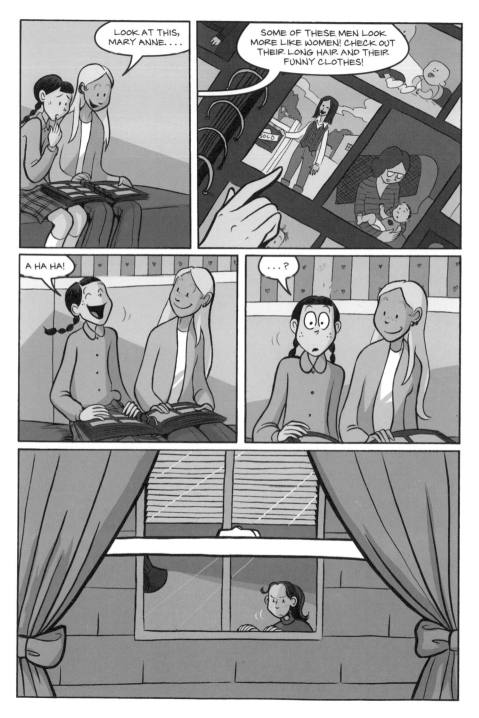

111

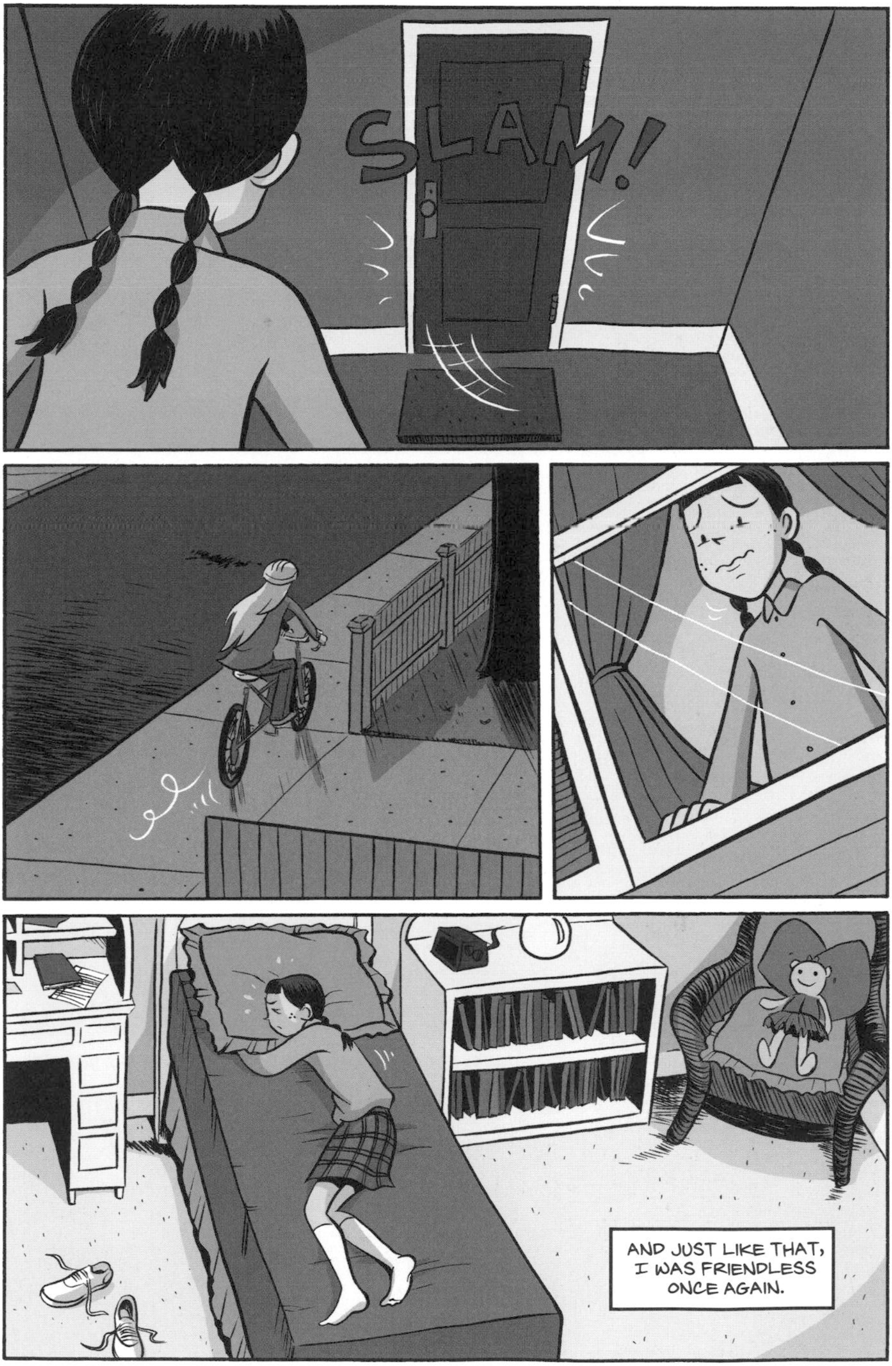
SLAM!
AND JUST LIKE THAT,
I WAS FRIENDLESS
ONCE AGAIN.

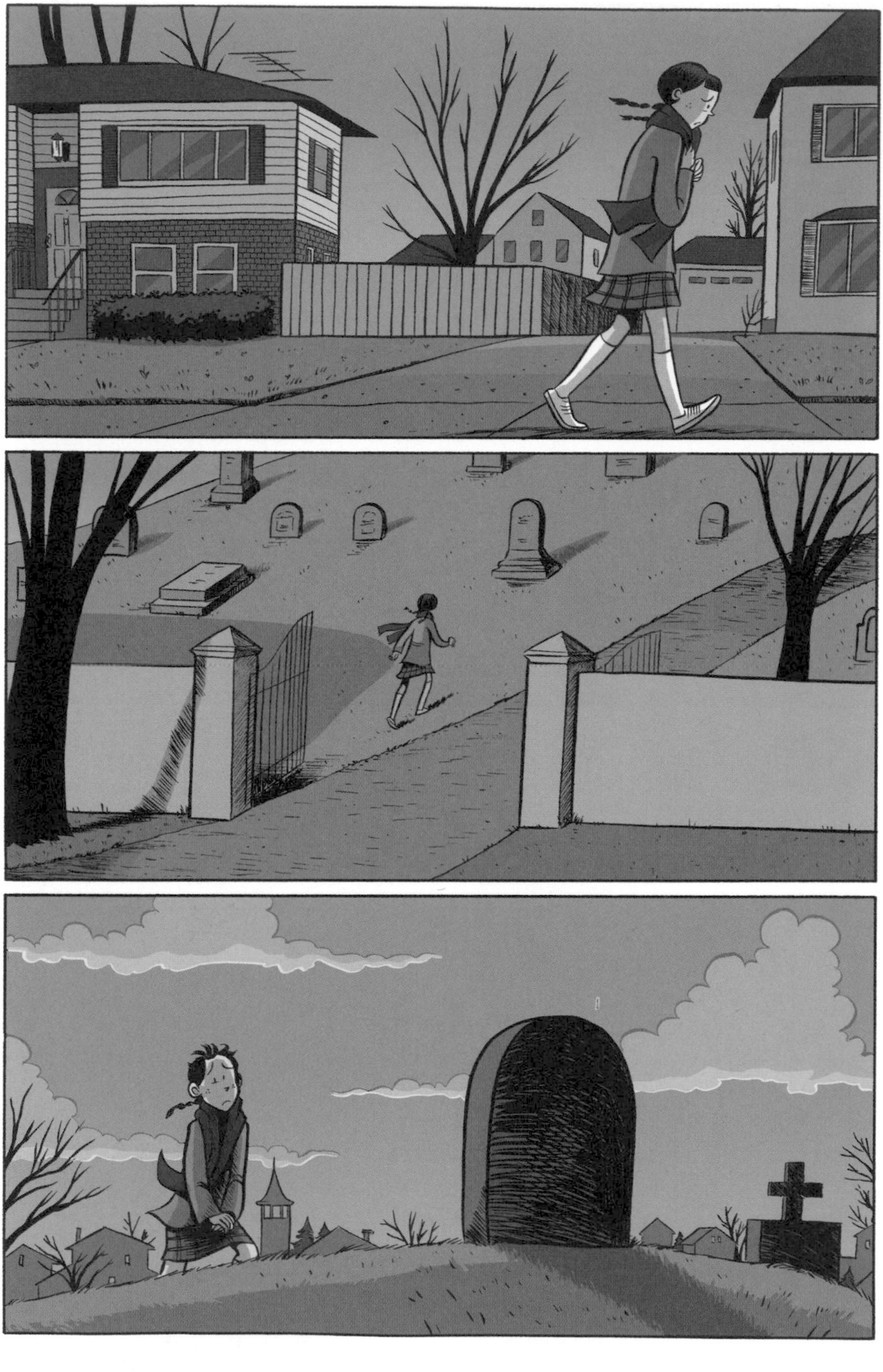

120

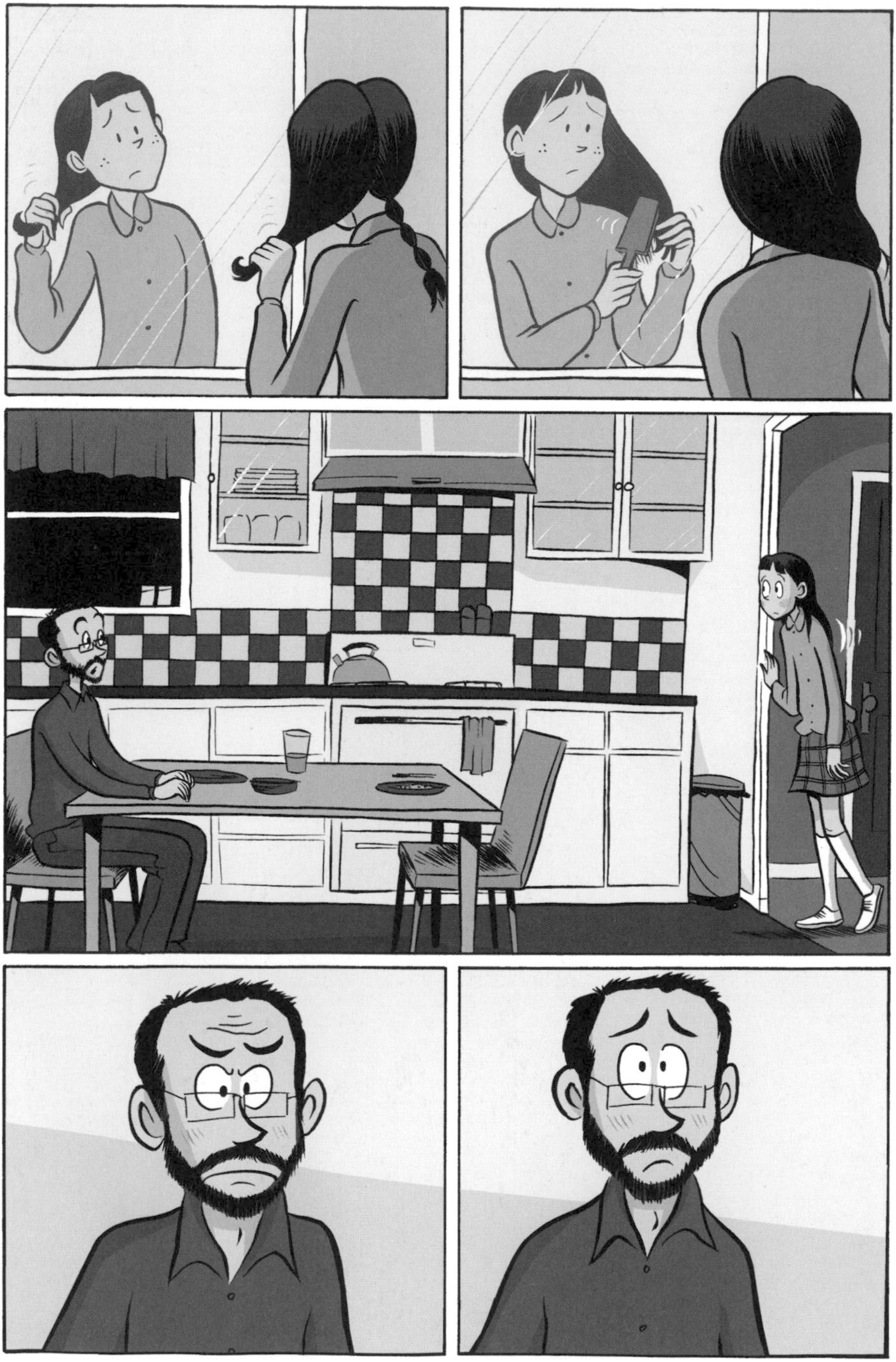

Sunday, February 8

   The members of The Baby-sitters Club have been
enemies for almost a month now. I can't believe
it. Claudia, Kristy, and Mary Anne — I hope you
all read what I'm writing, because I think our
fight is dumb, and you should know that. I
thought you guys were my friends, but I
guess not.
I'm writing this because tomorrow the four of
us have to help out at Jamie Newton's birthday
party, and I think it's going to be a disaster.
I hope you read this before then because I
think we should be prepared for the worst.
P.S. If anybody wants to make up, I'm ready.
                              Stacey

126

128

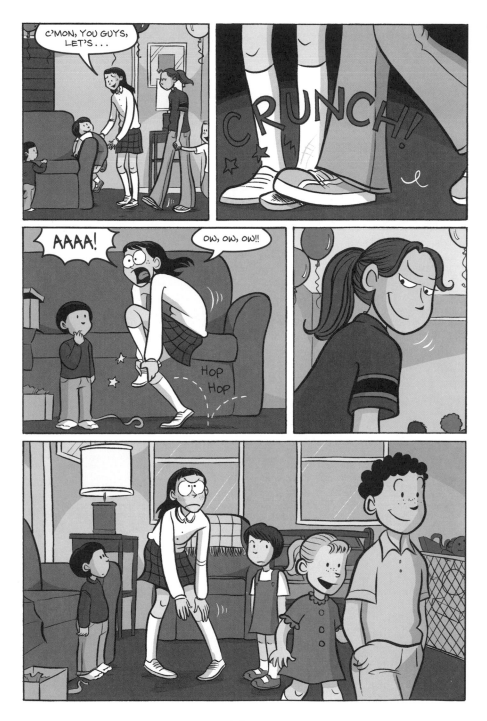

130

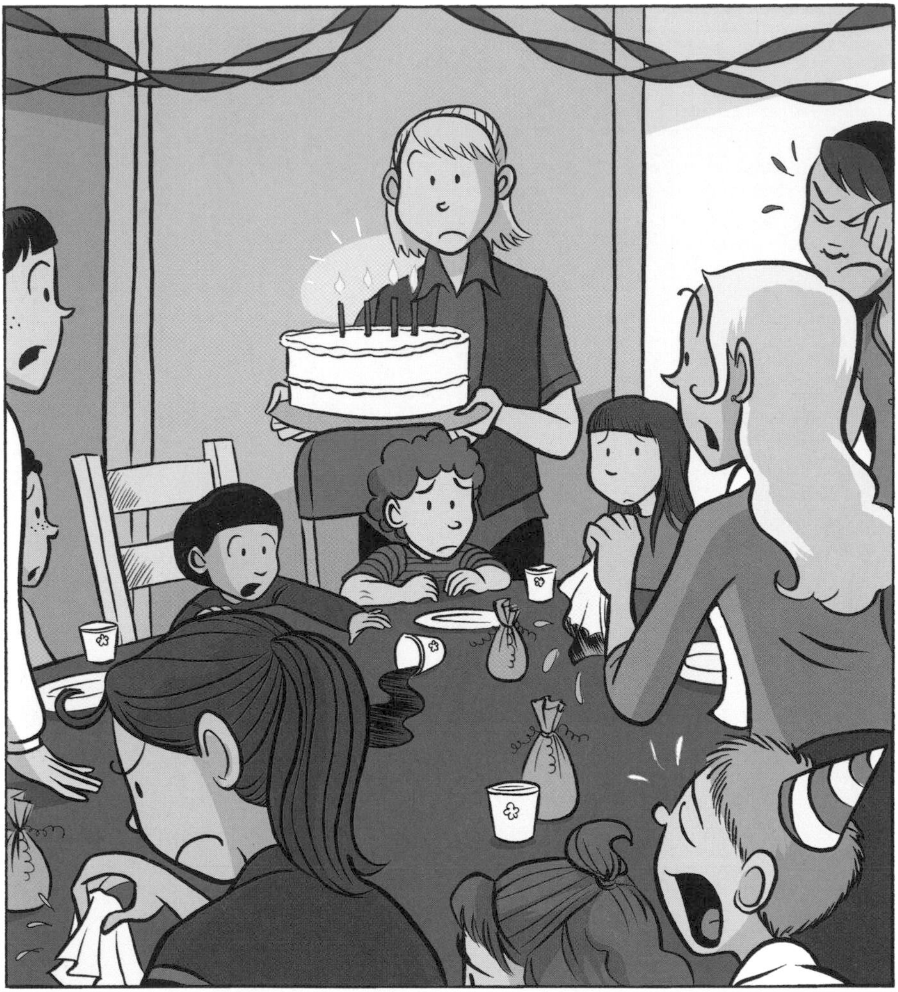

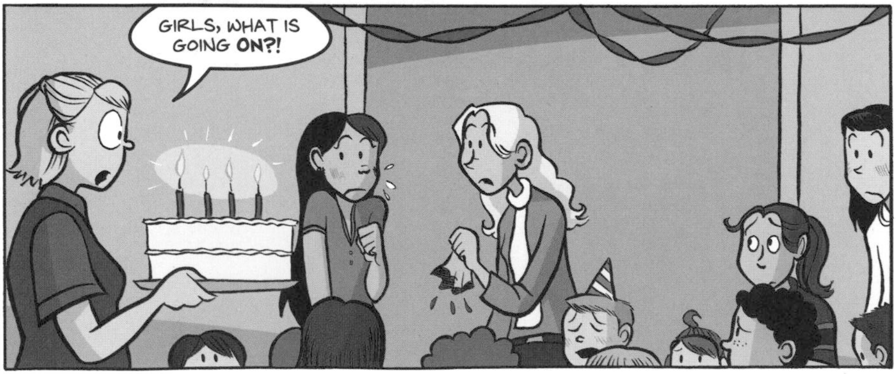
GIRLS, WHAT IS GOING **ON?!**

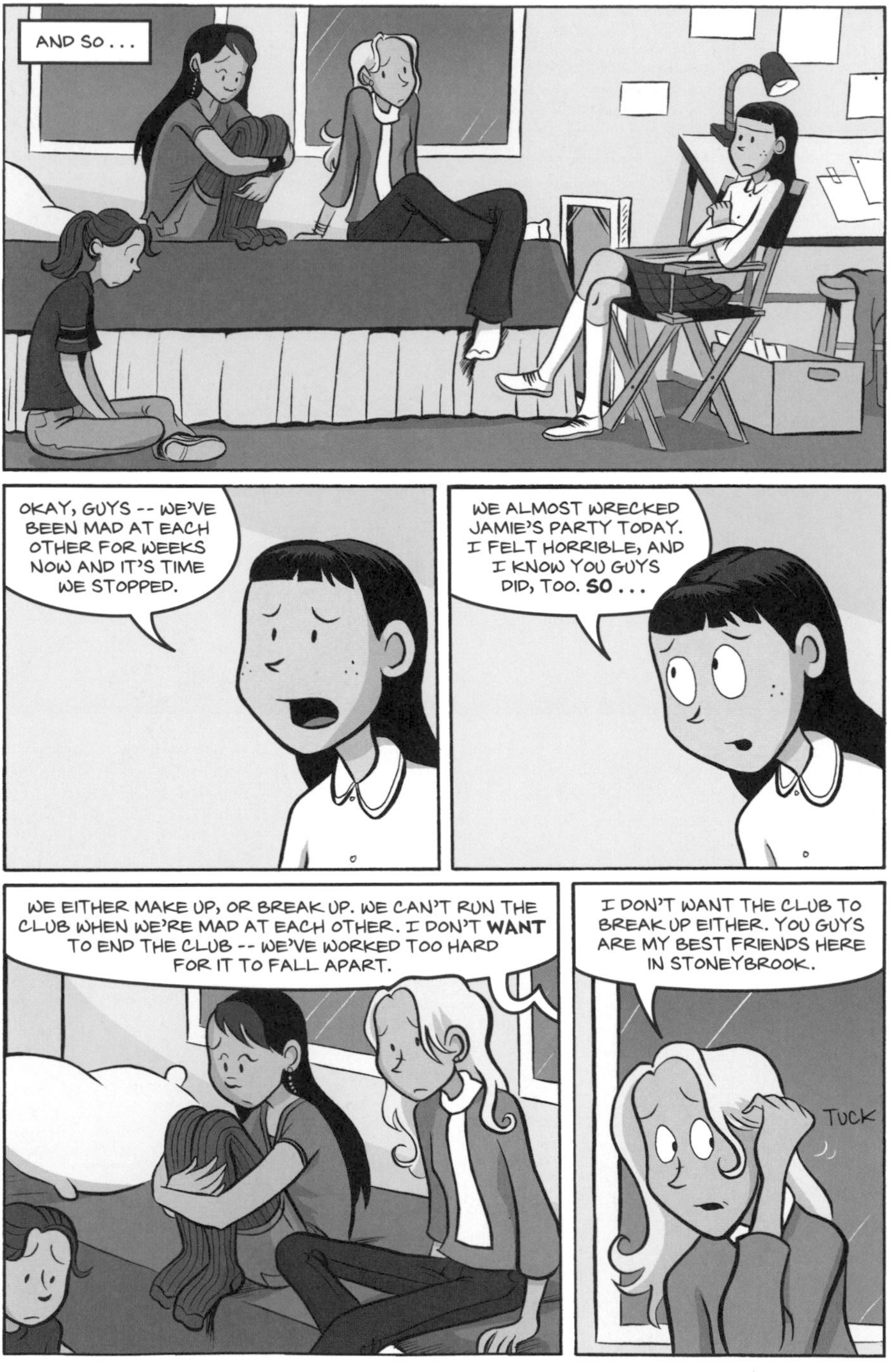
AND SO . . .
OKAY, GUYS -- WE'VE BEEN MAD AT EACH OTHER FOR WEEKS NOW AND IT'S TIME WE STOPPED.
WE ALMOST WRECKED JAMIE'S PARTY TODAY. I FELT HORRIBLE, AND I KNOW YOU GUYS DID, TOO. **SO . . .**
WE EITHER MAKE UP, OR BREAK UP. WE CAN'T RUN THE CLUB WHEN WE'RE MAD AT EACH OTHER. I DON'T **WANT** TO END THE CLUB -- WE'VE WORKED TOO HARD FOR IT TO FALL APART.
I DON'T WANT THE CLUB TO BREAK UP EITHER. YOU GUYS ARE MY BEST FRIENDS HERE IN STONEYBROOK.
TUCK

137

138

143

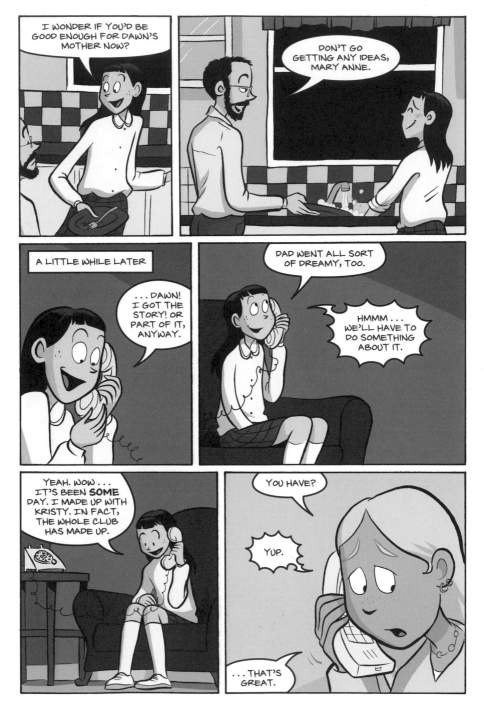

144

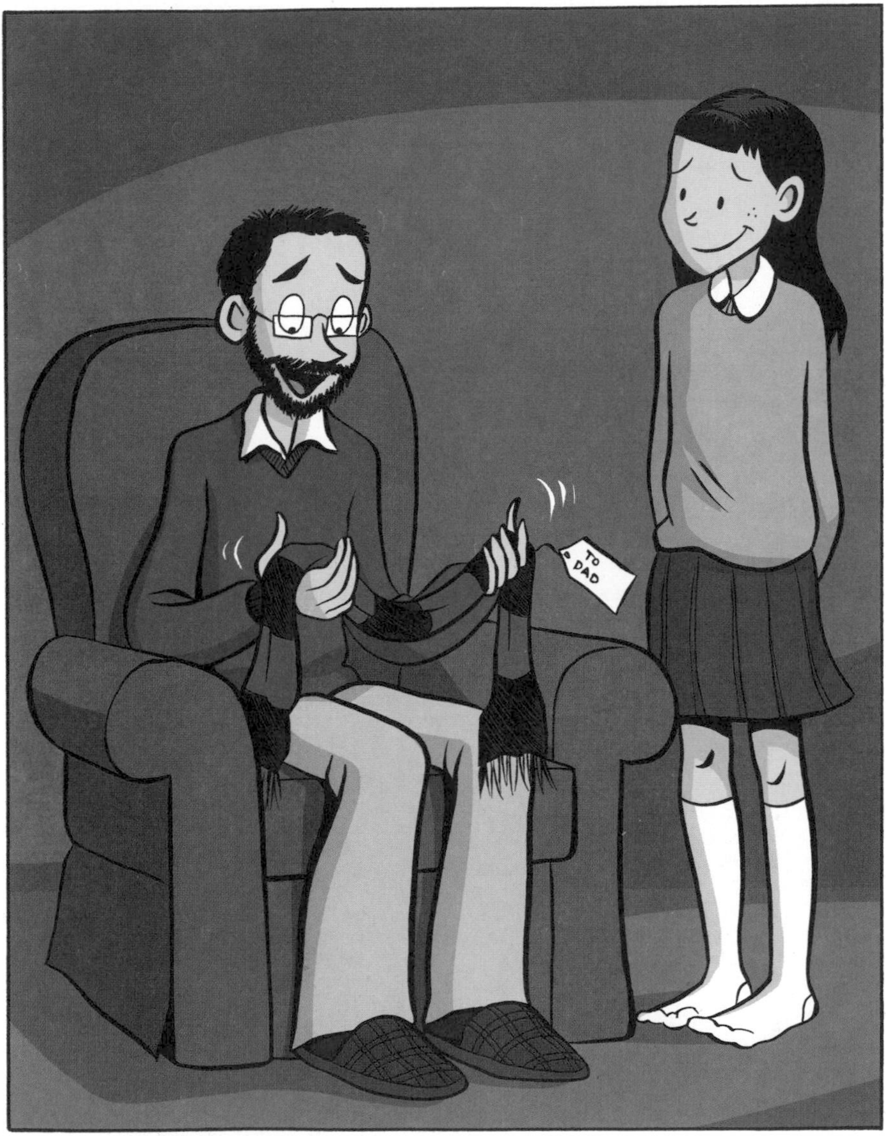
TO DAD

149

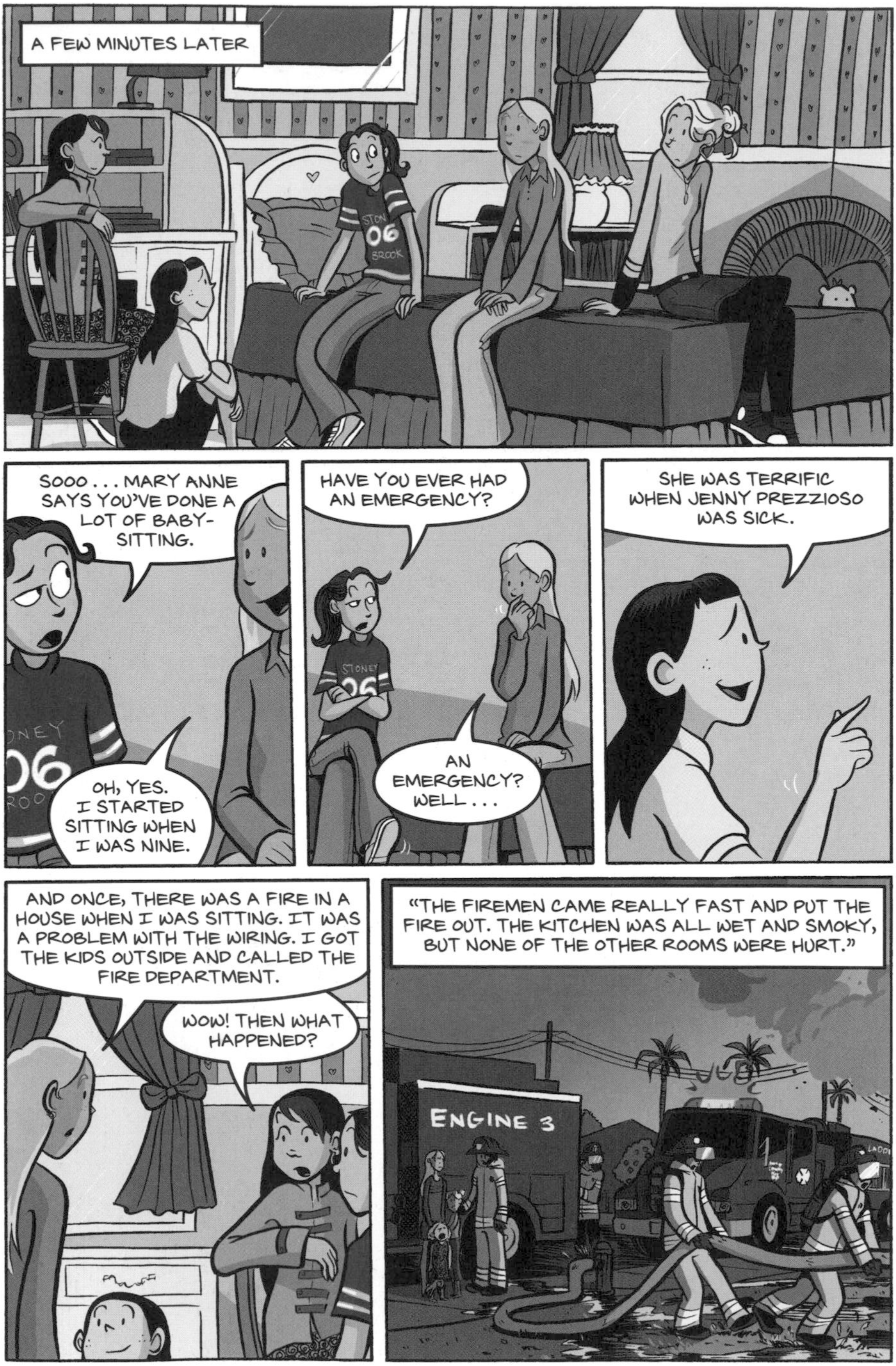
A FEW MINUTES LATER
SOOO . . . MARY ANNE SAYS YOU'VE DONE A LOT OF BABY-SITTING.
OH, YES. I STARTED SITTING WHEN I WAS NINE.
HAVE YOU EVER HAD AN EMERGENCY?
AN EMERGENCY? WELL . . .
SHE WAS TERRIFIC WHEN JENNY PREZZIOSO WAS SICK.
AND ONCE, THERE WAS A FIRE IN A HOUSE WHEN I WAS SITTING. IT WAS A PROBLEM WITH THE WIRING. I GOT THE KIDS OUTSIDE AND CALLED THE FIRE DEPARTMENT.
WOW! THEN WHAT HAPPENED?
"THE FIREMEN CAME REALLY FAST AND PUT THE FIRE OUT. THE KITCHEN WAS ALL WET AND SMOKY, BUT NONE OF THE OTHER ROOMS WERE HURT."
ENGINE 3

ANN M. MARTIN'S The Baby-sitters Club is one of the most popular series in the history of publishing — with more than 176 million books in print worldwide — and inspired a generation of young readers. Her novels include *Belle Teal*, *A Corner of the Universe* (a Newbery Honor book), *Here Today*, *A Dog's Life*, and *On Christmas Eve*, as well as the much-loved collaborations, *P.S. Longer Letter Later* and *Snail Mail No More*, with Paula Danziger, and *The Doll People* and *The Meanest Doll in the World*, written with Laura Godwin and illustrated by Brian Selznick. She lives in upstate New York.

RAINA TELGEMEIER is the #1 *New York Times* bestselling, multiple Eisner Award–winning creator of *Smile* and *Sisters*, which are both graphic memoirs based on her childhood. She is also the creator of *Drama*, which was named a Stonewall Honor Book and was selected for YALSA's Top Ten Great Graphic Novels for Teens. Raina lives in the San Francisco Bay Area. To learn more, visit her online at www.goRaina.com.

ALSO BY
RAINA TELGEMEIER

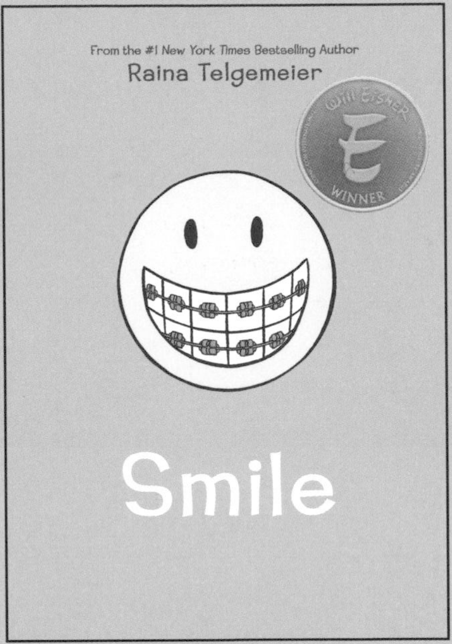

From the #1 New York Times Bestselling Author
Raina Telgemeier
WINNER
Smile

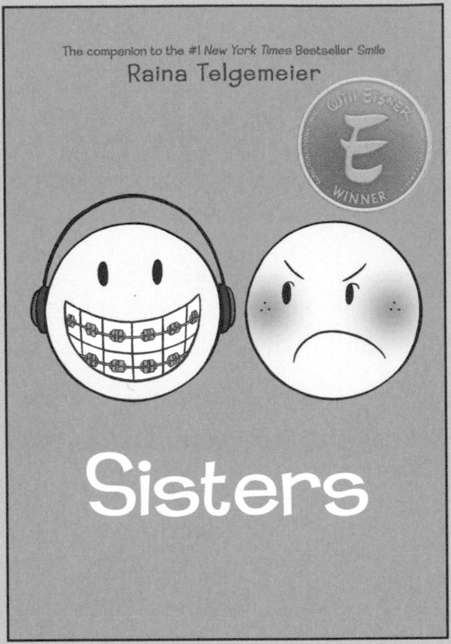

The companion to the #1 New York Times Bestseller Smile
Raina Telgemeier
WINNER
Sisters

This is the true story of how Raina severely injured her two front teeth when she was in the sixth grade, and the dental drama — on top of boy confusion, a major earthquake, and friends who turn out to be not so friendly — that followed!

Raina can't wait to be a big sister. Amara is cute, but she's also cranky and mostly prefers to play by herself. Their relationship doesn't improve much over the years, but they must figure out how to get along. They are sisters, after all!